Laird's Darkness

HIGHLANDER OF THE ISLES
BOOK 2

KATY BAKER

© Copyright 2026 by Katy Baker
Text by Katy Baker
Cover by Kim Killion Designs

Dragonblade Publishing, Inc. is an imprint of Kathryn Le Veque Novels, Inc.
P.O. Box 23
Moreno Valley, CA 92556
ceo@dragonbladepublishing.com

Produced in the United States of America

First Edition February 2026
Trade Paperback Edition

Reproduction of any kind except where it pertains to short quotes in relation to advertising or promotion is strictly prohibited.

All Rights Reserved.

The characters and events portrayed in this book are fictitious. Any similarity to real persons, living or dead, is purely coincidental and not intended by the author.

AI Statement: No AI or ghostwriting was used in the creation of this story, or any story, published by Dragonblade Publishing. All text, structure, content, ideas, and concept are 100% human generated solely by the author whose name appears on the cover. It is prohibited to use this material, or any copyrighted material, for AI engine training.

ARE YOU SIGNED UP FOR DRAGONBLADE'S BLOG?

You'll get the latest news and information on exclusive giveaways, exclusive excerpts, coming releases, sales, free books, cover reveals and more.

Check out our complete list of authors, too!

No spam, no junk. That's a promise!

Sign Up Here
www.dragonbladepublishing.com

Dearest Reader;

Thank you for your support of a small press. At Dragonblade Publishing, we strive to bring you the highest quality Historical Romance from some of the best authors in the business. Without your support, there is no 'us', so we sincerely hope you adore these stories and find some new favorite authors along the way.

Happy Reading!

CEO, Dragonblade Publishing

Additional Dragonblade books by Author Katy Baker

Highlander of the Isles Series
Laird's Curse (Book 1)
Laird's Darkness (Book 2)

Chapter One

ROSE MACFINNAN PERCHED on the arm of the sofa and stared at the bit of paper in her hand. Stark black letters stared right back at her, cold and formal. How had it ever come to this?

Her eyes scanned the letter for the umpteenth time, even though she could recite by heart every single word printed on the page. A heavy feeling formed inside, like she had a bowling ball sitting in her stomach. This was it. It was over.

"That's the last of them! Thank the Fates!" said a bright voice, snapping her back to the present. Her younger sister, Elise, walked into the living room, and Rose hastily stuffed the paper into the back pocket of her jeans and forced a smile.

"That's great. Thanks for helping me out today."

Elise shrugged. "Can't think of a better way to spend a Sunday morning than helping my big sister brew up cough mixture." She frowned, screwing up her face. "Oh, wait. Yes, I can." She began ticking things off on her fingers. "Sleeping late. Going to a coffee shop. Binge-watching something on TV. In fact, pretty much anything else."

Rose raised a sardonic eyebrow. "Yet here you are anyway."

Another shrug. "What can I say? I must be a sucker for punishment."

Rose shook her head, a smile curling her lips. "Yeah, that must be it."

She felt a swell of affection for her little sister. Elise was the wild child of the family, with her pink hair and free-spirited ways, but she had a heart of pure diamond, no matter how hard she tried to hide it behind flippant remarks and sarcasm. To be honest, Rose envied her. She'd never been able to emulate her younger sister's confidence or easy charm, the strength or presence of their elder sister, Sarah.

When they'd lost Sarah to cancer, Rose had tried her best to fill the hole she left behind, to become the big sister Elise needed and the wise aunt that Sarah's daughter, Jenna, needed, but she had a nagging feeling she'd never quite managed either. Like with most things in her life, Rose had fallen short.

Elise wiped her hands on a tea towel and dropped into a chair, pushing her pink-tipped hair out of her eyes. "Are you all right?"

"I'm fine," Rose said quickly. "Why wouldn't I be?"

"Dunno. You seem a little… distracted. You've barely said a word all morning."

Rose waved a hand. "Just tired, that's all."

Elise snorted. "That's hardly surprising, is it? You've been running around all summer treating summer colds, measles, chicken pox, and Fates-alone-knows what else. You're not as young as you used to be."

Rose gave her a flat look. "Elise, I'm thirty-seven. I don't need you wheeling me to an old-folks' home just yet."

Elise grinned. "You know I'm only kidding. But seriously, you work too hard."

Rose sighed. How many times had they had this conversation? "Elise, I'm a MacFinnan spellweaver. It's my *job* to help people."

"We are *both* MacFinnan spellweavers," Elise corrected. "And yes, it's our job to help people, but it is *not* our job to drive ourselves into the ground doing so. When was the last time you had a holiday? Heck, when was the last time you even took a day off?" The mischievous grin was gone, and Elise looked serious all of a sudden. She leaned forward and took Rose's hand. "I'm worried about you. You're driving yourself too hard. If Jenna were here, she'd say the same thing."

"But she's *not* here, is she?" Rose snapped. "And with her gone, it's even more important that I keep on top of things."

Jenna, their niece, and fellow MacFinnan spellweaver had lived nearby until recently, just on the other side of the lake behind Rose's house. But she'd just got married and now lived all the way over in Scotland. And several hundred years in the past to boot. Rose tried not to think about that. It made her head hurt whenever she did.

Elise sighed. "Has anyone ever told you how stubborn you can be?"

"Yes. You have. Many times. It must be a family trait."

"Touché," Elise replied with a smile. She climbed to her feet. "Just think about what I've said, will you? You can't keep putting everyone before yourself, Rose. You deserve to be happy too. Especially with what you've been going through this past year."

Rose opened her mouth and closed it again. She didn't have an answer to that.

Elise put a hand on her shoulder. "I'll call you later, okay?"

Rose caught her hand and squeezed it. "Thanks, Elise."

"Don't thank me. I'm just looking out for myself. I don't want you driving yourself to exhaustion and leaving me to do all the work, do I?"

She gave another lazy grin, then sauntered out the front door, letting it bang closed behind her and leaving Rose alone in the echoing house.

For a moment, she stared at nothing, mulling over Elise's words, then she took a deep breath, gave herself a mental shake, and hauled herself up. Her soft shoes made no sound on the polished boards as she went into the kitchen. The counter was filled with small brown bottles, each carefully labeled and dated. The smell of the cough syrup she and Elise had spent the morning brewing—honey, lemon, and various herbs—filled the kitchen with its heady aroma and brought back memories of when their mother had taught them the recipe when they were just girls.

She smiled, remembering. Sarah, calm and authoritative, Elise, a brat likely to throw a tantrum if she didn't get her own way, and herself the rule follower who listened closely to everything their mother told them and obeyed her instructions to the letter. Happy memories.

She ran a finger along some of the bottles, checking the stoppers were in tight. It was September, and already the days were starting to cool. She and Elise had made the cough syrup in preparation for the maladies that winter inevitably brought and the people who always sought her help—usually those without the money to pay for medication.

When they turned up at her doorstep with coughs and colds, she'd give them the syrup and tell them to take it three times a day, and they would leave happy, thinking it was the mundane ingredients of the syrup that healed them. In fact, it wasn't, it was the MacFinnan magic that she and Elise wove into each and every bottle, but people didn't need to know that. There were fewer and fewer believers these days, and so she'd had to come up with increasingly inventive ways to mask her gifts.

Satisfied that the syrups were all in order, she crossed to the kettle and filled it. As she waited for it to boil, she pulled the piece of paper from her back pocket and read it again. The words printed across the top stood out starkly, broadcasting Rose's failure.

Decree Absolute.

It was done. Over. She was no longer married. She wasn't sure what she was supposed to feel about that. Relieved? Upset? Angry?

But all she felt was empty. Numb. She had wanted to make her marriage work, she really had. It was a wry joke in her family that MacFinnan spellweavers were usually too much for any normal man to handle and this had been borne out in the case of her parents and her elder sister, all of whom had gotten divorced, but she'd been determined to buck the trend. Why couldn't she be both a spellweaver *and* a wife? Why couldn't she live both her magical life and a normal one? She'd been so determined she could have it all.

She'd been wrong.

She and Dennis had gradually drifted apart, and for the last year, the only times she'd seen him had been in the lawyer meetings they'd both been required to attend. It had been amicable, without animosity on either side, and there were no children involved, but that didn't make it any easier to bear.

She sighed, Elise's words ringing in her head. *You can't keep putting everyone before yourself, Rose. When was the last time you took a holiday?*

She couldn't remember. Five years? Longer? She crumpled the bit of paper in her fist. It was probably not since she and Dennis had gone camping for their honeymoon—all they'd been able to afford.

Dropping the paper into the bin, she spun on her heel and marched resolutely into the study. Seating herself at her antique computer, she fired it up and opened the internet. She wasn't sure what she was looking for, so she typed in, *great holiday vacation spots*. A huge list of hits appeared on the page, too many to take in at once. She scrolled until something caught her eye.

Italy.

As she clicked on the link, images of vibrant-blue seas, crumbling castles, and olive groves filled the screen.

Oh yes, that looked like her kind of place all right. She had a bit of money from the divorce, so why shouldn't she follow Elise's advice and take some time for herself? A bit of time to de-stress and think about what she wanted to do with the next chapter of her life?

Her finger hovered over the *book now* button, but she hesitated. What would happen to her patients while she was away? What if Mrs. Carlton's bad leg got worse? What if Michael Chapman's gout came back?

She shook her head, imagining what Elise would say if she could hear her thoughts. *Just book it! They will be fine!*

Her finger was just about to press the button when a sound caught her attention, pulling her head around to look through the window. It sounded like splashing and was coming from the lake behind her house. This was not unusual, of course, as numerous youths liked to swim in the lake during the summer, but this sounded different. To Rose's highly tuned senses, this sounded like somebody in distress.

She rose from her seat and rushed out the back door, taking the steps down from her porch two at a time. Hurrying along the path, she pushed through the little gate and all but ran down to the lakeshore.

Sure enough, when she arrived, she found the surface choppy and disturbed, as though something had been thrashing around in it recently, but she couldn't see any sign of a person.

No. Wait. There. Over on the jetty. A woman was sitting on the edge of the platform, legs dangling over the side. Her arms were wrapped around herself as if she were cold and her long hair was plastered to the sides of her head.

Rose hurried around the shore towards her. "Hello!" she called, waving a hand. "Are you all right?"

The woman didn't respond.

Rose padded along the jetty, the boards making hollow thumping noises beneath her feet, and crouched by the woman's side.

"Is everything okay?"

The woman slowly turned to look at her. Rose gasped. The woman's skin was as smooth as alabaster, with full lips and a straight nose. But this wasn't what had made Rose gasp. It was the woman's eyes. They were pure silver, with no iris or pupil at all.

Rose scrabbled backwards. Now that she was closer, she could feel power emanating from the woman in waves. The hair on the back of her neck stood on end.

"Who are you?" she whispered.

The woman smiled, revealing perfect white teeth. "My name is Lir, goddess of the sea. And I need yer help."

Chapter Two

CAILEAN MACNEIL WRUNG out the sweat-sodden cloth, dipped it in a basin of cool, clean water, and pressed it against Drew's damp forehead. It didn't seem to be making any difference. His old retainer and friend was getting worse. Drew had thrown off the blankets that the healers had placed over him, and sweat streaked his limbs and torso.

Despite the cool September breeze coming in through the open window, he was burning up, the fever chewing through him as it had already done to so many others.

Helpless frustration welled up inside Cailean. He was the laird of this island, damn it! He should be able to do something to help his people. But in this, he was as helpless as a newborn babe.

He clenched his fists, trying to curb the anger that rose inside him like boiling oil. He'd tried everything. He'd brought healers from all over Barra, tried every remedy they knew, but nothing worked. The sickness was getting worse, and Cailean's rage and frustration increased with each new report that came in.

"I'll give him more willow bark," Maggie said from Drew's other side.

Cailean nodded. Maggie's wrinkled face was drawn and haggard. Like him, she hadn't been getting much sleep. He knew the castle healer was as frustrated as he was. She held a mortar and pestle in her hands, grinding down more ingredients for remedies.

"Yer heathen concoctions havenae helped in the least," said Sister Beatrice, the castle's other healer, who was folding sheets by the door. "Only the Good Lord can save him now. I'll say more prayers."

"Oh, because they've done the world of good so far, ye mean?" Maggie retorted. "Yer Christian god seems to have forgotten our little corner of the world!"

They fell to arguing, and Cailean sighed. Maggie and Beatrice were sisters, both healers in their own way, but had taken vastly different paths in life. Maggie was steeped in the old ways of gods and goddesses of field and furrow, Beatrice in the ways of the Christian god. Both thought their way was right and other wrong.

Cailean didn't care one way or the other. He'd never held much faith in deities who seemed to care little for what happened to the mortals who venerated them. All he cared about was finding a way to save his people. Until now he'd always done that with a sword in his hand and a command on his lips. Norse raiders? He'd drive them off. Disputes among his people? He'd knock the leaders' heads together until they saw sense.

But this? Swords and brawn were no use against this enemy, and the bickering of his two healers wasn't helping any.

"I need some air," he muttered, heaving himself to his feet.

He left Drew's sickroom and made his way through the castle until he reached the main doors. Stepping outside, he stopped, sucking in a lungful of the sea air and trying to calm the tempest of emotions raging inside.

It was a cloudy, cold day, and the breeze coming in off the ocean held hints of the winter to come. If they couldn't find a way to combat this illness, how many of them would make it through that winter?

"Papa!"

He turned just as a small body cannoned into him, wrapping skinny arms around his waist.

He gave an "oomph" and then a laugh, returning the fierce

hug. "What's this for?"

Catriona looked up at him, her freckled face breaking into a grin. "No reason. Just havenae seen ye since breakfast, is all."

As usual, Catriona's red ringlets had come free of the plait that he'd tied them in. And, as usual, there was a mischievous glint in her eye. He raised an eyebrow at his daughter.

"Dinna give me that. I know that look when I see it."

Cat blinked, feigning innocence. "What look?"

"*That* look. That look that says ye've done something ye shouldnae and are being extra nice so I dinna notice. Come on, out with it. What have ye done now?"

At nine years old, Catriona MacNeil was a handful. Tall for her age, and with her mother's fiery coloring and temperament, she had seemingly limitless energy and was always getting herself into some scrape or another. She could usually be found with the other local children swimming in the coves that dotted the shore, fishing in the inland lochs, or climbing the trees that blanketed the hills inland. She flatly refused to behave like a lady, to the eternal despair of Sister Beatrice, who acted as her tutor.

She shuffled her feet and looked a little sheepish.

Cailean crossed his arms over his broad chest. "I'm waiting."

"Well..." she began, drawing out the word.

She was interrupted by a sudden high-pitched yapping and a scrabbling against the door of the stable that lay on the other side of the courtyard. A second later, the door burst open and a black-and-white puppy came racing across the yard towards them.

"Ye were supposed to stay there until I'd spoken to him!" Cat cried as the puppy started dancing around her feet.

"So that's it!" Cailean thundered. "Ye've been and gotten one of Old Malcolm's pups after I expressly told ye no!"

Cat scooped up the tiny dog and backed away, holding him protectively. "Malcolm said I could have him! He's the runt of the litter and willnae be any good for shepherding anyway!"

"That isnae the point. The point is that ye disobeyed me."

To her credit, Cat looked suitably abashed. But a moment

later, her defiance returned. "He willnae be any trouble, and I'll train him myself. The kennel master says he'll help me, and he can sleep in my room. I'll clean up after him, I promise. Look, he already knows some commands."

She put the little dog down. "Patch, sit."

To Cailean's surprise, the pup did exactly that. He raised an eyebrow. "Patch?"

"That's his name. Because he's got a black patch over his eye. See? Can I keep him, Pa? Please?"

Cailean had been laird long enough to know when to pick his battles, and this was clearly a battle he was not going to win. He sighed. "Fine. But ye *will* train him. And ye will feed him. And ye will clean up after him. Clear?"

Cat cannoned into him again, throwing her arms around his waist. "Oh, thank ye, thank ye, thank ye!"

Cailean's annoyance melted away to be replaced by a warm, fierce love for this strong-willed girl of his. He wrapped his arms around her and kissed the top of her head. He would do anything, *anything* to protect her. But what if he couldn't protect her from this sickness? What if it came for her too?

A cold, visceral terror clutched at his insides, so strong that for a moment it took his breath. What if he lost her the way he'd lost her mother?

No, he thought. *I won't let that happen. I will never let that happen. I will die first.*

Cat looked up at him, seeming to notice his pained expression. "Are ye all right, Papa?"

He forced a smile. "I'm fine. Why dinna ye take Patch to the kitchen? I'm sure there were some sausages left over from breakfast. But after that, ye get straight to yer lessons, ye hear?"

Cat gave a little cry of delight and turned to scamper off across the courtyard, Patch running at her heels. Cailean watched them go, that terror clenching his gut again. He could *not* lose her. He just couldn't.

Taking a deep breath, he turned and strode away, out of Dun

Mallach's gates and onto the road that zigzagged downhill to the coast.

The village that hugged the slopes of the hill on which Dun Mallach was built was quiet at this time of day, with most folks either out fishing or else working the fields inland, so only a few oldsters were around, mending nets or sitting on the front step of their houses, watching the world go by. These few raised hands and called greetings as he strode past, which Cailean returned in kind.

But in truth, his mind was on other things. His thoughts churned, as turbulent as the winter seas. He strode down to the beach, sand and shingle crunching under his boots. The tide was out, and so the shore had become a long stretch of rock pools and sandbars, glimmering in the random shafts of light that occasionally broke through the overcast.

Cailean stared out to sea. The breeze streamed his hair and plaid out behind him and helped to clear his thoughts a little. This was where he always came when he wanted to be alone or needed to think. The smell of the sea, the bite of the wind, the endless horizon, they all helped to soothe his turbulent emotions.

But not today. Today his thoughts wouldn't settle, going round and round and round, with no solution presenting itself. In his mind's eye he saw Drew's fever-ravaged face. He saw the countless others who had already succumbed to the sickness. What was he to do? What *could* he do?

If he had been a religious man, he might have fallen to his knees and prayed. He might have given offerings to the old gods as Maggie did, or prayed to the Christian one as Beatrice wanted him to. But Cailean had long since lost all faith in gods. His loss of faith had started when they took his wife from him, leaving his daughter without a mother, and it had only increased when the sickness began taking his people and the gods stood by and let it happen.

It was once said that the Kingdom of the Isles—Barra, Skye, and Islay—was protected by an ancient magic and that it would keep harm from coming to the people of the Isles. If that were so, Cailean had never seen any evidence of it. Barra had been beset by raiders, savage storms, and now the sickness.

Oh aye, he no longer had any faith in gods.

He felt his hands curling into fists and the old, familiar anger forming in his gut. Anger at the gods. Anger at the hand fate had dealt him. But mostly, anger at himself.

These were *his* people. It was his duty to save them.

But he didn't even know where to begin.

ROSE STARED AT the silver-eyed woman. "I beg your pardon? Did you just say you're a *goddess?*"

Was she a little unhinged? A goddess? Seriously?

The woman cocked her head and regarded Rose with those disconcerting silver eyes. "Do ye have a problem with yer hearing? Aye, I am the goddess Lir, and as I said, I need yer help."

She had a strange, lilting accent. Scottish? And those eyes... They were like pools of quicksilver, and they seemed to see right into Rose's soul. She swallowed. She had the strangest feeling that the woman wasn't unhinged at all. She had the strangest feeling that those eyes weren't some fancy contact lenses made for show.

She got the feeling that this was *real*.

She had always known about the other world, of course. Her mother and grandmother had taught her all about gods and spirits and the creatures that walked the world beyond the knowledge of humanity, but she'd never actually *met* one before.

And now here she was talking to a goddess.

"There's nothing wrong with my hearing," she replied. "I... um... I'm just a little... surprised."

Lir studied her. "Ye are Rose MacFinnan, are ye not? A MacFinnan spellweaver?"

"Yes, but—"

"Good," Lir said, cutting her off and rising gracefully. "Then ye are the one I need. Come. We must be going. Time is short."

"Going? What do you mean? Going where?"

"To Barra, of course. In the Isles of Scotland. There is somebody there who needs yer help. In fact, many people. Help that only a MacFinnan spellweaver can give." Those silver eyes intensified as Lir stared at her. "And not just any MacFinnan spellweaver. But *ye*, Rose MacFinnan."

Rose held up her hands and backed away a step. "Hang on. Barra? Scotland? I can't just up and go to Scotland! I've got responsibilities here! You'll have to find somebody else."

"There *is* nobody else. Ye are needed, Rose MacFinnan, needed in a way ye never have been needed before. The question is: Will ye answer that call as yer ancestors before ye have always done?"

Rose opened her mouth and closed it again. Was it really just moments ago she'd been looking at holidays on the internet? How had everything turned so surreal in such a short space of time? She heard Elise's voice in her head.

You can't keep putting everyone before yourself, Rose.

But someone needed her. She couldn't ignore that. She'd never been able to. She'd been given her powers for a reason, and that reason was helping others.

Really? A traitorous little voice spoke in the back of her head. *To the point where you sacrifice everything? Even your marriage?*

She squashed the voice. She would *not* go there. She opened her mouth, fulling intending to say, *Sorry, I can't. I'm going to Italy.*

But what actually came out of her mouth was, "Of course I'll come to Barra. Although I'll need to book an air ticket."

What? Why had she said that? Elise would be furious! But how was she supposed to stand aside when a *goddess* had come asking for her help?

I'll just do this one task, she told herself. *Then I'll take a break. I'll go to Italy. I will.*

A smile curled Lir's mouth. "I knew I had chosen right in ye,

Rose MacFinnan. Yer name will be whispered through the ages."

"Right. Whatever. I'd better go pack and book my air ticket."

Lir caught her arm. The woman's fingers were as cold as ice. "There is no need for that. I will take us to Barra."

Rose blinked. "Um. You will?"

Lir's smile widened. "I *am* a goddess. Follow me."

She strode off along the jetty, her feet leaving wet prints on the wooden boards, halting at the end where it jutted out over the water. She glanced over her shoulder. "Well? Are ye coming?"

Rose licked her lips, glanced back at her little house, then at Lir. *Oh, heck*, she thought. *What have I just agreed to?*

She moved along the jetty until she stood next to the goddess. "Why do I get the feeling I'm not going to like this?"

Lir laughed softly. "Dinna worry. It will be over in a heartbeat. Take my hand."

Rose did so, wincing at the cold smoothness of Lir's skin.

"Ye may wish to hold yer breath," the goddess instructed.

Then she jumped off the jetty, dragging a startled Rose with her. Rose had time for a single yelp before she plunged into dark, bitterly cold water—

—and came up coughing and gasping.

Lir still had hold of her hand, and Rose clasped it tightly as though it were the only thing stopping her from drowning.

"You... you... could have warned me!" she gasped, thrashing around with her free hand.

Lir bobbed a few inches away. She seemed amused. "Did I not warn ye to hold yer breath?"

Rose scowled and flicked wet hair out of her eyes, looking around. As she did so, she realized things had changed. There was no sign of her house, the jetty, or the jogging path that led around the lake. Instead, she could see sand dunes rising beyond a rocky shore and could hear the hiss of waves lapping against it. The water tasted salty.

The sea. This was the sea, and that shore was... what? Barra? Had she really traveled so far in the blink of an eye?

Lir released Rose's hand and began swimming away from her. She moved with the grace of a dolphin, leaving Rose to flounder and flap behind her, doing her best to follow.

A wave of relief went through her when she felt the bottom under her feet and was able to clamber out onto the shingle beach that bracketed the shoreline. She collapsed in a heap, staring up at the cloudy sky and listening to the rapid thump of her heart.

What am I doing? she thought. *I'm Rose, the sensible MacFinnan, remember? This is the sort of crazy thing Elise would do.*

She struggled into a sitting position and found Lir standing just in front of her, hands clasped demurely at her navel. "Welcome to the Kingdom of the Isles, Rose MacFinnan," she said formally. "Or more accurately, the island of Barra."

Lir held out a hand, which Rose took, allowing Lir to pull her up. She got her first decent look at her surroundings. Beyond the dunes, the ground rose steeply into a series of hills, on the tallest of which sat a large complex of stone buildings with towers and crenelated walls. Pennants flew from the top of the towers, and a large gate tower guarded the entrance.

Rose stared at it. Wait. Was that a *castle*?

Then her eyes were drawn to something else. A village hugged the knees of the hill on which the castle sat, flowing down in tiered rows, with a zigzag path weaving its way through. But it wasn't a normal village with shops and cars and roads, oh no. This looked like something straight out of a painting. The buildings were constructed of timber, with thatched roofs and wicker fencing around cottage gardens. Rose made out gaggles of geese and chickens meandering between the buildings and even a couple of pigs wallowing by the side of the path.

There wasn't a car, nor a café, nor a tarmacked road in sight.

A horrible suspicion began to form at the back of her mind. She whirled on the goddess. "Lir, where have you brought me?"

"Barra, as I said."

"Really? Then why does everything look so strange? This place looks nothing like any Scottish settlement I've ever heard of."

Lir shrugged. "That's because ye are out of yer time. This is the year 1493."

Rose goggled. She felt her jaw drop. She must have heard wrong. Lir hadn't just said it was 1493. Had she?

"You're joking, right? Please tell me you're joking."

"I dinna joke, Rose MacFinnan."

Rose turned in a slow circle. Out on the sea she spotted a fishing boat but it wasn't a metal-hulled one with a motor, but carved from wood with a basic sail and two paddles. To the west she saw a line of people working in a field. There was no sign of machinery, just wooden hoes that they were using to clear the ground.

No, she thought. *This cannot be happening.*

She pressed a hand to her forehead, suddenly dizzy. "I did not agree to this! I agreed to travel to Barra, not travel through time!"

The goddess cocked her head, seeming puzzled by Rose's outburst. "Does it matter? These people need yer help. What difference does the time period make?"

Rose stared at her incredulously. "Are you serious? It makes every difference! How the hell do you expect me to survive in 1493? I would never have agreed to come if I'd known this was what you meant!"

"Would ye not?" Lir replied, narrowing those strange silver eyes at her. "Are the people of this time not worthy of yer aid?"

Rose felt a flicker of anger. "You're trying to trap me with words and I won't have it." She lifted her hand and pointed a finger at the goddess. "You brought me here under false pretenses. Take me home. Now."

Lir said nothing and it was difficult to gauge emotions on that silver-eyed face. But for a moment, Rose thought she saw regret, sadness, and something else flicker across her smooth features. Fear?

"If ye wish it, I will take ye back," the goddess said softly. "But ye are needed here, Rose MacFinnan. Sorely needed. I wouldnae have come to ye otherwise. We can never know where our destiny will take us and perhaps this is where yer destiny lies. Perhaps it is here that ye will find what ye are truly looking for. Have ye considered that? But if ye choose it, I will take ye home and ye will continue yer life as if ye had never met me. Is that what ye wish?"

Was it? Did she want to go back to her life? Back to her divorce and her empty house and her holiday for one?

No, she realized suddenly. It wasn't.

Perhaps it is here that ye will find what ye are truly looking for.

What *was* she looking for? She had no idea. All she knew was that TV dinners, making winter cough syrups, and coming home to an empty house was *not* it.

And just like that, her decision was made.

"No," she breathed. "That isn't what I wish. I'll stay. I'll do what I can to help these people."

Lir's eyes lit up and she took Rose's hands in both of hers. "Then ye have my thanks, Rose MacFinnan. *He* willnae accept my help. Perhaps he will accept yers."

Then she released her hands and walked back towards the sea.

"What do you mean?" Rose called after her. "*Who* might accept my help?"

Lir didn't answer. She climbed up onto a long a spur of rock that stuck out into the sea and carried on walking. Waves crashed against the sides of the rock, sending spray across its surface.

"Wait!" Rose cried. "You haven't told me what I'm here to do!"

She hurried after the goddess, reached out a hand to grab Lir's shoulder, but suddenly caught her foot on a loose rock. Her ankle twisted and she went staggering sideways.

She had time for one terrified scream before she hit the water and went under.

Chapter Three

CAILEAN HEARD A scream in the distance and his head snapped in that direction. He spotted a figure in the distance out on the rock spur—a woman?—for an instant before it went tumbling into the sea.

Adrenaline shot through him and he was off and running before he had time to think. He ripped off his plaid and his shirt as he pelted down the sand and shingle to the water's edge and finally kicked off his boots as he launched himself into the waves.

Cold and darkness hit him like a slap but he didn't let that slow him. He knew these waters as well as anyone alive and if he didn't reach that woman soon, the current here would dash her against the rocks like a piece of flotsam. He would be damned if he would lose anyone else.

He moved with sure, powerful strokes against the current, and as he neared the rock spur, he dived, eyes open and searching the dark, thrashing waves. Long strands of kelp waved about, obscuring his vision, and the sea seemed angry today, determined to push him back towards shore.

There!

He saw the flash of a pale arm in the darkness. He kicked downwards, powering towards it. A woman was hanging in the water, eyes closed, dark hair waving like the kelp forest around them.

He got one arm around her waist and kicked upwards with everything he had. She was a dead weight pulling him down, but he clung on grimly, determined that the sea would not have her. Little dots began to dance in front of his eyes and his chest felt like it might burst as he powered up, up, up, until finally, he broke the surface in an explosion of water.

He heaved in a great breath, filling his lungs with sweet, sweet air, and then rolled onto his back, trying to keep the woman's head above water.

Her eyes were still closed and she didn't appear to be breathing. But a moment later, her eyes flew open, a great gout of water exploded from her mouth, and she sucked in huge ragged breaths. She began struggling, her arms flapping around and her legs kicking, threatening to send them both under again.

"Be still!" Cailean growled. "Dinna fight me or ye'll drown us both!"

Her eyes swiveled towards him and widened. "W-what?" she managed to gasp.

"Try to relax," he told her. "I've got ye. I'll get us both to shore."

She seemed to understand. She stopped struggling and he was able to get a better grip around her waist. Swimming on his back, he pulled her behind him, keeping her head on his chest to keep it out of the water, and they began to make progress against the choppy waves. The woman began kicking her legs to aid him and it was not long before Cailean felt the seabed under his feet and was able to drag them both up onto the beach.

He released the woman and collapsed onto his back, chest heaving and muscles screaming. The woman rolled onto her side and began retching, bringing up seawater and fighting to regain her breath.

"Are ye hurt?" he asked her.

She retched a bit more before rolling onto her hands and knees. Her hair, dark as a moonless night, fell forward to curtain her face. Her sodden clothes—an odd pair of trews and a shirt like a man's—clung to her slim frame. She said nothing for several moments as she got a hold of herself but finally turned to face him, brushing the hair out of her eyes.

Cailean blinked. He didn't recognize her and he would *definitely* have remembered this woman. Around his own age, she had high cheek bones, smooth skin, and bright blue eyes that looked as big as saucers.

"I... I... I'm okay," she gasped, her voice hoarse from swallowing seawater. "Thanks... for pulling... me out."

"Ye are welcome, lass."

He didn't recognize her accent. Not Scots or Irish. She wasn't a local then. No wonder he didn't recognize her.

She looked around as if searching for something. "Where is she?"

"Where is who?"

The woman braced her hands on the sand and pushed herself unsteadily to her feet, turning her head this way and that. "Where did she go?"

Cailean clambered up, water dripping from his hair and down his chest. He looked around. There was nobody else in sight. "Who are ye looking for?"

"Lir, of course!" the woman cried as if this should be obvious. "She was here literally a moment ago. She's the one who brought me here and I'll be damned if I'll let her just disappear on me without a so much as a by-your-leave!" She cupped her hands around her mouth and bellowed, "Lir! Where are you! Come back here this instant!"

Cailean took a step closer. "Lass, there is nobody else here. Ye were alone when ye went into the water."

She whirled to face him. "No, I wasn't! I was with Lir! She can't have just vanished!"

Cailean was struggling to keep up. "Lass, who are ye? And who is this Lir?"

"The one who brought me here. She said she was going to being me to Barra but never mentioned anything about bringing me through time. Oh, Elise will never let me live this one down!"

Her words made no sense at all. Had she hit her head on a rock when she fell into the water?

He tried a different approach. "I'm Cailean MacNeil, laird of this island. What is yer name?"

This seemed to calm her a little. She blinked at him. "I'm Rose. Rose MacFinnan."

He started in surprise. MacFinnan. He'd not heard that name in a long time. There had been no MacFinnans in the Kingdom of the Isles in centuries, but the name had taken on something of a legendary status. The magic that was said to protect the Isles had been created by MacFinnan spellweavers.

And then something else registered. Lir. Where had he heard that name before?

"How did ye get here?" he said, looking around warily. "I canna see any ship."

"I didn't come by ship. Or by air. Lir brought me. From the twenty-first century. She said you needed my help."

Cailean stepped back. He felt suddenly as if the sand he was standing on was shifting beneath his feet. Lir. *Now* he recognized the name. She was said to be a goddess of the sea and once the patron goddess of the Isles. And she'd brought this woman from the *future*?

Rose MacFinnan. The goddess Lir. Everything slotted into place.

"You're a MacFinnan spellweaver," he breathed.

"That's right," she said, smiling wryly as she looked down at herself. "And what I want right now is to weave a spell that will dry my clothes. Unfortunately, I don't know any clothes-drying spells. Not high on my ancestors' lists of priorities, no doubt."

Cailean did not reply. His thoughts were spinning.

A MacFinnan spellweaver.

Had Lir heard his plea? Had She brought this woman here to help them?

He hardened his heart. No. He had *not* asked Lir for help, nor did he want it. He and his people would find a way through this without the intervention of gods or spellweavers. He didn't trust any of them. Where had the MacFinnan spellweavers been when the sickness started? Where had they been when children and oldsters fell ill?

Where were they when Mary died?

Back then he had prayed, given offerings, done everything he could think of to get someone, anyone, to intercede and save his wife. They had not. So why should he accept their help now? He knew all too well that those with power always wanted something in return for their aid. What did this spellweaver expect from him?

A sudden shout rang out from the dunes above. "My laird! Was that really who I think it was?"

The voice was laced with excitement and as Cailean turned, he saw Maggie hurrying towards them. She was sprightly for her age and held up her skirts on one side like a girl as she skidded down the dunes and puffed right up to them.

"I felt it!" she said, her eyes alight with excitement as they fixed first on Rose and then on him. "A surge of... something. Then when I looked out of the window, I saw Her standing on the beach. Was it really Her? Was it Lir? Has she come to save us?"

Cailean scowled. "No. But she brought us a visitor."

"Hi," Rose said, holding out her hand. "I'm Rose MacFinnan. A pleasure to meet you."

Maggie's eyes widened as she took Rose's hand in both of hers. "MacFinnan? Did ye say MacFinnan? As in MacFinnan spellweaver?"

"That's the one."

"And Lir brought ye here?"

"She did." Rose smiled wryly. "And then promptly disappeared on me. Cailean here saved me. I would have drowned without him coming to rescue me. Not exactly how I planned my arrival."

Maggie's mouth formed a surprised little O. "Lir be praised!" she cried. "And ye too, my laird! Ye have brought a MacFinnan spellweaver to save us!"

"I have done no such thing," Cailean snapped. "And she isnae staying. She's going right back where she—"

Ignoring him completely, Maggie linked her arm through Rose's and led her along the dunes and onto the path to the keep, keeping up a steady stream of dialog as she went.

Cailean glared after them. Why did he feel like those sands were shifting beneath his feet again? With an annoyed grunt, he strode after the two women, catching them up in a few strides.

"Wait," he snapped. "I didnae give permission—"

"Maggie!" somebody shouted. "Is it true? Was it her?"

A crowd had gathered at the base of the hill, clearly alerted by Maggie on her way down to the beach, and now they swarmed around the three of them, all eager to get a glimpse of Rose.

"Aye!" Maggie replied. "It was Lir! She and the laird have brought a MacFinnan spellweaver to save us!"

"Bless ye, laird!" someone shouted.

"We never doubted ye!" shouted another.

Cailean ground his teeth. He wanted to tell them all that this was nothing to do with him, that they should not be putting their faith in something so nebulous. But they wouldn't listen. And could he blame them? Suddenly, they had hope. Suddenly, they had something to believe in.

It was more than he'd been able to give them over these last few months.

He glanced at Rose. She'd gone very pale, her eyes wide, as she took in the crowd. She didn't look like some all-powerful spellweaver sent by a goddess. She looked like a woman out of her time, frightened and bewildered by all the attention.

An unexpected wave of protectiveness welled up inside him. He stepped closer to her side and bellowed, "Out of the way! Back, all of ye!"

They obeyed his command, making room on the path so that

he, Rose, and Maggie could walk unhindered.

"Thanks," Rose muttered from the side of her mouth. "That was a bit... intense."

"Aye," Cailean replied. "My apologies. They are excited, that's all. MacFinnan spellweavers are something of a legend in these parts."

Rose raised an eyebrow. "No pressure then. I don't even know what's going on here, let alone whether I'll be able to help."

"Oh, ye will, my dear," Maggie said from Rose's other side. "Lir wouldnae have brought ye here otherwise."

She spoke with total confidence, her faith in Lir unshakable. Cailean envied Maggie's faith. It had been a long time since he'd believed in anything.

As they walked up the winding path that led through the village and up to the gates of Dun Mallach, villagers came out of their houses to stare. Rose smiled and waved at them but most didn't return the gesture, too awed by the prospect of a MacFinnan spellweaver in their midst.

Finally, they reached the castle gates and the guards stepped aside to let them through. Cailean indicated for the gates to be shut behind them, keeping the crowd out. Maggie excused herself to go and check on Drew and, no doubt, to gossip to everyone in the castle about Rose's arrival.

"Wow," Rose muttered, craning her head back to look up at the keep. "This really is a castle. A real, proper castle."

"Aye," Cailean replied, feeling a flush of pride despite himself. "This is the seat of Clan MacNeil. Welcome to Dun Mallach."

⇶⫷

THIS WAS ALL happening *way* too fast. Less than half an hour ago she had been making a cup of coffee in her kitchen and thinking about her divorce. Now, she'd met a goddess, traveled back in time, fallen into the sea to be saved by a strapping Highlander, had a crowd of people gawping at her like she was a fairground attraction, and now, to top it all, she was in a castle. A real, medieval castle complete with battlements and guards on the walls. It was too much.

"I need to sit down," she muttered, folding her legs and lowering herself to the cobbles.

A heavy hand settled on her shoulder and Rose jumped, looking up to find Cailean standing over her.

"Are ye well, lass?" he rumbled. "Do ye need to see a healer?"

She snorted. "That would look good wouldn't it? The healer needing to see a healer the minute she arrives? No, I'm fine. Just a little… disorientated."

That was as understatement. She felt like she'd landed on another planet. Why had she listened to Lir?

"Aye," Cailean muttered, scrubbing a hand through his thick, dark hair. "Ye aren't the only one."

Rose studied him. He looked to be in his thirties, and his chest was broad and well-muscled, as though he liked to work out. Her mouth went a little dry and she forced her gaze to his face. His shoulder-length hair was dripping water down his shoulders and when it was dry, she guessed it would be a rich shade of brown. And his eyes… they were deep and dark beneath heavy brows. Right now they were full of wary suspicion as he watched her.

Rose swallowed. She got the impression this man was not someone you wanted as an enemy.

"You act as though you didn't know I was coming."

"I did not. The first I knew was when I saw ye fall off the rock."

Rose frowned. "But you're the laird, right? Aren't you the one who asked Lir for my help?"

His expression darkened, something like anger flashing in his dark eyes. "I wouldnae ask Lir—or any of the gods for anything. Not if my life depended on it."

She suddenly remembered what the goddess had said to her. *He willnae accept my help. Perhaps he will accept yers.*

Was Cailean MacNeil the person she'd been referring to?

She opened her mouth to speak but her words were drowned out by the sudden sound of excited yapping and a shout of, "Papa!"

She turned her head just as a young girl and a black-and-white dog came zooming across the courtyard and skidded to a halt in front of her and Cailean. The girl looked to be around nine years old and had bits of hay sticking out her hair and rips in her dress.

"Catriona," Cailean said in a low voice. "Ye are supposed to be at yer lessons."

"I was!" the girl replied, looking between Rose and her father. "But then Maggie came in and said we had a visitor and Sister Beatrice said I could come look and... and... and..." She trailed off, a little breathless. "Is it true?" she asked excitedly. "Are ye really a sorceress? Have ye really come to save us?"

"Catriona," Cailean growled. "Ye are being impolite."

"It's all right," Rose said. She turned to the girl. "Catriona, is it? I'm Rose. It's a pleasure to meet you. I don't know about 'sorceress,' but I'm here to help. I'll do whatever I can."

She didn't like making promises like that, especially before knowing the full extent of the problem, but the hope shining in the girl's eyes made her want to say something.

"I knew it!" Catriona cried, clapping her hands together. "I told Patch just this morning that something would turn up, didnae I, boy?"

"Dinna get ahead of yerself, lass," Cailean said. "Nothing's been decided."

"Have ye seen the stables yet?" Catriona said. "Or the kennels? Or the pond? How about the kitchens? Cook makes the best oat cakes ye've ever tasted!"

Rose laughed, holding up her hands. "Whoa! No, I haven't seen any of that. I've only just arrived."

"Then Papa and I will show ye around! Willnae we, Papa?"

"Not yet, we willnae. Our guest is wet and cold and no doubt tired from her journey. Perhaps she might like to change and rest first?"

Rose would indeed like to change first, but Catriona had other ideas. "But there's no time!" she cried, taking Rose's arm. "Sister Beatrice is already looking for me. Dinna make me go back to Latin today, Papa, please!"

The pained outrage on the girl's face was enough to make Rose laugh. "We couldn't have that, could we? I think a tour is just what the doctor ordered."

Catriona beamed, stuck her arm through Rose's, and led her off, a frowning Cailean and a capering Patch following close behind.

Rose was led through the big doors into the main keep where she found an echoing entrance hall just beyond, decorated with hangings in the same tartan color that made up Cailean's plaid and that of many of the people she'd spotted so far. Beyond this, a long corridor led deeper into the castle and she could hear the sounds of a busy household: people talking, dogs barking, the chink of pots and crockery.

"This way!" Catriona said brightly.

Rose was given a whistle-stop tour of the keep, then the kennels, the stables, the storehouses, and the kitchen, which was a large building separated from the rest of the keep to reduce the risk of fire.

Rose took it all in as best she could but the more she saw of the place, the more she felt like she'd stepped into a dream. It was so far removed from everything she was used to she kept thinking she would wake up in a moment and find it was all a dream.

But everything felt all too real. The smell of baking bread that tingled her nostrils. The weight of Catriona's arm through hers. The glowering presence of Cailean behind. The sound of the sea crashing against the shore in the distance.

Oh, yes, it felt all too real all right.

They were just crossing the courtyard, heading back to the

main keep when a stern voice rang out behind them.

"Catriona MacNeil, stop right there!"

Catriona froze, wincing as though a lash had struck her across the back. Rose turned to see a formidable-looking woman in a nun's habit striding across the courtyard towards them.

"I've been looking everywhere for ye!" the woman snapped. "I said ye could go for a few moments to greet yer father and his guest. I did *not* say ye could be gone for over an hour!"

"Sorry, Sister Beatrice," Catriona said, looking sheepish. "I... um... lost track of time."

"Lost track of time, my eye!"

"It's my fault," Cailean said, stepping smoothing up to his daughter's side. "I said she could give our new guest a tour."

"Humph." The nun put her hands on her hips and glared up at Cailean, not in the least intimidated by the man's size. "Be that as it may, my lord, how am I supposed to teach her to be a lady with constant interruptions? I have a hard enough task as it is!" She took a deep breath and turned to Rose. "But I'm forgetting my manners. Ye must be Rose. I'm Sister Beatrice. Welcome to Dun Mallach. Now, if ye will excuse us, my unruly pupil and I have Latin verbs to catch up on. Catriona, this way."

Catriona shot Rose and her father a pleading look as Sister Beatrice took her by the arm and led her away, Patch dancing along at the girl's heels.

Rose watched them go and blew out a breath. "Phew. Please remind me never to get on *her* bad side."

Cailean snorted. "If ye figure that one out, please let me know. Seems I'm *always* on Sister Beatrice's bad side."

Rose raised an eyebrow. "You? With your sunny disposition and charm? Never."

He scowled but she thought she detected amusement in his dark eyes. "I get the feeling ye are making fun of me, lass."

She smiled sweetly. "Wouldn't dream of it." She took a deep breath and let it out slowly before straightening her shoulders. "Now, shall we start at the beginning? Why don't you tell me why a goddess thinks I might be able to help you?"

Chapter Four

*Y*OU CAN'T, CAILEAN almost said.

The words danced on the edge of his tongue, the all too familiar unease with anything mystical welling up in him, but he bit back the words.

Rose watched him steadily, awaiting his response. She had a disconcerting gaze—clear and direct as though she could see right into his soul.

He blew out a breath. "There is a sickness on Barra, one that is afflicting my people badly. We have tried everything, every healing technique my people know of but naught seems to make a difference."

As he spoke, the fear he usually kept so tightly controlled bloomed in his gut like a poisonous flower. What if it could not be stopped? What if this were a curse from the old gods as Maggie claimed or a punishment from the new one as Beatrice believed? What if there was nothing any of them—not even a MacFinnan spellweaver—could do?

Rose rested her hand on his forearm. Her touch was warm and soft and sent a strange little tingle up his arm.

"What are the symptoms of this sickness?"

He cleared his throat, resisting the urge to step away, break the contact. He wasn't used to being touched. "Fever to begin with, then delirium, seizures, and finally death."

Her eyes narrowed and she cocked her head in thought. "Has it ever afflicted the island before?"

"Not in my lifetime although there are accounts of such things in the past. Do ye know what it is?"

She shook her head. "Not without examining the patients, although I've treated things before that sound similar."

She sounded so calm. So assured. Could she really help them? He felt a strange sensation uncurl in his chest and it took him a moment to realize what it was.

Hope.

He stepped back, wiping the back of his hand across his forehead. "Aye, well, before ye do anything, getting into dry clothes is probably in order."

She laughed softly, a light sound like spring rain on a pond. "Yeah, I'm not sure the drowned-rat look will catch on."

It looked just fine on her in Cailean's opinion. Her damp clothes, though odd, clung to her in all the right places.

He coughed. "Come with me."

He turned and led her through the doors into the main hall of the keep. It was quiet at this time of day, but come evening it would be boisterous and full to the rafters—even more so than usual he suspected as everyone would want to get a look at their unexpected guest.

He called over a maid. "Mable, escort Rose up to one of the guest rooms and see she has everything she needs. When ye are ready, come find me and I will take ye to the infirmary," he added to Rose.

She nodded. "I will." She hesitated for a moment and then said, "Thank you, by the way."

"For what?"

"Rescuing me."

He flashed an amused smile. "I wasnae about to let harm come to a MacFinnan spellweaver, was I? Ye might have turned me into a toad."

She waggled her fingers. "If you don't behave, I still might."

He found himself grinning despite himself. Rose MacFinnan had an easy-going, down-to-earth way about her that was impossible to dislike. She was, he realized, nothing like what he expected. Warm, funny, and bonny to boot.

"I'll leave ye to it."

He turned and strode away. It had been a most strange day. He needed to work off his pent-up energy. He took the steps down to the courtyard two at a time and strode towards the armory, shouting for some of his men to attend him.

He felt the need to swing a weapon.

ROSE SOON REALIZED that Dun Mallach was a maze. She'd followed Mable up two flights of steps, through several long corridors and numerous small antechambers, and she no longer had any idea where she was.

The place was large and drafty, but scrupulously clean, with tapestries on the walls and runners along the floors taking away some of the austereness of the stonework. It looked, Rose thought as she trailed along behind Mable, like something straight out of a Hollywood movie set.

Mable finally stopped outside a large, shiny wooden door. "Here we are," she said, giving a curtsey. "The best guest room in the castle, Lady MacFinnan." She clasped her hands in front of her and stared at the floor, clearly nervous.

Rose stifled a sigh. Was this how things were going to be? Didn't these people realize that she was just plain old Rose MacFinnan, a thirty-something divorcee who lived alone, ate microwave dinners, and loved detective movies?

"There's no need to curtsey," she said Mable. "And please call me Rose. Lady MacFinnan makes me sound like some old spinster."

Mable looked up and managed a small, shy smile. The girl

looked to be around seventeen or eighteen and had flaming red hair tied back with a scarf. "As ye wish... Rose."

She opened the door and Rose followed her into what could only be described as an apartment. It was not a room but a suite of rooms, decked out with dark wooden furniture and upholstered in the same-colored plaid that Cailean wore.

"Oh my," Rose said, looking around at the opulent sitting room. Beyond, she spied a bedroom, and a smaller room with an iron tub which she guessed must be the bathroom. "This is gorgeous. Tell me you have a coffee maker and it will be perfect."

"A what?"

Rose waved her hand. "Never mind."

Mable crossed to a large trunk. Flipping open the lid, she began taking out various items of clothing, holding them up, and glancing at Rose, and then either putting them back or laying them on a chair in response to a set of criteria she didn't bother to explain.

"Would ye like me to help ye dress?" she asked when she was finished.

Rose eyed the clothes Mable had picked out. There was a long, royal-blue velvet dress, a corset to go underneath, several petticoats, and some undergarments made of linen.

Oh, hell. Was she really expected to wear that? Why hadn't she insisted she go back to her house and pack some things before following Lir? She *really* had not thought this trip through.

"Um... I think you'd better," she replied. "Otherwise I'll be here until midnight."

She peeled off her sodden clothes and dropped them into a basket by the door then dried herself with a large cloth that Mable handed her, before gingerly beginning to don the clothes provided. They smelled of lavender and, to her surprise, fit Rose perfectly. Mable clearly had a good eye for such things.

"You seem to know what you're doing," Rose observed as she held up her arms to allow Mable to tie up the bodice of the dress.

"Aye, my mother was maid to Lady Mary, the laird's wife, and I was in training to take her place."

"Lady Mary? I've not met her yet."

Mable didn't answer for a moment but then said quietly, "I'm afraid Lady Mary passed. Four winters ago."

Rose put her hand over her mouth. "Mable, I'm sorry. That was insensitive of me."

Cailean had lost his *wife*? Catriona had lost her *mother*? And here she was, griping about having to wear unfamiliar clothes.

A sudden wave of compassion went through her. What must it be like for Cailean trying to raise a daughter alone as well as lead his people? No wonder he was a little surly.

Finally, Rose finished dressing and did a little twirl, determined to lighten the mood. "Well? How do I look?"

There were no mirrors in the room, for which she was grateful. She suspected she looked ridiculous. Dresses were *not* her thing. They were impractical and just got in the way. Most of the time she could be found in a flannel shirt and a pair of dungarees.

"Beautiful, my lady... um... Rose," Mable replied.

Rose grinned. "Flattery will get you everywhere." She clapped her hands together. "Right. I'd better go and find Cailean."

"I'll show ye."

Together, the two women left the room and made their way back through the keep. Mable said not a word the whole time and Rose was content to look around as they went, taking everything in. It wasn't every day you found yourself in a real Scottish castle.

They stepped outside and Rose saw that the clouds had cleared a little, letting through the late afternoon sun. The breeze was blowing from inland, bringing with it the scent of late flowers and also something colder—the smell of snow from up in the mountains, perhaps.

Autumn had just been taking hold of the landscape when she'd left home but here, at this more northerly latitude, it had already begun to bite, and from here she could see that the hills beyond the keep were turning to golds and browns. Winter would not be far behind, and the last thing these people needed was a sickness sweeping through their population right when they should be gathering in the harvest and laying down stores to see them through that winter.

From somewhere nearby she heard a rhythmic clack-clack-clack, like the sound of wood striking wood. It was towards this sound that Mable led her.

They passed through a gate and came out beyond the walls, into a wide square of flattened grass with wooden seats along one side, although nobody was sitting in them right now. A large rack stood at one end full of weapons: spears, swords, bows, and horrible-looking spiky things that Rose had no name for.

The clacking sound was louder here and she tore her gaze away from the weapons rack to find two men to her left maybe twenty paces away. They were both stripped to the waist and were fighting with staffs—the source of the noise. She didn't recognize one of the men—he was older, with black hair turning to silver—but the other she most definitely recognized.

Cailean hadn't noticed her and Mable standing there, his attention fixed wholly on his opponent. He'd tied his hair back with a leather band and his smooth features were set in a fierce scowl of concentration as he hit and parried and danced, moving as lightly as a ballet dancer, despite his size. And *nobody* should be allowed to have a body that fine, all smooth skin and sculpted muscle. Rose found herself staring and pointedly looked away.

Cailean's opponent suddenly noticed the two women standing there. He backed away and hoisted his staff to rest on his shoulder, nodding towards her and Mable. Cailean turned. His gaze met hers across the distance and damn her if she didn't suddenly feel a tingle run all the way down her spine.

Cailean tossed his staff to the other man. "Good session, Brock."

"Was it?" Brock replied, catching Cailean's staff. "Yer footwork is slow today, my laird. And yer balance could do with some work."

Cailean smiled wryly. "Brock, according to ye, my balance could *always* do with some work."

"Just so. I'll expect ye back here in the morning for another session."

Cailean inclined his head. "As ye say, weapons master."

Brock grunted, hoisted both staffs across his shoulders, and walked off, nodding to Rose and Mable as he walked by. Cailean picked up his shirt from where he'd dropped it, pulled it over his head, and then walked over to them.

"Rose," Cailean greeted them stiffly. "Mable."

Mable dropped a curtsey. "My lord. Lady Rose asked to see ye."

His deep gaze moved to Rose. "My thanks, Mable. That will be all."

The girl curtseyed again and hurried away, leaving Rose alone with Cailean. Silence descended and Rose cast around for something to say.

They ended up speaking at exactly the same time.

"Thank you for lending me the clothes."

"Ye are happy with yer room?"

"Ye are welcome."

"It's very nice. Thanks."

Silence descended again. Rose shifted her feet uncomfortably.

"Um… you said you'd show me the infirmary?" she prompted.

He blinked. "What? Oh, aye, I did. This way then."

They did not turn back towards the castle but took a path that skirted the outside of the training square and then across a small stream via a wooden bridge onto a flat area beyond that was bordered by stunted trees that had clearly been battered by the wind.

Within the protection of these trees, and therefore sheltered from the wind a little, sat a long gray building with a thatched roof. Smoke rose from a chimney at one end.

"My father built the infirmary away from the main keep," Cailean explained as they walked up to the door. "To limit the spread of disease."

Rose nodded, approving of such precautions. "Is the sickness infectious?"

"Not as far as we can tell. That is one of the strange things about it. There seems to be no rhyme nor reason to who gets it and who doesnae. There have been many instances where one family member falls ill but nobody else in the household does."

Rose digested this in silence, filing it away with the rest of the information she'd gleaned so far.

Cailean pushed the door open. Beyond, Rose found herself in a dim, cool room filled with the scent of lavender and comfrey from bunches that hung from the rafters. Even so, it was not enough to hide the stench of sickness and it smacked into Rose like a hammer blow.

There were six beds in here but only one was occupied. Two women were standing over the bed and Rose recognized Maggie, the woman who'd met her on the beach, and Sister Beatrice in her white nun's habit.

They appeared to be arguing, both gesticulating wildly, but they straightened as they heard the door open.

Maggie's face lit up when she spotted them. "Rose! My laird! Welcome, welcome. Come to see the patient?"

"Aye," Cailean said, walking over to the bed and looking down at the figure lying in it. "Any change?"

"None," Sister Beatrice said. She glanced at Rose, her welcome a little cooler than Maggie's had been. "I've been saying prayers for him."

Maggie snorted. "And a lot of good that has done him! Ye can cease yer prattling now, sister; we have a MacFinnan spellweaver to fix things."

Maggie gestured for Rose to approach. Rose walked over to stand next to the bed. Maggie and Beatrice hovered on the other side, watching her. One with excitement, one with suspicion.

Rose pushed their presence out of her mind and concentrated on her patient. A man was lying on his back, unconscious. He was big-boned and must have once been hale and vigorous, but now he looked as though he was being eaten alive. His skin was so sallow that it looked like melted wax draped over his skull and his breathing rattled alarmingly.

"Can I have a chair?"

Cailean brought over a stool and Rose lowered herself into it.

"What's his name?"

"Drew," Cailean replied. "Drew MacRae, castellan of Dun Mallach."

Rose pulled back the sheet. Taking Drew's hand in hers, she gently spoke. "Drew? My name is Rose and I'm here to help you. Can you hear me?"

There was no response. She looked at Maggie and Beatrice. "How long has he been unconscious?"

"On and off for days now," Maggie replied. "Sometimes he wakes up but when he does, he doesnae make any sense. Ranting and raving about evil spirits and the like."

"What treatments have you tried?"

"Everything," answered Sister Beatrice. "Willow bark to bring down his fever. Garlic and echinacea to fight infection. A hundred other things besides. You name it, we've tried it. But nothing seems to work. If Drew's sickness follows the same path as the rest, he'll soon start having seizures, and then there will be naught anyone can do."

Rose nodded. "I'll need some things before I get started. Maggie, Beatrice, could you bring me some warm honey? And perhaps an infusion of comfrey? Cailean, I'll need fresh bandages and boiling water."

The three of them left and Rose breathed out slowly after they'd gone. The truth was, she didn't need any of the things she'd listed but she didn't need them hanging around watching either. What she needed was peace and space and a chance to figure out what was wrong with Drew MacRae.

She placed her hand on the man's forehead. It was hot to the touch and as dry as a bone. Not a good sign. She placed her hand against his chest, feeling his heartbeat. It was weak and stuttering.

Damn. She didn't have much time.

Closing her eyes, she slowed her breathing, taking deep, long breaths through her nose, letting them out through her mouth. Slowly, she began to slip into that meditative, almost trance-like state she did when accessing her power. Inch by slow inch, she became aware of the thrum of her power inside her, running through her body like lines of golden thread. She tapped into one of these threads and sent a tendril of it spiraling into Drew's body. She felt the heat in him immediately, burning through his tissues, scouring him from the inside. He was filled with infection and if that infection reached his brain and the seizures started, she knew there would be nothing she could do for him.

The first thing to do was to break his fever and draw the heat out of him so his immune system could start its work. She opened her eyes and looked around. A bowl of water sat on the floor by Drew's bed with several flannels next to it. Dipping her finger in, Rose found the water to be ice cold. Perfect.

She lifted the bowl into her lap, keeping her right hand submerged in the water. She placed her left palm on the hot skin above Drew's chest. Letting her eyes slide closed, she accessed her power once more, mentally weaving a spell designed to drain the heat from Drew's body. She felt a tingle in the palm of her left hand, the one pressed to Drew's chest, and her skin began to heat. Focusing her will, she drew the heat out of Drew's body, moving it up her arm, across her shoulders, then down her right arm, using her own body as a conduit. Finally, the heat was expelled through the fingers of her right hand and out into the bowl of cold water.

The door opened behind her and she heard a gasp, but she didn't allow her concentration to waver. Bit by slow bit, the heat in Drew's body began to lessen and the temperature of the water to increase. It was no longer cold now but tepid, like a bath left to cool for too long. But, she didn't stop. Slowly, carefully, she drew the heat, away from his organs, out of his muscles, cleared it from his blood.

Only when the water was so hot it was in danger of scalding her skin did she stop. She removed her hands, broke her contact with Drew's body, and brought her awareness back into her own. Exhaustion swept through her and she slumped forward, the bowl tumbling from her lap to shatter on the flagstone floor. Scalding water splashed across the stone, sending up a gout of steam.

She began to topple off the stool but strong hands caught her before she could hit the floor and she found herself looking into Cailean's dark eyes.

"Easy, lass," he rumbled.

"It's all right," she said, her voice hoarse. "I'm okay."

"Nay, ye are not. Ye can barely hold yer head up."

All right, so she wasn't exactly okay, but it wasn't anything she wasn't used to. She took several deep breaths then waved a hand. "Don't worry. This is normal. It will pass in a minute."

Cailean said nothing but neither did he release her. Her vision swam and she had to admit to herself that his hands on her shoulders were the only thing keeping upright.

After a moment, her vision steadied enough for her to be able to raise her head. Maggie and Beatrice were standing by the door holding the supplies she'd sent them to fetch, staring at her with awestruck expressions.

She ignored them. Instead, she focused her attention on her patient. A thin sheen of perspiration now covered Drew's body and Rose allowed herself a tiny flush of satisfaction. Good. That was good. Sweating indicated that the heat trapped inside Drew's body was now escaping, his temperature was coming down, and the infection beginning to lose its hold.

"Is he cured?" Maggie asked.

"No," Rose replied. "Not quite yet." She took a deep breath and straightened on the stool, pushing away from Cailean's support. "Stage one complete. Now time for stage two."

Cailean stepped back a pace but did not retreat. He was watching her intently, concern etched on his handsome features. "Stage two?"

She nodded. "The hard part. I might lose consciousness. If I do, can you make sure I don't bang my head?"

Cailean's expression tightened. "I willnae let any harm come to ye, lass. I swear it."

Rose met his dark gaze. She suspected he did not make such promises lightly, this laird of Barra.

Taking a breath, she laid a hand on Drew's forehead again. This time, as she sent her awareness spiraling down into his body, she wasn't looking for anything wrong. This time, she was searching for something *right*. His own immune system. Like a cable jump-starting a car engine, she sent a burst of energy through his system, jolting it into action. Now it would take over the fight, locating the infection within his body and fighting it off. After this was complete, she poured energy into him, shoring up his body's natural defenses and giving it the strength it needed to heal.

Slowly, Drew began to respond. His lungs begin to expand and contract more fully. His blood began to flow more freely. His heart, so weak to begin with, found a steadier rhythm.

Finally, Rose slowly withdrew her power and blinked her eyes open. She was surprised to find herself slumped against a hard, warm body. The body smelled of leather and sky and wind and there were arms around her too, strong as tree roots.

Cailean. She was slumped against Cailean, her forehead resting on his shoulder. Had she passed out? Sometimes she became so engrossed in a healing that she lost track of herself. Usually Elise or Jenna were there to pull her back. This time, it seemed, it had been Cailean MacNeil.

She breathed deeply, inhaling the scent of him, and then slowly lifted her head. His face was only inches from hers, dark eyes intense as he studied her.

"How... how..." She moved her jaw a few times, working up enough saliva to speak. "How long was I out?"

"Only a few minutes, lass," Cailean replied, his voice rumbling in his chest. "Might I suggest a sturdier perch next time? One where ye aren't so likely to fall and crack yer bonce?"

"Noted," she said with a weak smile.

With some effort, she got her hands against Cailean's hard chest and used it to lever herself up to a sitting position. The room swayed and for a second she thought she might pass out again. But it slowly passed and she was able to concentrate on her patient.

Drew MacRae was awake. He still looked weak and a little befuddled, but there was already more color in his cheeks and the look of death had retreated from his features.

Maggie and Beatrice were busy fussing around him like mother hens, mopping his brow and getting him to drink some water.

"I canna believe it," Maggie said, her awestruck gaze flicking to Rose. "Ye did it. Ye really did it."

Rose shook her head. "That remains to be seen. I've kick-started his own healing processes, that's all. We'll need to keep a close eye on him the next few days to make sure there's no relapse."

Sister Beatrice nodded. She looked as wide-eyed as her sister. "We will, have no fear of that. Thank the Lord for sending ye to us, my dear."

"What...?" Drew slurred, his voice as dry and whispery as burned parchment. "What happened?" His eyes rolled in his head, taking in the people clustered around him.

Cailean moved to stand over the bed. "Ye have been ill, my old friend," he said gently. "But ye are on the mend now. All will be well."

"Ill?" Drew replied, his voice a little stronger. "I canna be ill! Who will arrange the castle rota? And make sure the guards get paid?"

A faint smile curled Cailean's lips. "Dinna fash, man. Yer duties are being attended to. Did ye really think we would do aught else after the service ye've done this clan?"

Drew ran his tongue around his cracked lips. "When can I go home?"

"When we say ye can," Beatrice said sternly. "And not a moment before."

Drew turned a pleading look on Cailean. "Dinna leave me with these two, my lord. They are terrifying."

Cailean snorted. "Ye must be feeling better if ye are making jokes."

"Who said I was joking?"

Rose levered herself up from the stool. "I'll be back to check on you later," she said to Drew. "Try to get some sleep."

Drew's hand snaked out from beneath the sheet and found hers. His grip was weak but insistent. "It was ye, wasnae it?" he whispered. "I heard yer voice. Ye were calling me from the darkness! Ye brought me back!"

Rose smiled. "I'm just glad I could help. Rest now. I'll see you later."

She patted him on the shoulder and turned to leave. She stumbled, her legs weaker than she expected, but Cailean caught her arm and steadied her.

"Easy, lass. We dinna want to have to put ye in the bed next to Drew's, do we?"

"Oh, I don't know," she said with a smile. "It might be nice lying in bed and having someone look after me."

He raised an eyebrow. "Trust me, ye do *not* want Maggie and Beatrice looking after ye."

"We heard that!" Maggie snapped.

Cailean winced. "Come, let's make our escape while we can."

He led Rose out into the cool afternoon. The wind had changed direction again, this time blowing from the sea, and the salt-laden breeze was invigorating. Rose took a deep breath through her nostrils and allowed it to settle all the way down into her lungs.

Her exhaustion dissipated just a little and she turned to face seaward, squinting against the wind, and gazed out over the vast expanse of ocean to the horizon. What lay beyond that horizon? she wondered. What new experiences and adventures awaited someone with the courage to look? She had never had that sort of courage. Her life had revolved around her small community, her husband, her sister and niece, her patients. That was it. She'd never wanted more.

But now look at her. She was many miles and many years from home, surrounded by people she didn't know. She tried not to think about it. If she did, she might pass out again.

"I'll need to see Drew again first thing in the morning," she told Cailean. "And I'd like to sit down with Maggie and Beatrice and make some notes on what they've found so far."

"Aye. Tomorrow." He glanced at where the sun was dipping towards the horizon. "The evening meal will be served soon. I can have it brought up to yer room if ye would like some privacy. Or ye can join us in the great hall and meet my people if ye'd prefer. But I warn ye, ye will likely be stared at like some wonder at a fair. Anyone would think they've never met a woman from the future before."

Rose snorted. "The coward in me would like nothing more than to hide in my room all night. But if I did that, my sister would never let me live it down. I think I'd quite like to meet the rest of your people."

"Ye would? Well, dinna say I didnae warn ye." His expression was mock-serious, his eyes flashing with humor. She found she quite liked this more playful side to him.

"I'll take my chances."

"This way then."

Together, they set off back to the keep.

Chapter Five

CAILEAN'S INSTINCT HAD proven to be correct when he'd thought the great hall would be busy tonight. In fact, *busy* was not the word. *Packed to the rafters* would be a more apt description.

Word of the arrival of a MacFinnan spellweaver had spread across the island like wildfire and everyone it seemed, from toothless old grannies to rough-mannered sheep farmers, suddenly had business in Dun Mallach.

Every bench was full, every table laden with food, and the great hall echoed with the clamor of excited chatter, good-natured banter, and the occasional argument. He had not seen the great hall so busy in years, nor his people so full of excitement.

He glanced to his left where the source of that excitement was sitting. Rose MacFinnan was listening patiently as Catriona kept up an endless stream of chatter about things that a nine-year-old found extremely important. The dressmaker's cat was about to have kittens. A lad down in the village had given her a bouquet of daisies. The hilarity when Malcolm Tanner had fallen in the river and had to be rescued by his da.

Rose listened to it with infinite patience, exclaiming in all the right places and sharing Catriona's outrage that Malcolm Tanner had accused *her* of pushing him in the river. Cailean suspected there might be a bit of truth in that.

Catriona had taken to Rose immediately, seeming not the least intimidated by the fact that she was a terrifying MacFinnan spellweaver out of legend.

The same could not be said of his people. Just as he'd warned her, they'd gawped when he'd introduced her and even now covert glances kept being aimed in her direction. If she was bothered by it all, she didn't let it show.

A small black nose suddenly appeared from beneath the table and Patch darted out, snaffled a bit of chicken that Catriona held out for him, then darted back under the table.

"Catriona," Cailean said, turning a stern gaze on his daughter. "What have I told ye about feeding that dog at the table?"

She had the decency to look abashed. "I tried to leave him in my room, Da, but he kept crying and scratching at the door."

"That's because ye are treating him like a bairn and not a dog. Why canna he live in the kennels like all the other hounds?"

Catriona looked mortified. "Because he wouldnae like it! He'd cry all night! If ye make Patch sleep in the kennels, then so will I!"

Cailean rolled his eyes. She did have a flair for the dramatic. "He's a *dog*. He would probably love it in the kennels with his own kind."

But Catriona was having none of it. She turned to Rose. "Tell him, Lady Rose! Ye know that Patch would hate sleeping in the kennels, dinna ye?"

Rose held up her hands. "Whoa! Leave me out of this one. I'm not stupid enough to get involved in an argument between father and daughter. Although…"

She reached down and scratched Patch's ears and the pup went up onto his hind legs with his front paws in her lap, tongue lolling out of his mouth in ecstasy. "He might get bullied by the older dogs, and I'm sure he would miss Catriona."

Catriona turned to face Cailean with a smug expression of triumph on her face, as though the word of a MacFinnan spellweaver settled the argument.

Oh, wonderful. Just what he needed. Winning an argument with his daughter was hard enough; it would be doubly hard now she had an unexpected ally.

"We'll discuss this another time," he growled but Catriona only grinned, knowing she'd won this battle.

He sighed and took another swig of ale. For the thousandth time, he wished Mary was still here. He missed her with an ache that never seemed to lessen, no matter the time that passed. She would have known how to handle Catriona's demands. Mary had always been better at standing up to her than he had and had teased him mercilessly at how easily their daughter was able to twist him around her little finger.

Over on the left side of the hall, his warriors were crowded around their table, drinking and singing and bantering the way they always did. He wished he could join them. He wished he could get blind drunk with them like he'd done when his father was still the laird and he didn't have the responsibilities he carried now. He wished that, just for an evening, he could forget the cares that hung around his neck like a mill stone and relax.

Rose suddenly yawned hugely, making Catriona giggle.

"Oops," Rose said. "I think it's time I went to bed. If I stay up any longer, I think I'll end up face-first in this pie."

Cailean waved Mable over. "Escort the lady Rose to her room, would ye?"

As Rose scraped her chair back and followed Mable out, Cailean couldn't help watching her go. Watching the way her midnight hair cascaded down her back. The way her hips moved as she walked.

"I like her," Catriona announced, breaking him from his thoughts. "She's nice." She pressed her hand against her mouth, suppressing a yawn.

"Aye," Cailean said. "Perhaps she is, but she willnae be the only one with her face in her pie if ye dinna get to bed soon. It's way past yer bed time."

"But I'm not tired, Papa," Catriona protested. Another huge yawn cracked her face, putting the lie to those words.

"Come," he said, pushing his chair back. "Bed. I'll take ye."

With a huff, Catriona hopped down from her seat, and took the hand Cailean held out to her. Ella, Catriona's maid, came forward, but Cailean waved her back and told her to stay and enjoy the feast—he would take his daughter up to bed tonight.

With Patch trotting along at their heels, they left the great hall, made their way through the keep and then up the main staircase. Catriona's feet began to drag with tiredness so he hoisted her into his arms and carried her, and for a wonder, she made no complaint.

Catriona's chambers were next to his own where he could keep a better eye on her, and as he nudged the door open, a wave of warmth hit him from the fire that burned merrily in the fireplace.

Patch jumped onto the bed, turned in a circle a few times, then settled down with his head resting on his paws. Cailean resisted the urge to order him off. Catriona would have him back on the bed the second he was out of the room, anyway.

He gently lowered Catriona onto the bed and then sat down on the end of it. "Make sure ye brush yer teeth before ye go to sleep and change into yer nightgown."

She rolled her eyes at him in an imitation of Mary that was so accurate it made his chest ache. "Papa, I *do* know. I *am* nine, ye know."

He smiled, feeling a sudden rush of love for his girl. "Aye, ye are growing up, my little lass. Ye will be an adult before I know it."

Catriona made a face. "Ugh. I hope not. Adults are so dull."

Cailean laughed. "Aye, perhaps we are." He leaned down and kissed her on the cheek. "Good night, Catriona."

"Good night, Papa."

He opened the door but then paused as Catriona said, "Papa? Is Rose going to stay?"

"Nay, sweetling," he replied, looking back at her. "She's come to help us but then she needs to go home."

"Oh." She sounded sad at that. "I'd like it if she stayed."

"Well, she canna. She's got her own family to get back to."

"What family?"

Cailean realized he had absolutely no idea. He knew next to nothing about their guest. "Enough questions," he replied. "Go to sleep. And dinna forget what I said about brushing yer teeth."

He closed the door and padded silently down the corridor towards his own room. He was tired and his muscles ached. He wanted nothing more than to fall into bed and sink into oblivion for a few hours. Yet he suspected that wouldn't be easy. He felt wrung out and on edge and his thoughts kept going round in circles. The sickness. Lir's intervention. Catriona and his people.

Rose MacFinnan.

He stopped. To his left, a corridor led down to the guest quarters. He ought to carry straight on to his own rooms, go to bed, and try to sleep. That would be the sensible thing to do.

Instead, he found himself turning on his heel, striding down the corridor into the guest quarters, and stopping in front of a large, polished door. He rapped his knuckles lightly on the wood and heard footsteps approaching.

The door pulled wide, revealing Rose standing there, blinking in surprise. Her midnight hair was a riot of dark waves falling across her shoulders and her eyes seemed big enough to drown in as she gazed up at him in surprise. She was wearing a shapeless nightdress that covered her from neck to toes but candlelight was spilling from behind her, making the nightdress seem almost transparent and casting the curves underneath into stark silhouette.

Cailean's mouth went dry. What was he doing here? Why had he come?

"I... um..."

Oh hell.

He cleared his throat and tried again. "I... um... I just came to thank ye."

"Thank me?"

"For what ye did today. For helping Drew." *For bringing hope to my people and my daughter.*

Rose shook her head. "You don't need to thank me for that. It's why I'm here, remember?"

Cailean wondered about that. Why *had* she agreed to travel into the past to help people she'd never even met? What did she get out of it? In his experience people didn't do things without some kind of reward. So what was hers? She'd asked for nothing but Cailean wasn't stupid enough to think her help would come without a cost.

"Er... was there anything else?" she asked.

Aye, he thought. *I want to know what you're doing here. I want to know who you really are and why you came. I want to know why you make me do stupid things like come to your door when I have no reason to be here.*

But all he said was, "Nay. That was all. Sleep well, Rose MacFinnan."

"Sleep well, Cailean MacNeil."

He gave a curt nod then spun and strode away. As he reached his own rooms and closed his door, he got the feeling that sleep would be a long time coming.

CASTLES, ROSE HAD decided, were noisy, drafty places and they were nowhere near as romantic as the movies painted them.

As she lay in her ridiculously big bed, weighed down by the heavy brocade covers, she desperately wanted to sleep. But sleep seemed determined to elude her. It was late. The distant sounds of the feast in the great hall had dissipated some time ago, indicating that everyone had gone to bed. Yet that didn't mean the castle had fallen quiet.

There was the tramp of feet from the guards that walked the

battlements outside. There was the barking of dogs from the kennels when some noise disturbed them. There was the stamp and whinny of horses in the stables.

And within the castle itself *everything* creaked. The floorboards. The doorframes. Her damned bed, every time she so much as breathed.

It was most annoying. Although, she reflected, staring up at the ceiling above her bed and counting the cracks in the plaster for the umpteenth time, the castle noises were probably not the real reason she couldn't sleep.

Being in a strange bed and a strange time would probably account for that.

Oh, what she wouldn't give for her own bed and her own little house right now! It wasn't much, but it was hers and was comforting in its familiarity. And what she needed most right now was *definitely* a bit of familiarity.

Instead, the strange noises, the huge bed, the opulent room only served to remind her how far from home she really was.

Had Elise noticed she was missing yet, she wondered. Unlikely. Rose had disappeared many times before, called away abruptly by some emergency or other. No, Elise was probably not be missing her at all. In fact, it was unlikely that *anybody* was missing her. Certainly not Dennis. Her ex was no doubt off enjoying his single life.

She was feeling sorry for herself, but she allowed herself to wallow in it for a moment. After everything she'd been through today, she'd bloody well earned a few moments of self-pity!

I just came to thank ye.

Cailean MacNeil's words echoed in her head. He'd looked so earnest, almost unsure of himself, as he'd stood at her door earlier. She'd been surprised in the extreme when she'd found him standing there. Surprised by his presence, yes, but also surprised by the way her stomach had fluttered at the sight of him.

Why had that happened? Ridiculous.

Ugh. She thumped the bed with her fists. These thoughts were getting her nowhere. If she had her phone with her, she'd play the meditation recordings she used when she couldn't sleep, but in her rush to do what Lir suggested, she'd even left that behind.

Finally, her eyes drifted closed, only to be startled awake again what seemed like only a moment later by a furious pounding noise. She bolted upright and looked around wildly.

"What the—?"

It took her muzzy thoughts a moment to figure out that the pounding was somebody knocking on her door. She brushed her hair back from her face and blinked bleary eyes. Dawn light streamed through the windows, showing she'd been asleep for much longer than she thought. All night, in fact.

"Lady Rose?" came Mable's voice. "Come quickly! Ye are needed!"

The alarm in the girl's tone sent an equal spike of alarm through Rose's body. She threw back the covers and threw open the door.

Mable stood outside, wringing her hands. "My apologies, my lady," she said, forgetting that Rose had asked her to drop the formality. "But the laird sent me to fetch ye. I'm to bring ye to the infirmary immediately."

"What's happened?" Rose asked, her stomach dropping like a stone. "Has someone else fallen ill?"

"I dinna know. I was only told to fetch ye."

"Right. Give me a minute. I'll get dressed."

She cursed the fiddly nature of fifteenth-century clothing as she struggled into a dress, Mable doing her best to help her. When it was done, she grabbed her shoes, ran a quick hand through her unruly hair, and dashed out of the door behind Mable.

Even though it was barely dawn, the castle corridors were busy as they hurried through the keep then out to the infirmary.

The close-growing trees meant it was still dark around the

long building and candlelight glowed from the windows. Maggie was waiting by the door.

"What is it?" Rose called as she came in sight. "What's happened?"

"It's Drew," Maggie replied. "Come quickly!"

Rose followed as Maggie pushed the door open, and as she did so, Rose made out the sounds of a scuffle and a strange, high-pitched wailing from within. Stepping inside, it took a moment for her to figure out what she was looking at. Drew was writhing and twisting on the bed while Cailean did his best to hold him down. It was Drew who was making the strange, high-pitched wailing noise.

Drew's eyes had rolled back in his head, showing just the whites, and foam crusted at the corners of his mouth. Sister Beatrice hovered nearby looking worried and there was a red welt on her temple, perhaps where she'd been struck by Drew in his thrashing.

Rose rushed over to Drew's side. "Hold him down!" she cried. "Don't let him injure himself."

"What do ye think I'm trying to do?" Cailean growled. "Dance with the man?"

Rose placed her hand on Drew's forehead. His fever was back, worse than before, and as she sent her senses questing down into his body, she felt a roiling knot of infection within him, spreading its tendrils up into his brain, causing this seizure.

His sickness had not only returned, it had spread.

Damn it! What could she do? If this continued, the infection would burn through his brain and Drew would be lost. She bit her lip, thinking furiously.

There was only one thing she could try. She called on her power and wove a powerful spell, one designed, not for healing, but for stasis. It was a last resort, designed to keep a patient alive while a better, more permanent remedy could be found. Its equivalent in modern medicine was putting someone into an induced coma and it was a spell Rose used only reluctantly. Once placed, there was no guarantee that the patient would wake up.

She wove the spell and wrapped it around Drew's brain and organs, allowing it to sink deep into his tissues. Slowly, his seizure subsided and he became still, flopping back onto the bed.

He still breathed. His heart still pumped and his blood still flowed, but everything else, including the spread of the sickness, had been incapacitated. He would not get any worse, but neither would he get any better. It was a state of suspended animation and was a temporary measure at best.

Slowly Rose withdrew her power and slumped into a chair. "You can let go now," she told Cailean. "He's asleep. He won't wake."

Cailean glanced at her and then slowly released his grip on Drew.

Rose turned to Beatrice and Maggie. "When did this start?"

"About ten minutes ago," Beatrice answered. She had gone pale, making the red welt on her forehead stand out all the more. "He was fine last night. Sitting up, talking and joking. We thought he was on the mend, but then this morning, when the laird came to check on him and I shook him awake, he began thrashing around and moaning." Her eyes found Rose's. "Is it my fault? Should I not have woken him?"

Rose shook her head. "It's not your fault, Beatrice. It's the sickness, same as before. It's back, only worse. I don't understand it. How did it take hold again so quickly? And why wasn't he able to fight it off?" These last questions were muttered to herself.

She looked over at the two healers. "I need to see your notes," she said. "Everything you have on the sickness."

"Notes? Ye mean writing?" said Maggie. She tapped her head. "I dinna hold with such things. Everything I need is in here."

Beatrice rolled her eyes at her sister. "*I* kept notes," she said in an exasperated voice. "One of the first things we were taught in the convent was scribing. I'll get them for ye."

She crossed to a cupboard and took out a thick wad of parchment tied with string which she handed over. "Although I dinna know if ye'll find aught in here that will do any good."

"Thanks," Rose said, taking the bundle. "There might be something. I'm going to go and get some air while I study these but I'll be right outside. Call me if there's any change in Drew's condition." There shouldn't be with the spell she'd placed on him but Rose didn't want to take any chances.

Beatrice nodded. "We will."

"I'll escort ye out," said Cailean. He held the door open for her and they both stepped out into the cool dawn air.

The sun was just rising above the sea, making the waves shimmer like beaten gold and promising a fine day ahead. Even so, the air held a bite that was strong enough to make her shiver.

"Here."

Cailean threw his plaid around her shoulders and she took it gratefully. "Thanks." It smelled like rain on the ocean and the wind across heather. It was a scent she was coming to associate with him.

He didn't reply. He was staring out at the sea, his eyes far away. "Is there aught that can be done?" he asked at last.

She didn't need to ask what he was referring to. She opened her mouth to give the usual reassurances, the platitudes that had become so second nature they fell from her tongue before she even thought about them. But she stopped herself. Cailean deserved better than that.

"I don't know," she said softly. She stepped up to his side and laid a hand on his arm. He startled at her touch and turned to look at her. "But I promise you this. I will do everything in my power to find out what this sickness is and to stop it. You have my word on that."

Something flashed in his eyes, something she couldn't quite place. Then, to her surprise, he placed his hand over hers. "That's all anyone can ask of ye, lass."

In his eyes she saw a bone-deep weariness and was reminded again of the weight he carried—the weight of an entire clan. She sometimes found it exhausting trying to look after her little family and there were only the three of them—herself, Elise, and Jenna—so how much more taxing must it be to have the weight of an entire people on your shoulders?

Cailean's shoulders were broad, true, but nobody should have to bear the weight of such responsibility alone.

After a moment, he stepped aside. "I will leave ye to yer work," he said. "Send word if ye need aught."

She nodded and watched as he strode away. She sighed, blowing out a great breath. So much for this being a quick and easy task. Whatever this sickness was, it seemed it wasn't going to play nice.

She looked around, spotted a fallen tree trunk nearby, and perched atop it, pulling Cailean's plaid around her shoulders to keep off the morning chill. Carefully, she untied the string from around Beatrice's bunch of notes and examined them. Beatrice's handwriting was scrupulously neat and filled the page in orderly rows. There was only one problem: It was written in Gaelic.

She was sure Beatrice would be able to translate the pages for her if she asked, but there was no time for that. Instead, she tapped into her power, wove a spell, and the words on the page shifted and blurred, translating themselves into English.

This done, she leaned over the first page and began to read. It soon became apparent that this sickness did not follow the pattern of any epidemic she'd ever encountered. There seemed to be no pattern to who contracted the disease and who didn't. There was no correlation with either age or gender. Nor did there seem to be the usual seasonal pattern of the infection dying off a little in warmer weather and returning when the weather turned cooler. According to Beatrice's notes, the sickness seemed entirely random.

Rose put the pages to one side, frowning. No. She did not believe that. Every illness had a pattern. Every disease had markers that could be recognized, rules that it followed. She just had to figure out what this one's were.

Clasping the notes in her fist, she made her way back into the infirmary. There was no sign of Beatrice or Maggie, but she could hear their voices coming from a room at the back and smelled the scent of medicinal herbs wafting from the open door. No doubt they were busy preparing some treatment or other.

Good. It would give her the chance to examine Drew alone.

His condition hadn't changed, for which Rose was grateful. At least it meant her spell was holding. She seated herself on the stool and laid her palm on Drew's forehead. Closing her eyes, she sent her senses questing deep into his body. She traveled deeper than she'd gone before, beyond the stasis she'd placed him in, beyond the pump of his blood and the beating of his heart. She wanted into the core of him, to where the sickness was hiding.

Where are you? she thought. *What are you? Show yourself.*

She let her awareness expand, taking in not just Drew's body but the deep, almost invisible life force that powered it. Gradually, that life force became visible to her mind's eye, a myriad of glowing lines of light that spread through his body like tree roots and encased it in a cocoon of energy.

Then suddenly, something slammed into her. It was as sudden and shocking as a snakebite and with a gasp, she broke contact, snatching back her hand. Glancing down, she saw that her palm was red and angry, as if burned.

Perhaps hearing her gasp, Beatrice and Maggie came rushing in from the back room. Rose hastily curled her fingers, hiding her burned palm.

"What is it?" Maggie asked. "Is something wrong?"

Yes, there is most definitely something wrong, she thought. She swallowed thickly and looked up at the two healers.

"Other than the sickness," she said, "have there been any other strange occurrences recently? Anything out of the ordinary?"

Maggie glanced at her sister, a wary expression crossing her face.

"What?" Rose demanded. "What is it?"

"There are rumors of odd things happening around the

coast," Maggie said carefully. "Fishermen have reported the currents changing and taking them off course. There have been more storms than usual, and there was that incident over at North Cove."

"Incident? What incident?"

"All the fish there died. The local villagers went down to the beach one morning and found it full of fish floating belly side up. It was quite eerie by all accounts."

"When did this happen?"

Maggie shrugged. "A couple of days ago. Why? What has this got to do with Drew?"

Rose didn't reply. The burn on her palm was beginning to smart. "I don't know," she said at last. "I need to talk to Cailean."

She climbed to her feet and hurried out of the infirmary, glancing down at her palm. The skin there was red and puckered. Oh, yes, there was definitely something wrong here. There was more going on here than just a sickness.

And she was determined to find out what.

Chapter Six

THE SWISH, SWISH, swish of the brush and the repetitive movements as he groomed Arrow's tail helped to calm Cailean a little. The silver stallion, gifted to him from Jamie Donald, lord of the Kingdom of the Isles, bore it with relatively good grace, although he snorted and stamped occasionally to tell Cailean that it was high time he was taken for a run.

"Easy, lad," Cailean murmured. "I'll take ye out soon. I promise."

Around him, the stable hands were busy with their work: mucking out, grooming, feeding. They gave Cailean a wide berth, perhaps sensing that their laird was not in the best of moods this morning.

No matter what he did, he couldn't get the image of Drew's contorted limbs out of his head. Was that what lay in store for them all if this sickness couldn't be contained? Was this what lay in store for his daughter?

The thought twisted his stomach with fear, and his pulse ramped up a notch. *No*, he told himself. *It won't come to that. I won't let it.*

But the truth was, no matter his protestations to the contrary, this was one enemy he was helpless against. Swords and muscle were of no use. He could do nothing. Only Rose MacFinnan had a chance against this enemy.

His hand stilled, and he placed his palms flat against Arrow's sides as his eyes closed. He took a deep breath, trying to steady the thumping of his heart.

She had tried, and she had failed. What chance did any of them have if even a MacFinnan spellweaver could not help?

Ye shouldn't have put your faith in her, an insidious little voice said in the back of his head. *Or anything to do with gods and magic.*

When had he forgotten his own rule?

When Rose MacFinnan walked into your life, he answered himself. *And made you hope.*

He sighed. When would he learn his lesson?

"Over there, my lady," he heard one of the stable hands say suddenly. "Ye'll find him at the end."

He opened his eyes and turned to see the object of his thoughts standing in the doorway. Rose picked her way gingerly around the piles of hay and manure the stable hands were raking up and wove her way towards him. When she was a few paces away, he held up his hand to stop her coming any closer.

"Careful of Arrow. He can be a bit bitey."

Taking hold of the stallion's halter, he led him back into his stall, patted him on the flank, and then rejoined Rose in the aisle.

"That's a fine-looking animal," she said, watching Arrow tucking into the fresh hay in his feeding trough. "Even if he is a bit 'bitey.'"

"Aye, and as haughty as a prince," Cailean replied. "It was three weeks before I could even approach him." He cocked his head. "Is everything all right, lass? It's not Drew, is it?"

She shook her head. "Drew is as you left him. Maggie and Beatrice are watching him. It's just… just…" She trailed off, glancing down at the palm of her hand. There was a large red mark there, like a burn.

"What have ye done?" he asked, alarmed. "Here, that needs treatment."

He took her arm, led her over to the water trough, and dunked her hand into the clear, cold water.

She didn't protest but only smiled at him wryly. "I thought *I* was the healer?"

"Aye, well, in my experience, healers are not very good at looking after themselves."

She snorted softly. "You sound like Elise."

"Elise?"

"My little sister. She's always telling me I don't look after myself properly."

So, she had a sister? Cailean filed this little tidbit away. He pressed a little further. "Yer family must be missing ye. Yer husband? Bairns?"

A shadow passed across her face. "Perhaps they would be," she replied, "if I had either. But I don't. So they won't."

She wasn't married. Why was he so pleased by that?

He lifted her hand out of the water and carefully examined her palm. "That needs ointment. I know Beatrice has some comfrey—"

"Later," she said, gently extricating her hand from his. "I need to talk to you first."

He looked at her sharply, the tone of her voice sending a warning down his spine. "About what?"

She looked up at him, her eyes reflecting the dim light inside the stable. She took a deep breath, seeming to steel herself for what she had to say. "I don't think the sickness is a normal sickness," she said quickly. "I think it's being caused by... something else."

"Something else?" he said, frowning. "What do ye mean?"

She shook her head, frustration on her face. "I don't know yet, but when I examined Drew just now, I felt... something." She curled her fingers around her burned palm. "Maggie and Beatrice told me strange things have been happening around the island. They mentioned fish dying in droves?"

"Aye, up at North Cove."

"I want to see it."

"Dead fish? What have they got to do with any of this?"

She glanced at her palm again and then fixed him with a determined stare. "I don't know, but I intend to find out."

Cailean didn't reply, digesting this in silence. Two days ago, a villager from North Cove had arrived at Dun Mallach with an odd story about all the fish in North Cove dying. Cailean had his advisors take down the man's story, but with everything else going on, a few dead fish had seemed of little importance. Rose MacFinnan, though, obviously disagreed.

He scrubbed a hand through his hair. "All right. I'll have Cook pack something for breakfast and we can leave right away."

Her shoulders sagged, and she let out a long, slow breath. "Thank you."

"Don't thank me yet," he said wryly. "It's quite a way to North Cove, and the roads are bad. By the time we get there, ye might well be cursing me instead."

ROSE'S PREDICTION PROVED to be true. It had turned into a bright, sunny morning with a fresh breeze blowing in off the sea. If she didn't have so much playing on her mind, it could almost have been pleasant.

She and Cailean had left Dun Mallach behind, he riding Arrow, she riding a docile white mare called Snip, and they'd eaten breakfast as they rode.

Rose didn't know what the little pastries filled with nuts and raisins were called, but they were delicious, and she helped herself to four of them from the packet in her saddlebag as they wended their way along the coastline, heading north.

At first, the area around Dun Mallach had been heavily populated, and they'd passed through several villages where the inhabitants came out to call greetings to their laird and stare at the MacFinnan spellweaver in their midst. Rose did her best to set them at ease, waving and smiling, and calling out a hello to show she was just a normal person like them, but she wasn't sure she succeeded. Most of them stared at her with something approaching awe. This adoration was, she thought, going to take a bit of getting used to.

But as they'd traveled farther north, the settlements had become sparser and the country more rugged and broken. Here, the few settlements they spotted were farther inland and consisted of isolated crofts surrounded by rocky fields dotted with sheep and Highland cattle.

Cailean was a towering, silent presence at her side as they rode, his dark eyes scanning the terrain continually, as if alert for danger. He'd donned a huge sword, which he wore strapped across his back, and she knew he also had daggers tucked into the tops of his boots. He looked like a man expecting trouble.

But, she reflected, watching him surreptitiously as they rode, he seemed like a man who *always* expected trouble. He rarely smiled, but on the odd occasion when he let his guard down, such as around his daughter Catriona, he seemed a different man entirely, one whose eyes shone with amusement and whose warmth was plain to see.

She would like to see *that* Cailean MacNeil more often.

"How long until we get there?" she asked him.

He turned to look at her, one eyebrow raised. "That's the third time ye've asked that question."

"It is not."

"It is so, and the answer remains the same. We should be there by midday."

Midday? Aargh! That was ages away! Already her backside was beginning to ache from the hard saddle. While she enjoyed riding, and Snip was an exceptionally friendly and docile mount—a deliberate choice on Cailean's part, no doubt—her muscles were no longer used to riding, and she suspected she'd barely be able to move come the morrow.

This was your idea, she reminded herself. *So you'd better stop complaining. After all, the company could be worse.*

She found herself studying Cailean again. The sea breeze was sending his hair whipping out behind him in a dark cascade, and his cheeks had a faint blush from windburn. He rode his horse with the ease of someone who had grown up in the saddle and seemed utterly at home in this wild landscape.

"So," she said, looking around. "This is Barra, huh?"

Cailean followed her gaze, his dark eyes trailing the outline of the land. His harsh expression softened a little. "Aye. This is Barra. A more beautiful place ye willnae find in all of God's creation."

Rose had to agree. On a day like today, with the sun glinting off the sea to their right and the glens and hills to their left sparkling like emeralds, she could well understand why Cailean's voice throbbed with pride to call such a place home.

"And this must have been your stomping ground when you were a kid?" she said, giving him a grin. "Aww, I can imagine a little Cailean running around here looking cute."

"Cute?" he snorted. "Hardly. When I was a lad, I was a terror. I used to sneak away from my tutors at every available opportunity and spend my time out here hunting and fishing and exploring all the places I wasnae meant to go. The more forbidden or more dangerous, the better. I think I turned my parents' hair gray before its time."

Rose's grin widened. He *would* have been a cute kid, no matter what he claimed. With that thick, dark hair, those big eyes, and high cheekbones, he would probably have gotten away with murder. And as a young man, he'd no doubt had the lasses of Barra swooning all over him.

"Sounds like you were the opposite of me," she said. "Out of my sisters, I've always been the sensible one. While Elise was out causing mayhem and Sarah was busy putting the world to rights, I was usually at home studying. *I* wouldn't have snuck away from my tutors to go exploring. I would have been more likely to ask for extra homework. Yep. You could say I was the dull one. Still am, really."

"Dull?" Cailean said, his brows rising in surprise. "Nay, lass. Dull is the last word I would use to describe ye."

"Oh?" she said in a teasing voice. "Then how would you describe me? Charming? Absolutely bloody amazing?"

His dark eyes fixed on her face. "Aye, lass," he said softly. "I would describe ye as all of those things."

Rose went still. She'd meant it as a joke. She knew she was none of those things. But there was no amusement in Cailean's expression, no hint that he was teasing her. Her stomach fluttered.

"I never took you for a flatterer."

"I'm not. Just honest. And you missed something off your list. Stubborn. Why else would we be riding to a place in the middle of nowhere despite my protests?"

Rose laughed. "Oh, definitely stubborn. It's a family trait."

A small smile quirked the corners of his mouth. "Damn it," he said dryly. "*Two* stubborn women in my life. Managing one is hard enough. Have ye met my daughter, Catriona?"

Rose sucked her teeth. "Well, they say the apple never falls far from the tree. I wonder where she gets her stubbornness from?"

"Not from me, that's for sure."

"Oh?" Rose raised her eyebrows. "So you're blaming her mother then?"

It was the wrong thing to say. The moment the words were out of her mouth, she knew it. Cailean's expression, which had been relaxed and open, suddenly closed.

"Time is getting on," he said. "Come, let's pick up the pace."

He nudged his horse into a trot, and Rose cursed herself inwardly. Why had she said that? Why had she brought up Cailean's wife?

Idiot, she chided herself. *Think before you speak!*

They rode in silence, Cailean a glowering presence ahead of her, and he kept the pace such that it precluded any further conversation. Rose bumped along behind him, trying to remember her riding lessons and find the rhythm of her mount. She wasn't very successful. Snip might be a docile mount, but she still had a backbone like a saw and it felt like it was trying to snap Rose in half. Oh yes, she was definitely going to ache in the morning.

She could have cried with relief when they rounded a headland a long time later and Cailean announced that they'd arrived. He pulled his mount to a halt, and Rose let out a long, grateful breath.

"Remind me to strap some cushions to the saddle the next time we go riding," she muttered, leaning forward so she could rub her backside. "Or better yet, knock me on the head and wake me up when we get there."

Cailean glanced in her direction. "I dinna have such a death wish that I would ever knock a MacFinnan spellweaver on the head." He nodded at the scene in front of them. "But at least yer backside can rest now for a bit. This is North Cove."

Rose looked out. Ahead of them lay a wide horseshoe bay. A beach of sand so pale as to be almost white sloped down to the water's edge, and she could see layers of flotsam lying along the tide line, washed up at high tide. From this distance, she couldn't make out what the flotsam was. But she could smell it.

Rotting fish.

She pressed her sleeve across her mouth and nose. "Ugh. Lovely. Well? Shall we go and have a look?"

Cailean swung his leg over his horse's back and jumped down. He landed lightly for such a big man, and he turned in a slow circle, taking in the view from all angles before he answered her.

"Aye. There's nobody else here. It seems safe enough."

Rose wasn't sure what sort of danger he was expecting. Leaning forward and clinging to the saddle horn, she managed to swing her leg over the horse's back and slide ungracefully to the ground. Her knees buckled as her feet hit the sand, and she would have fallen had she not been clinging onto Snip.

"Are ye all right, lass?" Cailean asked.

She waved away his concern. "Fine. Fine. Nothing a Swedish massage and a few gin and tonics wouldn't mend."

He gave her a bemused look but didn't comment. From here, a series of sand dunes led down to the beach. Waves lapped at the shore with their incessant sigh and moan, and the wind was stronger, whipping her hair out behind her and filling her nostrils with the dead fish smell.

She put her sleeve over her mouth again and followed Cailean down the dunes and onto the beach. Just as she'd expected, the flotsam scattered along the tide line turned out to be dead fish.

They were everywhere, in all shapes and sizes. They formed a wide line almost the entire length of the beach, marking the extent that the water reached at high tide. Rose spotted more of them bobbing in the water, their silver bellies flashing in the sun.

Cailean's expression was troubled as he took in the scene. "I dinna like this," he muttered.

Rose was inclined to agree. Something didn't feel right, and it wasn't just the dead fish and the smell. Something felt... wrong. Unnatural. She studied the beach in both directions, trying to put her finger on what was bothering her.

And then it hit her.

"Where are all the scavengers?" she asked, turning to look at Cailean. "Where are all the gulls and crows and goodness knows what else that should be here feeding on all this? It's a feast too good to miss, but there isn't a single one. No creature would ignore a glut like this unless..."

"Unless they knew something was wrong with it," Cailean finished for her.

Rose nodded. In the wild, scavengers would leave carcasses of animals that had died from illness as they could smell the disease. Was that why there were no scavengers here?

Careful where she put her feet, Rose picked her way through the detritus and down to the water's edge. The soft hiss and sigh of the waves seemed a strange counterpoint to the death that filled the water. The waves were littered with tiny corpses bobbing in the surf.

"There must be thousands of them," Rose muttered, turning to Cailean. "Have you ever seen anything like this before?"

Cailean's eyes were troubled as he looked around. "Nay," he murmured. "Never. What could have caused such a thing?"

If this had been the twenty-first century, she would have suggested some kind of chemical spillage or other pollution. But there were no chemicals that could cause this in 1498.

She walked down to the water's edge, to where the sand was damp from the tide, and crouched. Careful not to let the water touch her as it came in, she held out her hand, hovering it just above the level of the waves, and closed her eyes.

As she opened herself up to her power, the sigh of the wind and the movement of the waves seemed to come alive. They whispered against her senses like living things. The beach, the rocks, the hills, all seemed to vibrate with a kind of energy. She could feel the life forces of the horses they'd left at the top of the dunes, stronger and more pulsing than those of the land.

And Cailean…

Cailean was a whirlwind of energy that buffeted against her senses like a thunderstorm. He was coiled power and unleashed fury; he was granite strength and burning heat. It took an immense effort to pull her awareness away from him.

She forced her attention to the waves, sent her mind skimming along the ocean bed, through the kelp forests that danced below the surface, between the rocks and little gaps where tiny creatures lived.

Then suddenly, she felt it.

A sense of wrongness permeated the waves like black ink spilled into clear water. It was dark, unnatural—and she had felt it before. It was the same thing that had burned her when she'd examined Drew.

With a gasp, she opened her eyes and rose but staggered with sudden dizziness. Cailean's arm shot out to steady her, his strong fingers closing around her upper arm.

"What is it, lass?" he asked. "What's wrong?"

"Dark," she whispered. "Something dark."

Cailean's hand rose to grip her other arm. Gently, he turned her to face him. "What do ye mean?"

She swallowed. Took a deep breath. Forced herself to look at him. "I understand now. Why my magic didn't work on Drew. Why none of Beatrice nor Maggie's remedies has helped. This is not a sickness, Cailean. It's a curse."

Chapter Seven

CAILEAN STARED AT her, unsure if he'd heard her correctly. A curse?

Rose had gone pale, and there was a thin sheen of sweat across her forehead. Whatever she'd sensed, it had affected her badly. Beneath his grip, he could feel her shaking. That alarmed him more than anything. What could be so bad that it would scare a MacFinnan spellweaver like this?

"Lass?" he said. "Rose. Look at me."

She licked her lips, sucked a breath through her nostrils before her blue eyes found his. "I felt it earlier when I examined Drew. I went deeper than before, and something didn't like that. It attacked me."

She pulled her right hand out of his grip and showed him her hand, where the puckered burn scar sat.

Cailean blinked, unease sliding down his spine. "Are ye saying *Drew* did that to ye?"

She shook her head. "Not Drew. The corruption inside him." She waved her hand at the cove and its multitude of dead fish. "The same corruption that did this. It isn't a sickness that is taking your people, Cailean. It's magic. Dark magic."

Cailean released her and staggered back a few paces. The beach beneath his feet felt suddenly like quicksand, and he was sinking, sinking, sinking…

He clenched his fists, closed his eyes. A curse. Dark magic. Anger flashed through him. Damn all the gods! How dare they?

He opened his eyes. "What is this magic?" he growled.

Rose wrapped her arms around herself. "I don't know yet. But it's not native to this island. It feels alien somehow. It's out of sync with everything else, slowly choking the islands like a vine around a tree. That's what happened here, I think. The curse overwhelmed the bay's life force and killed everything."

Cailean swallowed. "Is that what's going to happen to Barra?"

Rose met his gaze. Her eyes flashed, and he saw a glint of the power of the MacFinnan spellweavers. "No," she said, lifting her chin. "It isn't. Because we are going to stop it."

"We?"

"Yes, *we*. That's why I'm here, remember?"

"Lass, ye were brought here to cure a sickness. Now there is no sickness—"

"No. I was brought here to help a people in need," she cut in. "Regardless of what that help entails. I intend to discover what this curse is and end it." Her words were fierce, her expression defiant.

"Ye... ye would do that?"

"Of course." She looked a little puzzled by the question. "I'm a MacFinnan spellweaver. It's what we do."

No, he thought. *It's what you do, Rose MacFinnan.*

He stepped closer, so close she had to crane her head back to look up at him. The breeze whispered around them, and the waves lapped at his boots, but Cailean barely noticed. He stared down into her bottomless eyes.

"Thank ye, lass," he said softly.

Her lips parted, and a soft breath hissed through them. "I..."

She trailed off, staring up at him. In that moment, Cailean felt something shift inside him. He could not have named what it was, only that it felt... good.

Rose cleared her throat, stepped back. "Um. We'd better get back to Dun Mallach. I'm going to need a map of the island, and markers, and a list of everyone who has fallen ill."

"Aye. I'll send out riders to survey every settlement."

She nodded, then turned and began walking away. But she'd not gone more than three steps when she stumbled, almost pitching her face-first into the sand and dead fish. Cailean darted forward, got his hands around her waist and steadied her.

Her skin was waxy pale and there was a thin covering of sweat across her forehead. She was pushing herself too hard, he realized. She was exhausted. Her hands shook a little.

"I'm fine," she protested. "Honestly."

"Ye are a poor liar, Rose MacFinnan," he replied. "And I would thank ye to temper that MacFinnan stubbornness and let me help ye."

She shot him a flat look but clamped her lips shut and didn't protest as he helped her up the sand dunes to where the horses were waiting.

"Thanks, but I'm okay now," she said, pushing away from his aid. "The confrontation with the curse just knocked the stuffing out of me a little. I'll be fine from here."

He studied her. There were dark circles around her eyes, and she looked fit to drop.

"Ye are in no fit state to ride," he announced. "Ye will ride with me."

Before she could protest, he got his arms around her waist and hoisted her up into Arrow's saddle.

She yelped. "Wait! What are you doing?"

He swung up behind her, settling himself into the saddle. Reaching around her, he gathered up Arrow's reins.

"Dinna worry about Snip. She will follow us."

He nudged Arrow's ribs and sent the gelding off at a canter back towards the southern road, Snip following behind. Rose gripped the saddle horn but not before she was pushed backwards in the saddle so she was pressed right up against him.

The warmth of her body seeped into him, and that *something* he'd felt on the beach uncoiled in his belly again. He didn't know what it was.

But he knew he liked it.

ROSE DIDN'T SPEAK much on the way home. Her mind was awhirl with everything she'd discovered at North Cove. She glanced down at the burn on her palm. It no longer hurt and would probably heal without a scar, but even so, it was a reminder of all that was wrong here. Since the incident with Drew, she had suspected she was dealing with something other than an ordinary epidemic.

North Cove had only confirmed that.

She breathed deeply, trying to calm her racing heart as they cantered back towards Dun Mallach at a faster pace than on their way out this morning. Rose made no complaint about the pace. Nor did she complain that Cailean had taken it upon himself to have her ride with him without so much as a by-your-leave.

In truth, she was glad of it. She felt exhausted and wrung out, and there was something reassuring about the cage of Cailean's strong arms around her. He seemed as strong and solid as granite, and after the disquieting things she'd discovered at North Cove, that was exactly what she needed.

She had never sensed such malevolent magic as she had in the waters of the cove. During her work as a spellweaver, she had occasionally come across old magic, created for a dark purpose. But these were usually just weak curses set by someone with rudimentary gifts who wanted petty revenge for a perceived hurt. None of them ever held any real power.

But this...

This went deeper, further than anything she'd sensed before, and it was no third-rate village hedge witch who had set this. No, whoever or whatever had created this curse was powerful. Very powerful.

"Ye are quiet, lass," Cailean said softly.

Rose blinked, coming out of her reverie. She was leaning back against Cailean's warm chest, and she could feel his voice rumbling through his body.

"Am I? Sorry, I was just... thinking."

"Thinking? A dangerous pursuit, I'm told."

"Yeah, you're not wrong."

She bit her lip and then turned her head to look at him. His eyes, focused on the path ahead, flicked to her, and she could see that he was troubled, despite his light-hearted words. Who wouldn't be troubled after what they'd seen?

She kept herself busy by studying the landscape as they rode, looking for anything out of the ordinary, anything that might give a clue as to what was going on here. The villages were emptier than they had been on the way out, with most folks busy out in the fields or on the water. She spotted fishing boats on the waves and groups of children shrieking and laughing as they played on the beaches, in the water as often as out of it.

A pang of anxiety went through her. What would happen to those children, those fishermen, those women working the fields if she couldn't find a way to stop this curse-wrought sickness? In her mind's eye she saw this place deserted, the beaches wind-swept and silent, the villages empty and forlorn. A shiver slid down her spine.

No, she told herself. *I won't let that happen. I swore I'd find a way to help these people, and that's what I will do. Somehow.*

She was glad when they arrived back at Dun Mallach.

Cailean guided Arrow into the courtyard where he pulled him to a halt. Two stable hands came running to take hold of his and Snip's bridles as Cailean swung effortlessly down.

Then, before she could swing her leg over the saddle, he reached up, put his hands on her waist, and lifted her to the ground as if she weighed nothing at all.

Rose harrumphed as he set her on her feet. "Will you stop doing that? I'm not a sack of turnips."

Amusement danced in his eyes. "Are ye sure? Ye ride like one."

She didn't dignify that with an answer. Instead, she made do with a glare.

"Come," he said, ignoring her ire. "I have something to show ye."

Rose followed him into the keep. Once inside, he led her along the wide, echoing passage that ran the length of the interior. They passed doors and rooms she'd not yet seen, some open and some closed, until Cailean came to a halt in a small, round antechamber with three doors leading off it.

Reaching beneath his tunic, he pulled out a key on a string, and unlocked one of the doors. Within, Rose found a small, neat room with a single wooden desk and two chairs.

Cailean looked around the room, his dark eyes scanning the well-kept space.

"I havenae been in this room for a long time," he said, almost to himself. "This was my father's study. He used to spend hours in here studying languages and history." He smiled wryly. "And, I think, to escape the demands of the clan."

Rose examined the space. There were several bookcases filled with rolled parchments, a number of quills laid out neatly on the desk along with an inkpot. A huge leather-bound book stood open on a stand, which she guessed was a Bible. The place spoke of scholarship and learning, and although Cailean might not have been here in a while, somebody still obviously kept the place scrupulously clean.

Cailean crossed to the bookcase, knelt, and scanned the bottom shelf, running his finger along the line of documents until he found what he was looking for.

"Here." He carried the scroll over to the desk and unrolled it, pinning it down with the inkpot and several smaller books.

Rose joined him, peering at the document. It was a map. It showed Barra in a level of detail she hadn't expected. Settlements were clearly marked, along with topographical data like rivers and mountain ranges.

"My father employed Spanish mapmakers to document the island," Cailean said. "He spent time fostering in Madrid as a child and developed a taste for exploration while he was there. I think he would have loved nothing more than to be part of the expeditions that the Spanish and Portuguese have been sending out in recent years but alas, he was recalled to Barra when my grandfather became ill."

Rose thought about this. "If he'd stayed, he might have ended up being part of the expeditions that discovered the new world. Imagine that!"

Cailean glanced at her. "New world?"

Rose did a quick calculation in her head and realized she wasn't entirely sure if the Americas had been discovered yet. Damn. What were the rules about revealing future events? She waved a hand. "Never mind. This map looks like exactly what I need."

"What do ye hope to discover, lass?"

"A pattern, with any luck. I want to map where everyone has fallen ill. From what Beatrice and Maggie tell me, there is no pattern to *who* the sickness strikes. But is there a pattern to *where* the sickness strikes? If so, that might help me pin down the source of this curse. Then we can figure out what to do about it."

When Cailean didn't respond, she glanced at him and found him watching her with an odd, almost bemused look on his face.

"What?"

"Nothing," he replied, shaking his head. "It's just ye said it again. 'We.'"

"What's so surprising about that?"

He opened his mouth and closed it again. "I... I'm unused to receiving help unlooked for."

She got the feeling that this was a big admission for him. "Well you'd better get used to it," she said lightly. "Because I'm going to be around for a while."

He stared at her and Rose felt her breath quicken under his

scrutiny. "Aye," he said softly. "I think I could get used to that."

Then he suddenly cleared his throat and looked away. "I... I have to go train with my men. I'll have Beatrice and Maggie bring ye those lists of patients ye need."

He strode to the door, glanced over his shoulder at her for a moment, and then left, shutting the door behind him. Rose was left alone in the study. She blew out a breath and slumped into a chair. What a morning. What a strange, unsettling morning. First, the incident with Drew, then the scene at North Cove, and now... Cailean and the strange sensations he stirred in her.

She was staring at the map, chin resting on her hands, when there was a knock on the door a short time later. True to his word, Cailean had sent Beatrice and Maggie. They reported no change in Drew's condition, and with their help, Rose began marking locations on the map where the sickness was known to have broken out.

This was only a tiny amount of data, and she relied on the two women's memory of where their patients had come from, but it was a start. She'd ask Cailean to organize a more detailed survey of the island later.

Mable brought her a late lunch of cold meat pie which she ate hunched over the map. Her eyes scanned the markers she'd placed so far. There didn't seem to be any pattern to the locations. Yet. But she would find one, she was sure.

Finishing her pie, she leaned back in the chair and stretched her arms over her head. She was alone. Beatrice and Maggie had gone off on their own errands, and this part of the keep was quiet. The only sounds came from someone sawing a piece of wood outside and the tramp of feet from the floor above.

She rubbed her eyes which felt grainy from her lack of sleep. Late afternoon sunlight was pouring through the narrow, arrow-slit window and falling across the map on the desk. If she turned her head, from here she could see a tiny sliver of sea glinting at the bottom of the hill on which the keep stood and the tiny black dots of fishing boats out plying the waves.

She needed a break. A headache was starting to burn behind her eyes and there was a crick in her neck from staring at the map for so long. With a groan for her aching muscles, she stood and made her way out of the study, closing the door firmly behind her.

Stepping out into the sunshine of the courtyard, she closed her eyes and tilted her face up to the sun, enjoying the feeling of the warmth against her skin.

"Go on then! Fetch it!"

Her eyes popped open at the sudden voice. It was coming from around the corner. She heard excited yapping.

"Good boy!"

Smiling to herself, Rose made her way around the corner and sure enough, she found Catriona and Patch over by the curtain wall, engaged in a game of fetch.

Catriona hadn't noticed her yet, but Patch had. As Catriona threw a small leather ball for the little black-and-white dog, he suddenly lost all interest in the game and came zooming over to Rose instead, little tail whirling and tongue lolling out. Despite his diminutive size, he whacked into Rose's shins with enough force to knock her back a pace as he jumped up excitedly.

"Patch! Down! Bad boy!" Catriona called, marching over.

"It's fine," Rose said, crouching to scratch the little dog behind the ears.

"It is *not* fine," Catriona countered, scowling at Patch. "If he canna learn his manners, Papa will make me put him in the kennels. Do ye hear me, ye little scoundrel?"

Patch proceeded to roll onto his back, presenting his belly for a rub. Indulging the little dog, Rose said, "Oh, I think your papa's bark is worse than his bite. I don't think Patch will be going in the kennels any time soon."

"Aye, especially when he sees what I've taught him!" Catriona said, her voice bubbling with enthusiasm. "I'll show ye. Patch! Come here!"

The little dog jumped up obediently and Rose couldn't help

but smile as Catriona took Patch through his paces, making him sit, lie down, and even give his paw. Roll-over proved a little too complicated and Patch, suddenly bored with this game, decided it would be more fun to play tug-of-war with the bottom of Rose's dress.

"Patch!" Catriona cried in mortification. She grabbed him while Rose pulled the material in the other direction.

But when the little dog finally let go, their momentum was enough to send them both staggering backwards where they landed on their backsides on the grass.

Rose couldn't help it. She felt a giggle bubbling up inside her and suddenly she was lying flat on her back on the grass, shaking helplessly with laughter. Catriona, with Patch sitting on her chest and licking her face, followed suit.

The tension lifted from Rose like fog burning off under the morning sun and she lost herself in the moment, laughing and laughing until her belly hurt.

CAILEAN WIPED THE back of his hand across his sweaty brow as he pushed open the gate and stepped into the courtyard. His chest was heaving and his sweat-soaked shirt clung to his chest and back. It had been a good training session but now he was badly in need of a wash and a change of clothes.

Hoisting his scabbarded sword over one shoulder, he began walking but froze as he heard the sound of laughter coming from over on the far side of the courtyard. He turned his head and spotted Catriona flat on her back, laughing her head off while Patch stood on her chest, tail wagging madly.

And she wasn't alone.

Rose was also sprawled on the grass, laughing as hard as his daughter.

He paused and watched them. He didn't know what the two

of them had been up to, but clearly they'd been having a good time. His heart swelled at the sound of their laughter. It was a rare thing these days and it washed through him like the wind blowing away the clouds on a gloomy day.

Rose clambered to her feet and held out a hand to help Catriona up. His daughter proceeded to instruct Patch on something—trying to get him to roll over by the looks of it. But the little dog was having none of it and just grabbed the bottom of Rose's dress and starting yanking it, which set Catriona off into another fit of giggles.

Cailean found an answering smile spreading across his face.

His daughter always seemed to find the joy in life, no matter how difficult things seemed to get. And since Rose had arrived, she seemed to smile and laugh even more than usual. Rose, he noticed, seemed to have that effect on people. Everyone around the castle seemed to walk a bit lighter, a bit straighter, as though a weight had been lifted from around their necks.

He would, he realized, have to include himself in that assessment.

Why? Was it simply because she was a MacFinnan spellweaver and he was falling victim to the same blind optimism he'd always been so suspicious of?

He didn't think so. It was more than that. It wasn't Rose's powers that made him feel this way. It was Rose herself.

Despite himself, his stomach did an odd little flip whenever he laid eyes on her. He hadn't felt this alive since... since...

Mary.

Thoughts of his wife flashed into his head and it was like being doused in cold water. A wave of guilt crashed over him. How could he be thinking such things about Rose?

Across the courtyard, Catriona suddenly looked up and spotted him. "Papa!" she cried, waving enthusiastically. "Come and see what Patch can do!"

Oh, how he wanted to. He ached to lose himself in the simple enjoyment of Rose and Catriona's company. But he couldn't.

Guilt pinned his feet to the ground.

Without a word, he spun and went back through the gate, letting it slam behind him. Lifting his sword from his shoulder, he bellowed for his men to attend him, to get ready for another training session.

The wash and change of clothes would have to wait.

Chapter Eight

ROSE RUBBED HER eyes. The little dots she'd marked on the map blurred and swam. She'd met with Beatrice and Maggie again earlier in the evening and now there were more markers on the map. Still she could see no pattern.

With a sigh, she pushed it away. It was late. Outside the window, all was black and the only illumination in the little study came from a single candle perched in a holder on the edge of the table.

"Time for bed," she told herself. "You can pick this up in the morning."

She hated the delay. Who was to say how many more people would get sick in that time? How many others would have to pay for her lack of progress?

But there was nothing she could do. She was so tired she could barely think straight and in her current state who could say she wouldn't miss a vital clue? She heaved herself up. Picking up the candle holder and shielding the flame with one hand, she let herself out. The corridors of the castle were eerie at night, lit only intermittently by candles in sconces along the walls.

She made her way through the keep until she reached the staircase that led up to the guest wing. Here, she paused. The door to the great hall lay on her left and it was slightly ajar. Firelight glowed within. Perhaps she wasn't the last person awake after all.

She stuck her head around the door and peered inside. It took her eyes a moment to adjust to the gloom. The tables and benches had been cleaned down and the floor swept but a fire still burned in the hearth, casting warmth and light through the room.

A figure was sitting by the fire, sprawled in a chair, staring into the flames.

From this distance the figure was nothing more than a silhouette, but even so, Rose recognized Cailean. Nobody else in the castle was as big as he was. His eyes were fixed on the dancing flames. A bottle dangled from one hand.

She ought to go to bed. She ought to turn around, hurry up the stairs, and leave Cailean to his thoughts. But she didn't. He'd been on her mind all afternoon.

So instead of retreating, she stepped silently into the hall. Her shoes made no sound on the flagstones as she wove through the tables and approached the fireplace.

"Couldn't sleep, huh?"

Cailean whirled at the sound of her voice. In a flash, he was on his feet, dagger in hand.

Rose swallowed thickly, eyes fixed on the glinting metal so close to her face.

Cailean's eyes widened as he realized it was her. He tucked the dagger back into his belt.

"Rose?" he growled. "What are ye doing here? Ye shouldnae sneak up on me like that! I could have hurt ye."

"Yeah, I noticed," Rose replied. Jeez, how did somebody so big move so fast? "I won't make that mistake again, believe me. Remind me to never get on *your* bad side."

"My... my apologies," he said, running a hand through his hair. "I hadnae realized anyone else was still awake."

He slumped back into the chair, indicating for Rose to take the other. She lowered herself into it, enjoying the warmth that washed over her from the fire. Cailean stared in the flames, saying nothing. After a moment, he took another swig from the bottle.

"Drinking alone, eh? Never a good sign."

His dark eyes flicked to her. "Nay, never a good sign," he agreed, his words slurring slightly. He was, she realized, a little drunk. Several empty bottles were scattered on the floor around him, enough to knock most people out.

He held the bottle out to her. "Drink?"

She reached out and took it. "Thought you'd never ask." Setting the bottle to her lips, she took a large gulp. And then nearly choked as her throat lit on fire.

"Ugh. You could have warned me it was whisky!"

He raised an eyebrow. "This is Scotland. What else did you expect it to be?"

Okay, he had her there. With a shrug, she took another long gulp. This time she managed not to choke and almost enjoyed the warm feeling that settled in her stomach.

"What are you still doing up?" she asked him.

"I could ask the same question of ye."

She took another swig of whisky. "Working. I lost track of time. How about you?"

Firelight danced in his dark eyes as he watched her. He was utterly still, most of him hidden in shadow. "Do ye ever wish ye could have yer time over and do things differently?" he asked.

Rose snorted. "All the time. If I had a penny for every mistake I've made, I'd be a very rich woman."

His lips curled in a wry smile. "Mistakes? A MacFinnan spell-weaver? I dinna believe it."

Oh, you'd better, Rose thought. *Because my life is full of them.*

Thoughts of Dennis suddenly crowded into her mind. She had barely thought about him at all since she'd come here, nor the wreckage of their marriage. But now she couldn't help herself.

If she could have her time over like Cailean said, would she have done things differently? Would she have given more time to her marriage and tried harder to make it work?

She took another swig of whisky. Already, she was starting to feel a little fuzzy around the edges. She normally avoided alcohol, and she knew drinking strong spirits was *not* a good idea. But she didn't care. The oblivion that drink could provide suddenly seemed very enticing.

Cailean had gone back to staring at the fire. There was something in his hand and he was turning it over and over without even seeming to realize what he was doing.

"What's that?" she asked.

"Hmm?" Cailean looked at her and then down to the object. It was a silver brooch in the shape of a lily, its gilded edges catching the firelight. He didn't answer for so long that she thought he wasn't going to speak at all.

"It was my wife's."

Rose sucked in a little breath. "Oh. Mable told me what happened to her. I'm sorry, Cailean."

His lips twisted into a grimace. "Dinna be. It was a long time ago."

Not so long that it doesn't still cut you up inside, she thought.

His dark eyes found hers. "How come ye are not married, lass?"

She winced. She fidgeted on her seat. "I was," she said at last.

His eyebrows rose in surprise. "Ye lost yer husband?"

She shook her head, not wanting him to misunderstand. "Divorced. He's still alive—but he's gone all the same."

Cailean studied her. She saw no judgment in his eyes, only understanding. "Perhaps that is worse. After all, death is not a choice."

She nodded, surprised by the insight. "Perhaps. It was all so clinical when it ended. Like closing a bank account."

Why was she telling him this? She'd not even discussed this with Elise so why was she opening up to Cailean MacNeil as though she'd known him for years?

The whisky, she told herself. *You know it wasn't a good idea.* She glanced at the bottle that she still held in her hand.

"Ugh. I'm too old to be drinking this stuff."

"Old? Hardly. And besides, it's medicinal."

"Is that right? Perhaps I'll add it to my treatments. If nothing else, it will make my patients more pliable." Rose stretched her legs out towards the fire, warmth curling around her ankles. "Remind me never to drink with a Highlander. You folks don't know moderation."

"Or perhaps we just have regrets to drown."

His words landed heavily between them. Rose took another swig from the bottle then passed it back to Cailean. "I'll drink to that."

He took it and raised it to her in salute. "Here's to regrets."

"And on that note, I think it's time I went to bed," Rose said. She climbed to her feet and staggered, her head suddenly spinning so much she had to steady herself on the back of the chair.

Cailean rose easily, not staggering at all, despite the amount he'd already put away. "Careful, lass. Falling flat on yer face on this floor isnae pleasant. Believe me, I talk from experience."

"I'm fine," Rose said, waving a hand. "I'm not drunk."

Cailean just raised an eyebrow.

"Fine! Maybe I'm a little tipsy but I'm perfectly capable of walking, thank you very much."

To prove her point, she pushed away from the chair back and began walking towards the door. The floor lurched alarmingly and her head swam. Oh, hell!

She put out a hand to steady herself on one of the tables, but missed, and went sprawling. But before she face-planted into the unforgiving flagstones, strong arms went around her and lifted her back to her feet.

She found herself looking up at Cailean. His big hands were gripping her hips and as he set her back on her feet, he did not let her go. To steady herself, she placed her palms against his chest, feeling the contours of his pecs beneath his linen shirt.

Her mouth suddenly went dry, and she had to swallow a few times before she could speak. "Not a word," she said. "MacFinnan spellweavers do *not* get drunk. And they certainly don't need help to stand from handsome lairds."

"Handsome, eh?" Cailean said, a ghost of a smile on his lips.

Peeling one of her hands from his chest, Rose poked him with a finger. It was like poking granite. "Don't let it go to yer head, buster."

"I wouldnae dream of it."

The flames in the fireplace cast flickering shadows across his face, accentuating the contours of his cheekbones and the gleam of his eyes. She found her gaze tracing down his face and coming to rest on his lips. They were full and smooth, parted slightly.

What would it be like to kiss those lips? Would they feel as silky as they looked?

"Rose." Cailean breathed her name softly and the sound of it sent a shiver right through her. Something sparked in his eyes as he looked down at her and for a second—just a second—she wanted to kiss him more than anything in the world.

He dipped his head slightly and she thought he was going to do just that. But in the next instant, he lifted his chin and took a deep breath, as though getting a grip on himself.

It broke the spell. Rose stepped back, putting space between them. "I... um... good night, Cailean."

He watched her for a moment, his face half in shadow. "Good night, Rose."

Before she could do something stupid, she turned and staggered from the room. She managed to make her way up to her chamber where she fell into bed fully clothed and sank into grateful oblivion.

Chapter Nine

IT WAS MIDMORNING by the time Rose woke the next day. She blinked gummy eyes open, yawned wide enough to crack her jaw, and then stretched her arms over her head. Then she went still, waiting for the hangover to hit her. What had possessed her to drink whisky last night?

But to her surprise, there was no headache and her stomach felt fine. Not entirely trusting this, she sat up gingerly, swinging her feet around and placing them flat on the cold stone floor. Nope. Not a hangover in sight. In fact, she'd slept so well that she felt great, far better than she had any right to.

The sea air must be agreeing with me, she thought. *Or this place.*

Or Cailean, a traitorous little voice whispered in the back of her head.

She shut that voice down immediately. She really did not want to go there.

A twinge of guilt went through her. She hadn't meant to sleep late as this meant she'd lost valuable time that could have been spent looking for the cure for the sickness. But there was nothing she could do about that now.

Someone, probably Mable, had been in while she slept and left a clean set of clothes, a basin of water, a stick of lavender soap, and a cloth on the stand by the window. Rose rubbed her face, pulled herself to her feet, and padded over to it. The water was freezing cold. She would like nothing more than a hot, steaming bath, but for now, she contented herself with a cold wash. Once this was done she even managed to get dressed without help, for which she felt ridiculously pleased with herself.

Maybe I'm getting used to this time, she thought. *Maybe one day I won't quite stick out like a sore thumb.*

She threw open the shutters onto another bright, breezy day. The sun was high in the sky. Oops. The MacFinnan spellweaver sleeping late? Not a good look. She blamed Cailean for that. If he hadn't plied her with whisky, she would have been up hours ago. No doubt *he* hadn't slept in, despite staying up late and drinking enough to sink a barge.

She pulled the bone comb Mable had provided through her hair, squared her shoulders, and strode out of her room. Today was a big day. Today was the day she would begin figuring out how to combat the curse.

She called in at the kitchen and begged some cold pie off the cook for breakfast and wolfed it down while on her way to the infirmary. Once there, she found that Drew's condition had remained unchanged, and also that three more people had been admitted overnight. An examination of each revealed they had the same sickness that Drew had, all burning with fever, all unresponsive to her questions.

A twinge of dread went through her. Whatever this sickness was, it seemed to be getting worse. All she could do was put them into the same comatose state as Drew.

Leaving the infirmary under Maggie's and Beatrice's supervision, she made her way to her study, lost in thought. As she pushed through the door, she jumped in surprise when she discovered somebody was already in there waiting for her.

Cailean was leaning over the desk, his palms placed flat on its surface as he examined the map spread across the top.

Rose stopped dead. "Cailean. You startled me."

He straightened, brushing a wisp of dark hair out of his face. He looked tired. There were dark circles under his eyes and beneath his plaid his linen shirt looked a little rumpled. Perhaps he had a hangover after all.

"My apologies," he murmured, his dark eyes finding hers. "But I thought ye would want this right away."

He had a leather satchel dangling from his hand which he placed on the desk and opened. He pulled out a thick wad of parchment.

"What's that?"

"The records ye asked for. From every settlement on Barra, detailing the numbers who became sick in each."

Her eyebrows rose. "You've collected all that already? But I thought that would take ages!"

"It did," he said, his voice sounding slightly amused. "I sent riders out yesterday, straight after we got back from North Cove. They worked through the night and have been returning all morning, the last of them around half an hour ago." He glanced at the wad of parchment. "I hope this provides what ye need, lass."

"So do I," she muttered.

He placed the bundle on the table. "Aye, well. I'll leave ye to it. Let me know if ye need aught."

He turned to leave, but Rose caught the sleeve of his shirt. "You know, this would go much more quickly if there were two of us working on it."

Anyone could help her with this task, of course. Maggie, Beatrice, even Catriona. But it was Cailean's company she wanted.

He glanced down at where her hand grasped his sleeve and then up into her eyes. She couldn't read the look on his face but something in the way he watched her made her heart beat a little faster. Oh hell. He was the laird for God's sake! No doubt he had a hundred things that demanded his attention—

"All right," he said softly.

He held out a chair for Rose then sank onto the stool opposite.

"So how do we do this?" he asked.

Rose took the bundle of folded parchment and split it into two piles, pushing one across the desk towards Cailean.

"Simple. For each settlement we need to count how many people fell sick and put a marker for each case next to the settlement on the map."

"To what end?"

"Like I said, I'm hoping it will show us a pattern. Is the sickness concentrated in one area? Are there places that have escaped it all together? That might allow us to find where the curse originates from."

His expression turned fierce. "Aye, I would dearly love to find the origin of this curse. And whoever who created it."

His voice was low and dangerous, leaving Rose in no doubt as to what he would do to such a person. Not for the first time, she found herself glad they were on the same side. Cailean, she suspected, would make a formidable enemy.

She did not reply. Taking a quill and dipping it in the inkpot, she read the first report then marked on the map where it recorded cases of sickness. In this way, each settlement on the map began to have a tally chart marked next to it, allowing her to see at a glance the concentration of cases across the whole island.

She and Cailean worked in companionable silence, neither speaking. Rose found herself glancing at him as they worked. It seemed odd watching him doing such a mundane, clerical task. To Rose's mind he was more suited to the outdoors, to the moors and mountains, the sea and the cliffs, rather than sitting in this cramped study, reading reports.

Still, she mused, being laird of this island undoubtedly involved much more of this kind of work than she realized. Cailean certainly seemed at home with it as he read each report carefully before adding his notes to the map.

Rose wasn't sure how education worked in this time, but it was clear that Cailean was well educated. Some of the books on the shelves were written in French and Latin, suggesting he could read both. She watched as he leaned forward and made another notation on the map. She couldn't stop a smile spreading across her face. The stool was way too small for his large frame, and he looked faintly ridiculous perched there with his knees practically around his ears.

"Something amusing, lass?" he asked, raising an eyebrow.

"Not at all. You carry on. After all, you look *so* comfortable."

Cailean glanced at the stool on which he perched. "I get the feeling ye are making fun of me."

Rose widened her eyes and put her hand over her heart in mock innocence. "Me? I wouldn't dream of it. But seriously, you could have had the chair. This *is* your study, after all."

"And ye are a MacFinnan spellweaver," he countered. "And ye've already threatened to turn me into a frog."

Rose laughed. "It was a toad, actually. And that was only if you didn't behave yourself."

His expression turned grave. "And have I? Behaved myself?"

Rose nodded somberly, mirroring his expression. "You have been the picture of the gentlemanly host."

Cailean blew out an exaggerated breath. "Thank goodness for that. I dinna much fancy life as a toad. Too cold and slimy. And besides, my people would likely skin me if I dared to offend a MacFinnan spellweaver. In case ye hadnae noticed, they hold ye in high esteem, lass."

Rose snorted. "Why do I get the feeling you're now making fun of me?"

"Not at all. They do hold ye in high esteem." His eyes met hers across the desk. "As do I."

Rose said nothing. It was there again, that something in his eyes that had been there last night. But last night he was drunk and he wasn't now. A tingling sensation went through her, and she felt heat rushing to her cheeks.

She cleared her throat and looked down at the map, suddenly realizing there were no more reports to read. The map of the island was now covered with lots of little tally charts. Rose swallowed. There were an awful lot of them.

She rose to her feet so she could get a better look at the map and Cailean came to stand beside her.

"So many," he breathed.

"So many," she echoed.

How was she supposed to fix this? The curse was a magic strong enough to affect an entire people and she was a thirty-something divorcee who just happened to have a few tricks at her disposal. How could she expect to make a difference?

A hand settling on her shoulder startled her out of her thoughts. She hadn't realized she'd closed her eyes or clenched her fists until Cailean rumbled, "Relax, lass."

She let out a slow breath, trying for a calm she didn't feel, and forced her attention back to the map. There were cases of sickness all over the island as she'd expected and they were concentrated along the coast, again as she'd expected considering this was where most settlements were found.

But there seemed to be more along the west coast and a cluster in one place in particular. Rose tapped the spot on the map.

"What is this place?"

"Hemkirk," Cailean replied. He frowned. "I dinna know why there's such a high concentration there. The place is tiny. Little more than a fishing hamlet."

"Then I think we'd better find out, don't you? We were looking for a place to start, weren't we? Hemkirk it is."

FOR THE SECOND time in as many days, Cailean found himself riding with Rose MacFinnan. He could have had some of his men accompany them, but he'd decided against it. They were needed back at Dun Mallach he told himself, although deep down he knew that wasn't the real reason he had left them behind.

He wanted to be alone with Rose.

As they left Dun Mallach and took the inland path that would take them through the heart of the island to the west coast, he wondered what in all the fates he'd been thinking. It was reckless to be alone with her after what had almost happened between them last night.

He glanced in her direction. She was riding by his side, keeping her seat with more confidence than yesterday although she kept grimacing from time to time as though she still had aching muscles.

To be honest, he would much rather have had her riding with him on Arrow but he could think of no good reason to suggest she do so, so she was mounted on Snip once more. The mare plodded docilely along by Arrow's side, content to follow the bigger horse's lead.

It was a good job Snip *was* so docile, he reflected, seeing as her rider was giving her very little guidance and paying her scant attention. Instead, ever since they'd left the castle, Rose's attention had been fixed on the map that she was holding awkwardly in front of her, arms wide as she held it out, studying it with fierce determination.

"It willnae change," he said. "No matter how much ye stare at it."

"No, but I might see something I've missed," she said without looking up.

"Lass, with the amount ye've been studying that map it's a wonder ye dinna see it in yer sleep."

She sighed. "All right. Point taken." She folded the map and twisted around to stow it in the saddle bag behind her. "Happy?"

"Very. At least now I dinna have to worry about Snip putting her foot in a hole because her rider's mind is elsewhere."

Rose gathered up the reins and patted Snip on the shoulder. "I wouldn't let you hurt yourself, would I, girl? No, I wouldn't. Good horse."

Snip tossed her mane, clearly pleased by the attention.

Cailean rolled his eyes. Between Catriona and Rose, he would be lucky to have any decent working animals left.

They were heading inland and the sea was now only a faint strip of blue along the horizon behind them. The interior of the island was made up of deep glens and rocky hills, with thick stands of forest dotted between. It was sparsely populated, being farthest from the sea that gave the people of Barra their livelihood, and the few roads were little more than shepherds' tracks.

Still, Cailean knew this place like the back of his hand although he'd not been out this way since the sickness had started and he realized that he'd missed the wide-open spaces and the endless skies. Although, he reflected, the sky did not look very welcoming today. The sunny promise of the morning had given way to clouds that filled the sky from end to end, like a blanket thrown over the world, heavy with rain.

The wind was blowing away from them though, and if they were very lucky, they might escape the downpour that threatened.

Luck, he thought sourly. *Hardly. Clan MacNeil seems to be fresh out of such a thing.*

"Do you know 'I spy'?" Rose asked suddenly.

Cailean glanced at her. "What?"

"'I spy'. It's a word game. You play it to pass the time. My sisters and I used to play it all the time when we were little and our mother had taken us on a long road trip. Stopped us getting bored and acting up. Come on, it's easy. You look around for something you can see, then say the letter it begins with. The other player has to guess what you've chosen. I'll go first."

A little bemused, Cailean watched as she looked around, eyes scanning the muddy path they were riding along and the damp vegetation to either side. They were passing through a wide valley, with bracken covered slopes. The bracken was already starting to turn brown with the turn of the seasons. Winter, he realized, would soon be upon them.

"Got it!" Rose said. "I spy with my little eye, something beginning with *f*."

"Ferns," he said immediately.

Rose frowned at him. "How did you get that so quickly?"

He quirked an eyebrow at her. "Lass, look around. There's naught else for miles."

She gave an annoyed little harrumph. "All right. You suggest a game."

"This is hardly my area of expertise," Cailean replied. "Although I do play a mean game of drafts."

"You do? Excellent! Then I challenge you to a duel when we get back to Dun Mallach."

She was smiling and, looking at her, Cailean felt that odd sensation inside him again, that seemed to come upon him whenever he was in her company. She was a MacFinnan spellweaver, a woman with incredible powers and carried the expectation of a whole clan on her shoulders. Yet here she was, getting excited at the prospect of a game of drafts. She was unlike anyone he'd ever met.

Despite himself, he smiled. "All right, ye are on."

"Excellent! It's a date!"

Cailean didn't know what a *date* was, but Rose's expression changed suddenly, as though she'd said something she hadn't meant to. Her cheeks colored and she cleared her throat.

"Well, I don't mean a 'date' obviously. I just mean… well… erm…"

"Aye, lass," Cailean cut her off. "It's a date."

Rose's eyes were a little wide. "Well, okay then." She blinked and looked away. "I don't like the look of those clouds," she blurted. "It looks like we are going to get a drenching."

Cailean licked his thumb then held it up, judging the wind direction. "We willnae. The wind is coming from behind us. If it holds course until we reach Hemkirk we'll be fine. If it doesnae…" He shrugged. "Then we *will* get a drenching."

"I hope you're right. I forgot my umbrella." He looked her askance and she waved a hand. "Don't worry about it. A modern invention to keep you dry."

He nodded. "We have something similar. It's called a hood."

Rose couldn't help laughing at that.

As it turned out, Cailean was right. The wind continued to push the clouds away from them and by the time they reached Hemkirk, they hung far out over the sea, looking black and angry. Cailean didn't envy any fishermen who would be caught out in that when the rain hit.

But the clouds above them began to break up, letting through shafts of intermittent sunlight as they rode down the hill towards where Hemkirk nestled along the shore in the distance. There was not much to the settlement. A deep natural harbor meant larger fishing vessels could dock here but the poor soil and sparse grass on this side of the island made it difficult to grow crops or graze livestock. As a result, the village was a fishing station and little else, and the few families who lived here traded their fish for the supplies they needed from elsewhere.

There were around ten houses, built of stone and turf to better endure the weather on this side of the island, as well as a wooden chapel with a crude cross attached to its roof. The people of Hemkirk had been some of Sister Beatrice's earliest converts and she slogged over here each Sunday to read mass.

Many of the fishing boats, which would normally be out on the waves at this hour, were still bobbing gently in the harbor and the only signs of life they saw was a sheepdog lying on the wharf with a bone between its front paws, gnawing hungrily.

The dog spotted them riding down the winding path and sprang to its feet, barking madly. The racket brought a few villagers out of their houses—mostly women Cailean noticed—and they watched him and Rose approach with wary expressions on their faces.

When they reached the group, Cailean pulled Arrow to a halt and looked around at the rag-tag group. There were a few younger children and older males but Cailean didn't see many youths or working-age men. Were they all out on the fishing boats? But if so, why were so many of the boats still in port?

He dismounted in order to seem less intimidating, Rose following his example. "Greetings," he said to the group. "Who speaks for this village?"

The villagers glanced among themselves before an old woman pushed her way to the front. She had long gray hair in two plaits in the Norse style and the weathered, leathery skin of someone who spent most of their time out of doors.

"I do. My name is Agnes. My husband was the headman of this village. Welcome to Hemkirk, Laird MacNeil." She looked him up and down with an appraising expression before her gaze flicked to Rose. "What can we do for ye?"

Her tone wasn't exactly suspicious, but it wasn't particularly welcoming either. The folks on this side of the island were notoriously independent and didn't take kindly to anyone poking their noses into their business. But he was still their laird and they were still his responsibility.

"We've coming looking for information," he said. "Information that might help us in the fight against the sickness." He indicated for Rose to step up beside him. "Rose here is a healer and is trying to track the source of the sickness."

Rose smiled around at them. "Hi," she said. "I'm Rose. Rose MacFinnan."

Her name had an instant effect on the crowd. A collective gasp went up and Cailean heard whispers of, "A spellweaver! Here! God be praised!"

They swarmed forward, surrounding him and Rose, all talking at once, all firing stories of the sickness at Rose and asking a hundred questions besides.

"Wait!" Rose cried. "One at a time!" But her voice was drowned out in the clamor.

"Quiet!" Cailean bellowed. The crowd fell silent and he addressed Agnes in a quieter voice. "Is there somewhere we can go to discuss this?"

The old woman nodded. "Aye. Follow me, my laird." She

eyed the rest of the crowd. "And the lot of ye will wait outside while I speak to the laird and the spellweaver."

She led them through the village, the crowd following behind, until they reached a stone house with a turf roof. It was slightly bigger than the rest, as befit the headman of a village. The door was low and Cailean had to duck as he followed Agnes inside.

Within, it was more homey than Cailean had expected, with a meticulously swept flagstone floor, thick hangings softening the stone walls, pots and pans and bunches of herbs hanging from the ceiling, and a fire burning merrily in the hearth. Thick beams held up a ceiling, so low that Cailen had to stoop. Above the hearth hung a wooden cross but also an offering woven out of strings of seashells and coarse grass. Like many of his people, Agnes clearly embraced both the old ways and the new.

Rose looked around with wide, curious eyes as she stepped inside. "Wow," he heard her murmur under her breath. "A real highland cottage. Elise is never going to believe this."

Agnes waved at the two driftwood chairs by the fire—the only seats in the place—but Cailean remained standing, indicating the two women to take the seats instead. Rose sat in one and Agnes took the other, perching on the edge and clasping her hands in her lap, looking a little nervous.

"Well?" she asked. "What help can I give the laird and a MacFinnan spellweaver?"

Rose glanced at Cailean and he signaled for her to speak. After all, she knew what she was looking for better than he did. Rose took out the map and another rolled up parchment from the saddle bag slung over her shoulder.

"I was hoping you might help us get to the bottom of a mystery," she said. "I've been trying to figure out if there is a pattern to how the sickness strikes. There seems to have been an unusual concentration of cases in Hemkirk and I'm trying to understand why."

Agnes went a little pale, and she clasped her hands together even harder. "Isnae it obvious why?" she said, her voice cold and bitter. "It is a punishment from the Lord. We've angered Him. We need to repent our sins if any of us are to be saved."

Rose's eyes shone with compassion as she studied Agnes's weathered face. "I'm so sorry that it hit this village so hard," she said softly. "And I'm so sorry you lost your husband. The sickness took him, didn't it?"

Agnes watched Rose, her eyes filling with tears, before nodding tightly. "Aye, it did. Along with over half the village. Now they all look to me for leadership but I'm just an old woman. I canna do anything! I canna help anyone!"

The façade of calm authority that she'd shown outside in front of her people cracked and now she just looked old and tired and very afraid. Rose reached out and clasped her hand.

"You're doing just fine. But if you can help me, I'm hopeful that you won't need to lose anyone else."

A faint spark of hope came into Agnes's eyes and she squeezed Rose's hand in return. Cailean crossed his arms over his broad chest and remained silent.

Rose unrolled a parchment on her lap. "This is a list of names I've compiled of everyone who has succumbed to the sickness in Hemkirk. I can't find any kind of pattern as to why these were affected and not others. There's no pattern in age, gender, or anything else that I can see. Sicknesses like these are normally contagious but there are numerous times in this case where one or two members of the same family have fallen ill but the rest haven't. Sicknesses also usually take the very young and the very old first, but again, the youngsters and the oldsters seem to have gotten away unscathed. I can't make sense of it. I was hoping you might see something that I can't."

She held out the parchment to Agnes who took it with a shaking hand. She glanced at names then back at Rose. "Could ye read it to me? I canna read."

Rose looked a little taken aback but recovered quickly. "Of course." She pulled her chair over beside Agnes's and began reading the names on the list one by one. It was a long list for a village so small and listening to it, Cailean couldn't blame Agnes or her people for their loss of hope. Perhaps they were right. Perhaps it *was* a punishment from God. What else could explain why so many here had been taken?

Agnes listened in silence as Rose read out all the names. "Is there anything that stands out to you?" she asked Agnes finally. "Anything that they all have in common?"

Agnes sat very still, her brow furrowed in concentration. "I dinna…" She began to shake her head and then stopped. Her eyes narrowed. "Wait… it canna be, can it?" She looked up Cailean and then at Rose. "I didnae see it before."

Cailean took a step closer, towering over the two seated women. "What?" he demanded. "What did ye not see before?"

"Those names ye gave me. They *do* have something in common." She glanced at Rose and then back at Cailean. "They all make their living out at sea. I dinna mean *from* the sea—we all do that, be that mending nets or gutting the catch when it comes in. I mean the ones who actually go out on the boats. Every single name on that list is a member of a boat crew." She wiped a shaking hand across her forehead. "That's why the children and the old havenae been affected."

"Because they dinna go out on the boats," Cailean breathed.

"And why family members haven't caught it off each other," Rose added. "Because it's not contracted from people. It's contracted from the sea."

Cailean felt something cold settle in his belly. The sickness came from the sea? The thing that they relied on for so much was slowly killing them?

He shook his head. "How can this be?"

"I… I don't know," Rose replied, looking a little shaken in turn. "But people need to be told. They have to stay away from the water. In fact, it would be best if everyone moved inland until this is over."

"Move inland?" Agnes said. "Stay away from the water? How

can we do that? We rely on the sea for our livelihood."

"She's right," Cailean said, feeling the words like weights on his tongue. "Such a restriction would never work. Too many people depend on the sea and its bounty to put food on the table."

"Even if it's killing them?" Rose snapped.

Cailean shrugged. "Even then. I dinna think they would ever be able to believe that the sea is the source of our woes. They would rather live in ignorance."

Rose pressed her lips into a flat line, clearly unhappy with this.

Cailean turned to Agnes. "But I want ye and yer people to leave here," he said. "Come to Dun Mallach. Ye will be housed and fed there until this is over. Ye have already lost too much. I willnae lose anyone else here to this sickness."

But Agnes only shook her head. "I thank ye for the offer, my laird, but my people willnae come. This is their home, all they've ever known. They willnae leave it and neither will I."

Cailean could force them if needed. He could have a contingent of warriors here in hours and have the people forcibly marched back to Dun Mallach for their own safety. But he knew he wouldn't. That would only turn them against him and besides, he understood all too well the ties a place could wrap around a person's heart.

He ran a hand through his hair and let out a long, slow breath. "All right. But if ye change yer mind, ye will have a place at Dun Mallach."

Agnes gave him a small smile, then climbed wearily to her feet and patted Cailean's hand. "Ye are a good man, my laird. I know ye will do everything ye can to see us safely through this. I knew yer father in my youth, and he would be proud of the man ye've become."

Cailean didn't know how to respond to that. He coughed. "Aye, well. We'd better be going." He placed his hand over Agnes's. It felt as frail as a bird's wing in his big paw. "But ye think on what I said. I mean it, Agnes. I dinna wish to lose any more of ye."

"I know. And I will. Ye have my word."

He squeezed her hand then pulled the door open, holding it open for Rose to proceed him.

Outside, the villagers were still gathered, but Cailean led Rose through them without a word. They mounted their horses and rode off, leaving Hemkirk and its beleaguered people behind them.

Chapter Ten

ROSE PINCHED THE bridge of her nose and leaned back on the stool after checking on her latest patient. She had a headache forming behind her left eye and no pills to help take it off. Perhaps she'd ask Maggie or Beatrice what they used for headaches in this time. Willow bark? Feverfew?

If she got the time, that was. Since they'd returned from Hemkirk, it seemed she hadn't had a moment to herself.

Seven more patients had arrived at the infirmary while she and Cailean had been away. All with the sickness. All with exactly the same symptoms as the others. And she'd been able to help exactly none of them. Like Drew, all she'd been able to do was put them into that comatose state that at least arrested the sickness.

She sighed, looking down at the figure in the bed. It was an elderly woman from the village, a warm old soul by all accounts who was much loved by her neighbors even though she had no family of her own. It was two of her neighbors who'd brought her up to the keep when she'd fallen ill. Now, she lay on the pallet as though asleep, but Rose knew she wasn't. If she placed her hand on the woman's forehead, she knew she would feel the sickness raging in her beneath the stasis she'd placed her in.

With a sigh, she rubbed the side of her face and closed her eyes. So far, she'd come up with no way to help these people. So much for the vaunted all-powerful spellweaver!

"Here," said a voice.

Rose looked up to see Maggie standing over her holding out a small pottery cup.

She took it. "What's this?"

"My own concoction. Good for aches and pains and a bit of a pick-me-up. Ye look like ye could do with it."

Rose smiled wryly then downed the concoction. It was bitter enough to make her wince, but she finished it all the same.

"There's naught else ye can do here," Maggie continued. "Why dinna ye go and get some rest? We'll call ye if aught changes."

With a grateful nod, Rose got up, squeezed Maggie's shoulder, and left the infirmary. Stepping out into the cool evening air, she paused for a minute to take a few deep, invigorating breaths. The wind had picked up and dark clouds were beginning to cover the sky. It looked like a storm was on its way. She began to walk off but paused when she spotted a figure coming along the path towards her.

It was Cailean. He'd changed out of his riding clothes and now wore a white shirt, with the plaid of Clan MacNeil draped over his shoulder, across his chest, and falling in waves to his knees. She caught a glimpse of bare, muscled thigh as he stopped in front of her.

Rose swallowed thickly, forcing her eyes upwards. "Maggie and Beatrice are inside if you're looking for them."

"I'm not. I was looking for ye."

"Oh? Why?"

"Catriona's orders. She was mighty disappointed when ye didnae come to dinner. She made me promise I would ensure ye take a rest."

Despite herself, Rose found herself smiling. "Did she now? Well, I suppose I'd better do as she says. The last thing I want to do is risk the wrath of a nine-year-old."

Cailean nodded sagely. "Most wise. Which is why I brought these."

He held up a small wooden case and a muslin-wrapped bundle that gave off a delicious smell.

"Drafts and pie. After all, didnae I promise ye a... what did ye call it? A date?"

Rose flushed. It was obvious Cailean had no idea what a *date* was or its significance, but that didn't stop heat rushing to her cheeks. Oh hell. Why hadn't she kept her mouth shut?

She nodded, not trusting herself to speak, and they returned to the keep and made their way to the study.

Once inside, Cailean pulled over a stool and perched on it while he set up the drafts board on the desk. Rose took the chair and munched on a bit of pie as she watched him.

Was this really the same gruff, taciturn man who'd pulled her out of the water when she'd first arrived? That man had been wary, suspicious even. Then he had *not* been the kind of man who would come check on her welfare.

But, she was beginning to realize, Cailean MacNeil was nothing like what she'd originally thought. He was far more complicated than the rough Highland laird he first appeared to be, and beneath the hard exterior was something far softer and far warmer.

Cailean MacNeil, she suspected, was the kind of man who would sacrifice everything for the people he loved.

"Are ye ready to play?"

His words startled her out of her thoughts. He'd set up the game and was watching her expectantly.

"Are you kidding? I was born ready."

"Is that so? Then ye can go first. But I warn ye, no funny business. I've been playing my daughter for years and have an eagle's eye when it comes to cheating."

Rose's eyebrows climbed her forehead. "Me? Cheat? How dare you? I'm hurt. I really am."

She smiled to soften the words before studying her pieces. Or, that's what she tried to do at any rate. But despite her best efforts, she found her gaze flickering to the man seated across from her.

Cailean sat hunched on the stool, chin propped on his hand. The candlelight cast golden highlights into his dark hair as it fell around his face in lazy waves.

"Ye canna make yer move unless ye study yer pieces first," he rumbled.

"I *am* studying my pieces," she protested.

"Really? It seems ye are more interested in yer opponent."

Rose scowled, annoyed that he'd noticed. "Don't flatter yourself, MacNeil."

His only answer was a broad grin. She reached out and moved one of her pieces. Cailean sucked his teeth then moved one of his own. Rose moved another of hers. Then Cailean jumped her piece and claimed it.

Rose sat back in the chair, narrowing her eyes at him. "That was underhanded."

"That was strategy. I said ye ought to be concentrating, didnae I?"

She forced her attention to the game. Did he know how much his presence was distracting her? Was he doing this deliberately? Damn it. She really needed to get a grip on herself.

She moved another of her pieces, but her attention was still more on her playing partner and the way the firelight flickered in his eyes than on the game. To make matters worse, as he leaned forward the collar of his linen shirt fell open, giving her a glimpse of the sculpted chest beneath. She swallowed. Oh hell.

As the game progressed Rose couldn't have named any of the moves she'd made since Cailean had sat down.

"Thanks, by the way," she said suddenly.

"For what?" he replied, a little startled. "Beating ye at drafts?"

"You haven't beaten me yet, MacNeil."

He laughed. "Ah! There it is, that famous MacFinnan fire the stories talk about."

"Yep. You better believe it." She hunched forward and studied the game's layout. Unfortunately, there was no way she could now win. Under her breath she muttered the words of a spell and several of the pieces changed color so quickly it was almost impossible to detect. Then she made her move, using the changed pieces to take several of his. It tipped the balance.

"Ha! I win!"

Cailean was not fooled. He crossed his arms over his broad chest. "Do ye think I'm blind, woman? Ye cheated."

"I did not! How dare you?"

"Lass, I have been schooled in cheating by the very best."

Rose burst out laughing. "Oh, all right! So I cheated a little. Happy now?"

He shrugged. "I dinna mind losing," he said softly, "if it means I get to hear ye laugh."

Rose went very still. Her eyes met Cailean's and she was suddenly unable to look away. Her heart began to beat a staccato rhythm that she was sure Cailean would be able to hear if he leaned a little closer.

Silence stretched between them, broken only by the howl of the wind rattling the shutters as the storm gathered. Rose was suddenly hyper aware of him, of the soft rise and fall of his chest, of the strand of hair falling across one eye that she longed to reach out and brush away.

"Cailean," she began, not sure what she wanted to say.

Somewhere outside a dog barked. Rose jumped and Cailean was off the stool and over to the tiny window in an instant, suddenly alert and tense.

Then his shoulders relaxed. "Uneasy because of the weather," he said. "Naught to worry about."

Rose stood abruptly, nearly upending the drafts board in her haste. One of her red pieces rolled across the desk and clattered to the floor. "I... I should go."

Cailean turned from the window. "Did I do something wrong?"

"No," she said quickly. A little too quickly. "Nothing like that. It's just that..." *What? I'm worried that if I stay in your company much longer, I'll do something I'll regret. I'm worried that when I'm near you I seem to lose all common sense.*

It was ridiculous. They barely knew each other and were from worlds so different they may as well come from different planets. So why did his presence light an ache beneath her ribs the like of which she'd never felt before? Not even Dennis had made her feel like this. *Nobody* had ever made her feel like this.

And it was terrifying.

"I... um... I think that's enough strategy for one night."

A faint smile curled his lips. "Aye. Cheating is hard work."

She gave him a flat look. "I'll ignore that."

"Let me walk ye up."

"You don't have to do that."

"I know. I want to."

She nodded, not trusting herself to speak.

The keep was quiet as they made their way up the stairs to the guest wing although the sound of hammering rain could now be heard on the roof. Outside, the dog barked again and this time she heard the annoyed voice of one of the wall's guards telling it to be quiet. A few candles burned in sconces, creating pools of candlelight amid the shadow.

She paused at the door to her room, one hand on the handle.

"Rose," Cailean said softly behind her.

She turned and found him standing closer than she expected, so close that she could feel the warmth of him. So close that all she needed to do was go up on tiptoes and her lips would touch his.

He reached out and his fingers brushed hers where they rested on the door handle. It was a light touch, no more than the brush of a butterfly's wing, but it was enough to intensify that ache beneath her ribs.

"Good night," he said, his voice thick.

She swallowed. Nodded. "Good night, Cailean."

He stepped back, his eyes lingering on her face, then turned and walked away. Only when he had disappeared from view did Rose turn the door handle and let herself into her room. She leaned back against the door, heart hammering. Against the back of her eyelids all she saw was Cailean's face and the way he'd looked at her just now. Looked at her like he wanted to...

With an effort, she pushed the thoughts aside, crossed to the pitcher, and splashed cold water on her face. This trip into the past was not working out how she thought it would. Instead of a quick, easy healing, it was getting more complicated by the moment, and she could feel the knot tightening around her.

The sooner she went home the better. For all their sakes.

Chapter Eleven

"Everyone ready?" Cailean shouted, scanning the line of men spread out along the half collapsed wall of the barn. "We move it on three. One. Two. Three."

He got his shoulder under a beam, and he and his men heaved upwards with all their strength. He felt his muscles straining, felt the veins standing out in his neck as it inched upwards until, finally, he and his men heaved the beam over and sent it crashing to the ground on the other side of the wall.

With a grunt, Cailean straightened, putting his hands on his hips and leaning back to stretch his aching muscles. It was still raining, cold, hard droplets that seemed determined to find their way down the back of his neck no matter what he did. He was soaked to the bone, his clothes clinging uncomfortably to his skin, and he kept having to shake his head to clear water from eyes.

Fine Barra weather, he thought wryly.

The storm that had threatened yesterday had finally broken in the early hours of the morning, thunder cracking so loudly that it woke him from sleep and lightning flashing so brightly that it lit the inside of the keep from end to end. He'd got up, checked on Catriona—who was busy trying to calm a terrified Patch—and then gone out into the lashing tempest to ensure there was no damage to the keep.

As it turned out, Dun Mallach escaped lightly, with only the thatched roof from a log store being ripped off, but the village had not been so lucky. At first light, several villagers had come to fetch him, and he and his men had hurried down the hill, taking in the damage as they went.

There was a lot. Roofs had been torn away. Fences had been toppled. Stores and belongings had been scattered everywhere. At first, as he surveyed the damage, Cailean had felt the cold hands of despair reaching into his soul. First the sickness, now this. Why were his people being punished so?

"All right," he shouted, snapping back to the present. "Abe, Colin, Malcolm, see if ye can get some more of this debris shifted. Dougall, Cam, Sean, with me. We need to get that tree shifted from Old Seamus's house."

His men fell into step around him as he turned and walked uphill to where a fallen tree had crashed right through the middle of a house. Old Seamus, the house's occupant, was sitting on an upturned barrel, looking slightly dazed. He was lucky to be alive. He'd stepped out of the house to take a piss right before the tree had toppled, otherwise, he'd have been crushed when it fell. Perhaps the old gods or the new had a soft spot for the querulous old man.

Cailean walked over and laid a hand on the man's shoulder. "How are ye holding up?"

The old man blinked owlishly before lifting his head to look up at Cailean. "Ach, dinna ye worry, lad," he said. "It'll take more than a bloody tree to get the best of me."

How true those words were. Seamus was the oldest man on Barra, and even though he was approaching his eightieth year, he was still sprightly and determined, and flatly refused to go live with his daughter and her family so they could take care of him. Still, he would have little choice now until his cottage was repaired.

"How's the ankle?" Cailean asked.

The old man waved away his concern. "It's naught. Just twisted."

"Even so, I'll have Maggie or Beatrice take a look at it just as soon as they get a minute."

He issued a few orders to his men, and they began tackling the fallen tree with axes. It was not large—a hoary old apple tree from the orchard at the back of Seamus's house—but its trunk had snapped clean in two and it had crashed right through the roof and taken half of the house's front wall with it. Aye, Seamus was a lucky man indeed.

Cailean stood back, surveying the village. It was a hive of activity, like a kicked ant's nest. The worst of the storm had blown through as quickly as it came and he could see the storm clouds slowly moving out to sea, but the rain was still lashing down and the wind had become gusting, veering around unexpectedly and making everyone's work that much harder.

Still, at least Catriona was safe up at the castle. He'd given her stern instructions to stay put and tasked the cook with keeping an eye on her to make sure she didn't try and sneak down to the village—which she would, given half the chance.

Rose was safely sheltered up there as well. His thoughts turned towards his dark-haired guest, and his stomach did an odd little flip as he did so. Had she gotten any sleep with the storm raging outside? Or had she sat in her room, frightened and alone?

He snorted, almost rolling his eyes at such a ridiculous thought. Rose MacFinnan frightened? He had yet to see her scared by anything. Even so, he should have checked on her. But cowardice had kept him from doing so, afraid of what he might do if he faced her again. Now his thoughts kept returning to her over and over, when what he should have been doing was concentrating on his duties.

He growled under his breath and ran a hand through his sodden hair, brushing it out of his eyes. He heard a commotion from uphill and turned just as he spotted a figure coming down the path. Cailean didn't need the sudden cry of "the spellweaver is coming" to know who it was. His body seemed to recognize her before his brain did as his heart seemed to stutter a little and a tingle went right through him.

"Rose," he breathed.

She stopped to talk to a few people and then carried on towards him as those people pointed out his location. She seemed almost to glide over the muddy ground, as though she was immune to the mess and chaos around her, despite the way her hair was sticking to her face and her dress whipping around her ankles.

She came to a halt in front of him. A large basket was clasped in her hands, packed with bandages and other medical supplies. Her cheeks were pink from the cold.

Cailean scowled at her, even though he wanted to grin like an idiot at the sight of her. "Ye shouldnae be here," he said. "The path is slick with mud, and half the hillside is ready to slide."

"And yet I made it," she replied with a light shrug. "You didn't think I was just going to sit by the fire when there are people out here who need my help?"

"That's *exactly* what ye should have done. Maggie and Beatrice can handle things. Ye shouldnae be putting yerself at risk."

Her nostrils flared, and annoyance flashed across her face. "Excuse me, laird." She slipped past him before he could say anything and knelt in front of Seamus.

Cailean turned and caught the grins of his men, who'd stopped working to watch their altercation. He rubbed his temple. "Back to work, all of ye."

Rose was talking quietly to Seamus, her voice soft and soothing in a way his could never be and, for a wonder, the old man didn't even grumble as she probed his ankle and then bound it tightly in a clean white bandage.

"Don't put any weight on it for the next few days," she told him before glancing at the ruined house behind. "Is there anywhere else you can stay?"

"I'm not going anywhere! I've lived here for sixty years and I'm not about to—"

"Aye," Cailean cut in. "He's going to stay with his daughter, whether he likes it or nay."

Seamus turned a glare on his laird. Left to his own devices, the stubborn old goat would no doubt continue as before, even though his cottage was little more than splintered bits of wood and tumbled stone. God save him from stubborn people who didn't know what was good for them! He wasn't sure whether he was thinking of Seamus or Rose.

"Come on," he said. "I'll take ye to Brina's house."

"I'm not some bairn who needs his arse wiped!" Seamus snapped. "I can make my own way, thank ye very much!"

Irritation flared in Cailean's stomach. He didn't have time for this. He opened his mouth, but before he could bellow at the old man, Rose stepped neatly between them.

"We know that. But if you try to walk on that ankle, you will only delay your recovery, and then it will take even longer before you can come home." She held out a hand. "How about the laird and I *both* escort you to Brina's?"

Seamus screwed his face into a sour expression but nodded tightly. He pointed a spindly finger at Cailean. "But nobody is carrying me!"

Cailean rolled his eyes. "Wouldnae dream of it. Ye are too spindly and full of thorns to attempt it, old man." He shouted to some of his men, who brought over a small handcart.

She and Cailean helped Seamus into the cart with a lot of puffing and swearing on the old man's part, and then Cailean took hold of the handles and began pushing it. Rose walked beside the cart, steadying the blankets she'd wrapped around Seamus's shoulders as they began their trek along the muddy trail.

ROSE SAW EVIDENCE of the storm everywhere. Fences were down, bedraggled chickens and goats wandering wherever they liked, thatch had been torn from roofs, overturned buckets and barrels, broken branches, and piles of sodden leaves lay everywhere.

The storm had been a wild one, all right. It had kept her awake most of the night, howling around the keep's walls like an angry spirit shouting to be let in. Although she had to admit it, she'd not been asleep, anyway. There was too much going around in her head for sleep to come easily.

She didn't look at Cailean as they made their way through the village, but she could *feel* him. His presence was like a lodestone, and she was sure she would be able to pinpoint his direction even with her eyes closed.

They finally reached Seamus's daughter's house, a large, ramshackle place that stood on the edge of the village and seemed to have escaped the worst of the storm's ravages. Seamus's daughter, a big-boned woman with flaming red hair, came hurrying up the path, wiping her hands on an apron and surrounded by a gaggle of excited children.

"Grandpa!" they cried, gathering around the cart and firing a hundred questions at Seamus.

Seamus, for his part, managed to crack a smile. "One at a time! I canna hear myself think with all yer caterwauling!"

"What have ye gone and done to yerself this time, Da?" his daughter asked, putting her hands on her ample hips and glaring down at the old man.

Seamus waved a hand. "Dinna fash, Brina. It's only a twisted ankle. But ye should see the tree that tried to kill me!" He turned to his grandchildren. "Enormous, it was! Came straight for me, it did, but yer old grandpa is too wily to be caught by any mangy old tree!"

The children gasped, wide-eyed.

Brina rolled her eyes. "Thank ye for yer help, my laird," she said to Cailean. "Please come inside."

Cailean helped Seamus out of the cart and into Brina's house, where he collapsed into a chair by the fire. Rose knelt to check the bandages while Cailean enquired after Brina and her family.

"Och, we got through unscathed, thank the old gods and the new," Brina said. "And the children thought it was all grand fun. My husband, Eoin, has gone to check on the boats. It was low tide though, so I'm hopeful there isnae too much damage."

Cailean nodded. "Aye. Let's hope ye are right."

Brina poured them both mugs of hot cider from a pot hanging over the fire, and Rose took hers gratefully. Her hands were red from the cold, and she enjoyed the heat that flowed into her fingers as she wrapped them around the warm cup.

"We've not had a storm like that in many a year," Brina said, taking a sip from her own mug. "Why, it was enough to almost make ye believe in the old tales again. Especially with the stormlights."

"Stormlights?" Rose asked, turning a puzzled glance on the woman.

"Ye didnae see them?" Brina replied. "Over by the headland? Like lightning but underwater. Blue, and green, and purple. Reminded me of the old tales my da used to tell me when I was a bairn. The bairns thought it was the sea god rising in anger again. They hid under the table!"

"No, we didnae!" the children piped up. "It was ye who was frightened, Ma!"

Cailean grunted noncommittally, but Rose straightened, curiosity prickling.

"There are old tales about sea gods?" she asked.

Seamus waved a hand. "Bah! Of course there are. What do ye expect from a people who depend on the sea? My old gran used to say the Kingdom of the Isles was watched over by a god and goddess. He ruled the sea, and she ruled the land. She loved her people and brought them good fishing and calm weather. But the god grew jealous, thinking she loved the people more than she loved him, so he cursed her."

Rose's grip tightened on her mug. "Cursed her how?"

"Who knows? But the old tales say the stormlights are his wrath rising, trying to draw her back—or punish her for leaving."

He shrugged. "Ye see? Naught but a child's tale."

Rose narrowed her eyes, thinking. "Is it?" she said softly. "Or is it something more? I wonder."

Cailean glanced at her. "What are ye thinking, lass?"

Rose blinked, clearing her thoughts. "I... um... nothing. Yet." She finished her cider and handed the empty mug out to Brina. "Thank you for the drink. It's warmed me up nicely. Try to keep your dad off his feet for the next few days if you can."

"I'm right here, ye know," Seamus grumbled.

Brina rolled her eyes. "Dinna ye worry. I'll make sure he behaves himself, even if I have to get the children to pin him down."

The children cheered at this and began hanging onto Seamus's arms. The old man struggled weakly, threatening them with dire retribution that went wholly ignored. Rose couldn't help but smile at the rough affection that so obviously tied this family together. Seamus, she was sure, would be absolutely fine.

But if the sickness came here... The thought of Seamus, Brina, and the children in a similar state to Drew made her stomach churn. She had to stop that from happening.

She and Cailean took their leave of Brina and her family and made their way back up to the village. They worked all morning, Cailean with his men clearing debris, shifting fallen trees, repairing damaged walls and roofs, while Rose took care of the injured—bandaged hands, cleaned scrapes, and stitched the odd gash caused by flying debris.

But all the while, her thoughts kept returning to Brina and Seamus's words. *The stormlights are his wrath rising, trying to draw her back—or punish her for leaving.*

Cailean called a break at midday. Rose finished cleaning a young girl's skinned knees and straightened, stretching out her aching back. Her dress was sodden, soaked with mud up to the ankles, and her braid was a wet lump hanging down her back. Oh, what she wouldn't give for a hot shower!

Cailean came to fetch her, and they walked back up to the

keep together, arms brushing occasionally. He looked as exhausted as she was—and as filthy. His clothes were caked in mud, and his hair slick and clinging to his neck. They walked in silence, too tired to speak.

But eventually Cailean said, "Ye looked at home today."

She glanced at him. "I did?"

"Aye. Like… like ye belonged. Perhaps ye didnae notice the way the people responded to ye, but I did. Ye are no longer a stranger, lass. Ye are one of us."

Rose blinked. *Ye are one of us.* She wasn't quite sure what to make of that. It felt kind of… nice.

"What did you make of Brina's tale?" she asked, changing the subject.

He shrugged. "Not much. One thing ye will learn the longer ye spend here is that there is an old wife's tale for everything. An old man gets a wart on his nose? It's because he stole a lobster from a sacred rock pool."

Rose laughed. "I take your point. But… I don't know… It felt like more than that."

"Then ye should speak to Maggie."

"Maggie?"

"Aye, she knows all the old tales, every rhyme and riddle this island has ever whispered. If one of them talks about a sea god and his stormlights, she'll know it."

Rose mulled over this in silence as they walked up to the gates of the keep. It was raining again, an annoying misty drizzle that turned the world to gray fog. She could hardly see anything beyond a few feet, cocooning her and Cailean in their own little world.

"I'll have Mable heat water for a bath," he told her, turning to face her as they paused just inside the gates. "We dinna want our MacFinnan spellweaver to catch a cold, do we?"

Rose's eyes slid closed. "A hot bath? That sounds like heaven."

He reached out and flicked away a stray strand of hair that

was clinging to her face. As he did so, his hand brushed her cheek, sending a thrill of warmth right through her.

"Thank you," she said.

His eyebrows rose. "For what? Thank Mable. *She'll* be the one hauling the water up to yer bathtub."

"Not that. Well, yes, that. But... I don't know." *For making me feel wanted*, she thought. *That I matter. For making me feel... alive.*

But she didn't say any of those things. Instead, she went up on her tiptoes and kissed him. It was only a light brush of her lips on his cheek, but the effect was instantaneous.

Cailean froze.

The rain began to fall more heavily, shimmering sheets that turned the world to opalescent gray, and a low rumble of thunder sounded over the ocean. Cailean hadn't moved, yet something had changed in him. Rose felt tension thrumming in the air between them like a bowstring pulled tight. And the way he was looking at her... Those dark eyes were full of something that made her heart pound so hard she could feel it in the base of her throat.

His eyes searched hers, storm-dark and unguarded.

And then he moved.

He stepped into her space with a suddenness that stole her breath, one hand threading into the wet tangles of her hair, the other gripping her waist like he couldn't bear the distance a moment longer. His mouth claimed hers without hesitation—rough, raw, full of all the things he hadn't said.

The kiss wasn't soft. It was heat and hunger and frustration, lips crashing together in a clash of need that made her gasp. She clutched at his shoulders, then slid her arms around his neck, pulling him closer as she matched the intensity, lost in him.

Her back hit the wall, stone scraping through the fabric of her dress, but she didn't care. The world narrowed to the heat of his body against hers, the taste of rain on his lips, the sound of his breath mixing with hers.

He kissed her like he'd been waiting for years. Like he might never get another chance.

And she responded instinctively, fiercely, her hands tugging at the hem of his tunic as her mouth opened to his. Their bodies aligned, pressed together, heat blooming even in the chill of the rain. For a moment, there was nothing else.

No duty. No storm. Just *this*.

Then—

"Papa!"

Cailean sprang away as if he'd been stung. They both turned and saw two figures emerging from the mist. They resolved themselves into Catriona and Patch. Catriona was holding a shuttered lantern against the mist and gloom while Patch padded along at her heels, looking like a bedraggled mop.

Cailean blinked like a man surfacing from a dream. "What are ye doing out here?" he asked roughly.

Catriona glanced from her father to Rose and back again. Rose felt heat flushing her cheeks. Oh hell. Had Catriona seen them? If so, she gave no indication.

Catriona rolled her eyes at her father as if this was a stupid question. "I'm looking for ye, of course. Cook has brought muffins and bannocks for toasting on the fire, and she even let me have a sip of hot mead!"

"Did she now?" Cailean rumbled, raising an eyebrow. "Well, I might just have to have a word with her about that."

"Oh, come on! It's freezing out here!"

The girl took one of Cailean's hands in hers, and all but hauled him across the courtyard to the doors of the keep. Cailean gave Rose a look over his daughter's head. It was a look of apology but also of something else, something unfinished between them.

Rose swallowed thickly. At the door to the great hall, she begged off, saying she was going to get out of her wet clothes, but in reality, she needed some space. Space to figure out what the hell had just happened between her and the handsome Laird of Barra.

And time to figure out if she wanted it to happen again.

Chapter Twelve

As Cailean stepped into the great hall, he was hit by a wall of warmth and noise. Voices raised in friendly banter mixed with the scent of wood smoke, damp clothing, and baked bread that assaulted Cailean's senses. Steam rose from people's cloaks as they gathered close to the fire, and, as Cailen stepped inside with Catriona at his side, he paused, feeling like he'd been gut punched.

This was how his hall had been *before*.

Before the sickness. Before everything went wrong. Full of laughter. Full of life.

Over at one of the tables, his men were waxing lyrical about the repairs that would be needed following the storm and one of them, Lachlan, was boasting about moving a broken roof beam single handedly, while everyone else jibed him for his tall tales. Cailean couldn't stop the smile that spread over his face. Funny how it took a crisis to make everyone pull together. It was at times like this that his people showed their true worth.

"There's Maisie!" Catriona cried, spotting one of her friends. She went racing over to join her, Patch at her heels.

Someone handed Cailean a tankard, and he nodded his thanks, though he didn't drink. It was good to see his people in good spirits again, but there was one person missing, and to be honest, his heart was not here.

It was still out there in the rain, tangled with Rose MacFinnan's hair, caught between her lips and the soft sound she'd made when he'd pulled her close.

His fingers closed around the tankard as the memory shot through him. What had he been thinking? Not thinking at all, just acting on instinct and oh, by all the hells, it had felt right.

He shook his head and pulled in a slow and deep breath, trying to clear the memory. But it wouldn't budge. A burst of heat shot through him as he remembered how her mouth had opened under his, warm and willing, how he'd felt her hands fisting in his tunic, her body arching towards his like she needed him as badly as he needed her.

If Catriona hadn't come when she had...

He ran a hand through his hair. What in God's name was he doing? He was laird. He had responsibilities. A daughter. A clan that needed him to be focused and determined, not distracted.

And yet... he didn't regret it. *Couldn't* regret it. The soft feel of her lips on his had made him feel something he hadn't in a long time. It had made him feel... alive.

"My laird?" said a voice, and he turned to find Cook holding out a platter of food. "Are ye coming to join us? Or are ye going to stand there scowling until ye frighten the bairns?"

He huffed a low laugh, took the platter of food, and made his way to the high table where Catriona and Maisie were busy feeding scraps to Patch. He sat down heavily, his eyes straying to the empty seat where Rose had sat the night she arrived.

Ach. This was no good. He pushed his platter aside, untouched.

"Domnall, Ewan," he called. "Attend me."

The men—two of his closest advisors—left their spots where they'd been talking by the fire and seated themselves across from him at the high table.

"Well?" Cailean said, placing his hands flat on the scarred tabletop. "Give me the worst of it."

Domnall rubbed his stubbled chin. Older than Cailean, he had skin like tanned leather and a shock of gray hair like some unruly bird's nest. "We're still waiting for reports to come from the more outlying crofts, but it seems the southern crofts were the worst affected, exposed as they are. We know of three longhouses completely down. A lot of livestock has been scattered. I've sent a contingent of warriors down there to help, and they'll do what they can."

Cailean nodded. "And here in the village?"

"Got away lightly, all things considered," Ewan replied, leaning his considerable bulk back in his chair and spreading his arms. "Old Seamus's house was the worst hit as ye know, but I'm wondering whether it's even worth trying to repair it since ye and Rose took him to stay with his daughter. It will only encourage the old complainer to try and move back in when we all know he's better off with Brina."

Cailean nodded. "Are the stores intact?"

"Mostly," Domnall replied. "We dinna seem to have lost any grain, but the thatch on the outer granary is damaged and will need replacing. The path out to the north road is a mire and will need clearing before any grain deliveries from the crofts in that direction can get through."

Cailean ran his hand down the side of his face. "Set any of the unoccupied youths to hauling timber for repairs. I'll have Beatrice organize the women to inventory what was lost and what's worth saving." He met the eyes of his two advisors. "Make sure the word goes out that any who have lost their homes are to come here. Nobody will go without food and shelter while I sit in this hall."

They nodded. "Aye, laird."

Cailean let out a slow breath. It felt strangely grounding, falling back into the routines of duty, of being the laird of his people. *This* he could do. *This* he'd been trained his whole life for. Give him storms or raiders or poor harvests any day of the week. This enemy, at least, he knew how to face, unlike the sickness, the faceless, nameless enemy that stalked his people and struck without warning.

He took a swig from his tankard, barely tasting the ale. Ewan and Domnall, perhaps sensing his mood, excused themselves, and he was left alone at the high table, Catriona and Maisie having disappeared elsewhere.

He swirled the ale in its cup, staring down into the depths as though he might find some answers written there. He was bone weary and longed for nothing more than retiring to his chamber to sleep. But he knew sleep wouldn't come. He was too wound up for that. Thoughts swirled around in his head just like the liquid in his cup, stirring up feelings he'd rather not examine too closely. The storm. The sickness.

Rose MacFinnan.

He sighed, resting his head against the back of his chair. When had he come to rely on her so much? And what would he do if she couldn't help them?

He closed his eyes. He dared not think about that.

ROSE SANK INTO the deliciously hot water, letting it lap all the way to her chin. She sighed in contentment, feeling the heat slowly unknot her tired muscles and chase away the cold that seemed to have settled into her bones. She ached all over, but it was a pleasant sort of ache, born from the knowledge that she'd done some good today.

And what a day it had been.

First there had been the village and its inhabitants, half wrecked by last night's storm, but pulling together all the same. The teamwork. The camaraderie, the determination to put right what nature had so casually ransacked. It had made Rose warm inside to see the way they had all worked together, and she had begun to understand the fierce loyalty these people held to each other and why Cailean loved them so much.

Ah, Cailean. She should *not* be thinking about him.

Yanking her thoughts away, she rested her arms along the rim of the metal bathtub and leaned her head back, allowing her eyes to slide closed. She owed Mable a debt of gratitude for arranging this. Hauling hot water up here was no mean feat, even though she'd roped in some of the stable lads to help her.

As Rose lay back, she listened to the faint sounds of the castle: voices down in the great hall, shouts from the battlements, the clop of a horse's hooves from the courtyard, the whine of the wind in the roof. Those sounds were starting to feel normal, which was something she never would have believed possible.

It was startling, she thought, how this place, these people, this time, was losing its strangeness and was starting to feel like… well, not home exactly, but something like it, even if there were no coffee, indoor plumbing, or hair straighteners.

Imagine that. She smiled wryly. Elise would be shocked.

She stretched out her toes, resting them on the far edge of the tub. The water was starting to cool a little, and she should probably have a scrub, wash her hair, and get out before it grew tepid, but she couldn't bring herself to move.

Just a bit longer.

She found her thoughts skimming over the events of the day. She could still hear Brina's voice as she asked them if they'd seen the stormlights over the ocean and she'd seen Seamus's serious expression as he'd told her of the child's tale of the sea gods.

It was nonsense. Or at least it *should* have been nonsense. But something inside her, some instinct, suggested that it wasn't. Old tales, she knew, often held a truth buried deep within them.

And then there was him. Cailean.

The memory of his mouth on hers struck like a match against her skin. The roughness of it. The *need*. The way their kiss had drowned her in one sudden rush of heat and hunger that she had been powerless to control.

She touched her lips without thinking, her fingers grazing the place where his kiss had lingered.

What was happening to her? Why was she allowing herself to feel these things? She was newly divorced, for pity's sake! This was the last thing she needed!

But she wasn't *allowing* anything. The things she felt in Cailean's presence were not a conscious choice. They were instinctive, primal almost, and she couldn't do a damned thing to stop them, no matter how hard she tried.

Damn it all!

Her calm broken, she washed herself and stood up, dripping. Grabbing one of the large cloths Mable had left as a towel, she wrapped one around her hair, another around her middle, and stepped out onto the cold stone floor. Shivering a little, she exited the bathing chamber and slumped into a chair in the bedroom that faced the roaring fire. Chin resting on her hands, she stared into the flames as if she'd find the answers to her conundrum written in the writhing orange tongues.

She was startled from her thoughts by a knock on the door. "Just a moment!" she cried, looking around for where she'd dropped her clothes.

The door swung open. Rose gave a little yelp and pulled the towel tighter around herself.

"Ach, dinna fash, lass," came Maggie's voice as she stepped inside, breezing in like the start of a storm. "Ye dinna have aught I havenae seen many times before."

The woman closed the door behind her and lowered herself into the seat opposite Rose, letting out a groan as she did so.

"Ah, that's better. My old bones do ache so in this damp weather." She fixed Rose with her piercing blue gaze. "The laird said ye wished to speak to me. That ye wanted to know about some of the old tales?"

Rose nodded, pulling the towel tighter. "It was something Seamus and his daughter said today in the village. They asked if we'd seen the stormlights out at sea and then told me a story about a sea god and goddess."

"Ah!" Maggie held up one finger. "Now that is an old tale,

older than the stones beneath this keep, almost as old as the bones of the island itself."

"Could you tell it to me?"

Maggie's expression shifted. She cocked her head at Rose. "It's a long time since anyone showed any interest in the old gods. Beatrice's new god's hold strengthens and the old ways are slowly being forgotten. Why the interest now?"

"Because I think you might be right," she said. "I think there *is* some truth to these old stories and that the sickness is something to do with the old gods, just like you claimed."

Maggie blinked, studying Rose closely. Then she breathed out slowly. "Then we are in bigger trouble than I thought. The old gods can be as capricious and cruel as they can be generous. Are ye sure ye want to go down this route?"

"I have to. Please. Tell me what you know."

She listened intently as Maggie began to speak in a low, rhythmic voice, relaying a tale similar to that which Seamus and his daughter had told her that afternoon but different in several aspects. In Maggie's story, there was no curse involved. Instead, when the god became jealous of the goddess's love for her people and threatened to hurt them, the goddess confined him in a prison beneath the waves. The stormlights were indeed the god's rage and grief leaking out from his prison.

When she finished, Rose didn't speak, and silence reigned in the room, the only sound the crackle and pop of the fire between them. A prison. And a god's curse leaking out from that prison. Was that what was powering the magic that was bringing the sickness?

"But why now?" Rose asked, looking up at Maggie. "If this tale is as old as you say it is, why has the sickness come into being so recently?"

"I canna answer that question," Maggie said, shaking her head. "Although the tale goes on to say that the goddess, saddened by the loss of her love, began to fail. While she lived, the prison stayed strong, but finally, she succumbed to her grief and died. Perhaps that is why the god's rage and spite now leaks out to curse us."

Rose's mind whirled with possibilities. Could this be it? Could this be the clue she'd been looking for? And if so, what could she do about it? They were talking about the power of a god! How could she hope to counter that?

But it was more to go on than she'd had to go on this time yesterday. Now, at least, she had a place to start.

And it started with finding that prison.

Chapter Thirteen

CAILEAN GLANCED AT the early morning sky. It was filled with dark-gray clouds from end to end and the wind was blowing in off the sea, bringing with it the scent of another storm on its way. Wonderful. As if they needed more rain and mud to contend with.

"Barrels of oats and spare blankets," he said to the man guiding the carthorses. "See that they are well tied down, Aiden. The last thing we need is losing half the load to a ditch."

As he watched the cart trundle out of the gate, he rubbed the back of his neck. His limbs felt heavy and his eyes grainy. Sleep had escaped him for most of the night and now he was paying the price. Perhaps he ought to have Maggie mix up one of her sleeping drafts. He winced at the thought. They tasted like horse piss, and he wasn't entirely sure that wasn't their main ingredient.

He was leaning down to check the straps on a bundle of wool blankets when he felt her.

He didn't see her, not at first, but he felt her nearby like a bonfire burning against his senses. He straightened, turned, and there she was. Rose was standing by the door to the keep, looking out over the courtyard. She'd bound her midnight hair back in a plait and wore a burgundy cloak pulled tight against the weather. To Cailean's eyes she looked like some untamed spirit of old—beautiful, wild. And very, very dangerous.

He passed a hand across his face, feeling his stomach tighten like it always did when he laid eyes on her. She was the main reason he'd lain awake all last night, her and the memories of their kiss.

Her eyes found him and she waved, breaking into a wide smile. Picking up her skirts, she hurried towards him.

"I need to speak to you," she said urgently. "I think I've found something."

Cailean glanced around at the courtyard busy with people loading and recording supplies.

"Not here," he murmured.

He led her across the courtyard, the two of them slipping into the blessed calm of the stable. Here, the noise from outside was muted, and the air was filled the contented munching of the horses in their stalls.

He turned to face her but didn't speak. Neither did she. Was she remembering what had happened between them yesterday just like he was? Was she hoping it would happen again, just like he was? Or, more likely, was she regretting it and hoping to forget it had ever happened?

With an effort, he fought the urge to reach out and touch her, forcing his hands to remain firmly by his sides.

Finally, she broke the silence. "I spoke to Maggie, like you suggested."

He felt an obscure kind of disappointment. *This* was what she wanted to speak to him about? He schooled his expression to one of mild interest.

"And what did Maggie have to tell ye?"

"She remembered the story. It's about a sea god, like Seamus said, but the curse happened a bit differently to the story they tell. The god was imprisoned and I think… I think that prison might be weakening and that's what's allowing his curse to leak out."

Cailean's clenched. Curses? Gods? Prisons. Surely not. "It's just an old story."

"It's not," Rose said softly, her tone gentle but firm. "You know it's not. Brina saw the stormlights and I've been speaking to others that saw them too. And remember, it was a sea goddess that brought me here. What if Lir is the goddess in the story?"

Cailean studied the wood of the barn wall, where time and the elements had turned the old wood silver. "If that's so," he growled, turning to look at her, "then why has Lir not fixed the mess she left behind? If this is the work of some jealous god, then why has she not countered it? Surely she has the power? Why has she chosen to let my people suffer? I will tell ye why. Because gods and goddesses care nothing for the lives of mortals. This is all just a game to them! We are just pieces on their giant board, and they move us around on a whim! Whether it be Maggie's old gods or Beatrice's new one, none of them can be trusted. I've said it all along!"

He was suddenly furious, shaking with rage. All the emotion he'd kept buried deep within himself for the last four years came racing to the surface. He saw Mary's pale face in his mind's eye, saw her lips muttering prayers that went unanswered, saw himself kneeling at the Christian altar and at the pagan shrine out by the loch offering anything, everything, if they would only save his wife.

But they hadn't. He'd lost Mary to the cold indifference of the gods.

He would not lose Rose too.

"Ye need to leave it," he said hoarsely.

"Why? What are you afraid I'll find?"

He studied her, dread clawing up his throat. *It's not what you will find that terrifies me*, he wanted to say. *But what will find you.*

But aloud all he said was, "Some things are best left buried."

"And some things should never have been forgotten," she replied, her voice rising slightly. "I *can't* leave it, Cailean. You know that. I can't stand aside and let people suffer while there is a chance I can help them."

Her cheeks were flushed, her eyes flashing with defiance and still—still—he wanted nothing more than to kiss her again. The ache of it nearly knocked him off balance.

He stepped closer. "Rose, I—" His words trailed off. What could he say? *Don't do this, Rose. Don't meddle in the business of the gods. Don't make me lose you too. I don't think I could survive it.*

Something twisted in his chest. Fear. Guilt. Desire. Gods help him, all three.

He sighed, his shoulders sagging. "All right," he breathed. "What do ye need from me?"

She smiled and it lit up the gloom of the stable like the morning sun. "I'll let you know as soon as I figure that out."

He cleared his throat and gazed at her. "Listen, Rose. I—"

The door swung open, and a stable lad came in leading Catriona's bay mare. The lad startled when he spotted Cailean and Rose standing there.

"Oh! My apologies, I didnae realize ye were in here, my laird."

Cailean bit back a snarl of annoyance and smoothed his face to calmness. "Dinna fash, lad. How is Parsnip's colic?"

"Much better," the stable lad answered. "She'll be right as rain soon I reckon."

"I'll... um... see you later," Rose mumbled.

Before he could say another word, she took the opportunity to slip away, leaving Cailean staring after her.

ROSE LET THE stable door swing shut behind her and stood staring out over the bustling courtyard, trying to let the cold air cool her heated skin. It didn't work.

Damn it. Why did this always happen when she was near Cailean MacNeil? Why did her thoughts turn to mush? She could still feel his gaze on her, like an electric current across her skin.

What do ye need from me?

Oh, that was a dangerous question for him to ask. *I need you to touch me,* she had wanted to say. *I need you to kiss me like you did yesterday. I need...*

God help her, what did she need?

To get a grip! she told herself fiercely. *That's what you bloody need!*

Taking a deep breath, she set off towards the keep, her boots squelching in the mud. She needed time to think, to figure out what was going on, to—

"Rose!"

The small voice pulled her from her thoughts. She turned to see Catriona pelting towards her, holding her skirts out of the mud with one hand while Patch barrelled after her, ears flapping wildly.

Rose laughed as Patch pounced on her hem. "Well, hello to you too!"

"We've been looking for ye!" Catriona said breathlessly, skidding to a stop. "Patch was missing ye."

Rose crouched to scratch behind the little dog's ears and take her hem out of his mouth. "Aww, did he? Well, I missed him too." She smiled up at the girl. "And you. Did the storm keep you awake?"

Catriona shrugged. "Patch didnae like it much but it didnae bother me. I've seen worse." She pursed her lips in thought. "Although, there were more stormlights than usual."

Rose shot to her feet. "Stormlights? You saw them too?"

"Aye. I think it means the sea was angry."

Rose said nothing. Putting an arm around Catriona's shoulder, she turned the girl and they walked off together, Patch darting between their feet and growling at a particularly bold chicken that dared cross his path. Catriona kept up an endless stream of chatter, telling Rose about the new pastries cook was making, the scolding she and her friend Maisie got for stealing eggs from Maisie's mother's chicken coop, how a lad called Arnulf had fallen out of a tree and injured his wrist.

Rose nodded and smiled, letting it wash over her, but she wasn't really listening, until quite casually Catriona said, "Are ye going to marry my da?"

Rose tripped over a stone and nearly went sprawling. "What?"

Catriona giggled. "That's what it means when grown-ups kiss, isnae it? That ye are going to get married? And ye and my da kissed last night! I saw ye. In the rain."

Rose stared at the girl, mortification stealing through her. Her cheeks blazed hotter than the hearth in the great hall. Oh God! Catriona *had* seen them! She worked her jaw a few times, but no words came out. She tried again. "Oh, Catriona, I—That wasn't—We didn't mean for anyone to see—"

"Can I be a bridesmaid?" Catriona interrupted, clapping her hands together. "And can Patch carry the ring? He would love that! Oh, oh, and ye can ride to the chapel on Parsnip! Her colic has almost cleared up now and I could deck her out in flowers, and I could make daisy chains for yer hair, and, and—"

"Whoa!" Rose said, holding up her hands. "Slow down! Things aren't that simple!"

"Why not?" Catriona replied, puzzled. "Ye like my da, dinna ye? And my da likes ye."

Rose blinked. "He... he does?"

"Of course he does. He hasnae been anywhere near as grumpy since ye arrived. In fact, he's only given me a scolding once *and* he didnae make me put Patch in the kennels. And if ye and Da get married, I'll get a new ma!" She bounced on her toes in excitement. "Wouldnae that be grand?"

Rose opened her mouth to respond—though she had no idea what words would come out—but was saved by a sudden shout from the gate.

Turning in that direction and squinting through the biting wind, she saw a group of people slogging up the hill towards the gates. They were dressed in traveling gear and were carrying bundles of belongings on their backs. There were even a few carts pulled by weary-looking donkeys.

An old woman led them, and it took a moment for Rose to

recognize Agnes, headwoman of Hemkirk.

Rose gasped. "They came!"

Catriona squinted at the newcomers. "Is that good?"

"Yes," Rose breathed. "That's very good. Come on."

She took Catriona's hand and started for the gates, Patch running ahead and barking his welcome.

The crowd had been stopped at the gates as the guards questioned them but, knowing full well who these people were, Rose pushed her way through to where Agnes was arguing with them.

"It's all right, Jonas," Rose said to the guard. "These are the people of Hemkirk. Laird Cailean has offered them shelter. You can let them in."

Jonas, a gangly youth who took his duties very seriously, looked dubious. But he also looked like he had no intention of arguing with a MacFinnan spellweaver.

The lad swallowed and then inclined his head. "As ye say, mistress."

He swung the gate wide and indicated for the newcomers to enter the courtyard. Rose took Agnes's arm and helped her inside while Catriona guided the families to an overhang where warm broth was already being handed out.

"You came," Rose said, unable to keep the surprise from her voice.

The old woman nodded. "Aye, although I wasnae sure we would. Some of us can be more stubborn than Albert's goats." She nodded and Rose saw Catriona and Patch trotting at the side of an old man as he led a couple of white goats towards the stable.

Rose tilted her head as she regarded Agnes. She looked tired, the skin of her face seemingly drawn too tightly over her skull. "What changed your mind?"

Agnes paused, looking uncomfortable and her hand rose to clasp the small woven charm that hung from a leather thong around her neck. "The stormlights."

Rose's breath hitched. "You saw them too?"

Agnes nodded and her voice dropped lower. "We could hardly miss them, lass. They lit up the bay from end to end, like it was on fire. It was terrifying. And then the lightning—lightning struck the beach and the islets out in the bay. Much too close to the village for comfort. After that even the most stubborn of the old fools decided we had to leave."

Rose blinked, digesting this news. "What does it mean?" she muttered.

"It means, lass," Agnes said, "that the old gods are waking. And some of us are finally starting to listen."

She turned away, joining the rest of her people who were being ushered into the warmth of the kitchen. Rose stood rooted to the spot, watching them go.

Catriona came bouncing up to her. "Did ye see the goats? One of them tried to eat Patch's tail!"

Rose barely heard her, her thoughts fixed on Agnes's words. Stormlights. Lightning. The bay at Hemkirk lit like fire. Could that be the key to all of this?

She turned to Catriona, crouching until she was at eye level with her. "I need you to do something very important for me."

Catriona's eyes lit up. "What?"

"I need you to help these people get settled. Make sure they get some food and are shown where they can put their things. And if you see anyone looking frightened or lonely, you take Patch over. He's good at cheering people up."

Catriona beamed, bobbing on her toes at being given such responsibility. "I willnae let ye down!"

Rose squeezed her shoulder. "I know you won't."

Straightening, Rose turned and made her way behind the stables to where a row of wagons was being loaded with supplies. Her eyes sprang to the man overseeing it all.

Cailean had rolled up the sleeves of his linen shirt and was busy lifting sacks of supplies and bundles of timber onto the wagons with his men. He hadn't spotted her, and his features wore an intense expression as he worked. His movements were precise and economical, the muscles of his arms and shoulders bunching and flexing as he heaved the sacks up onto his broad shoulders before depositing them into the wagon bed.

Rose found herself staring, mesmerized by the flex of his shoulders, by the way his hair brushed his neck as he moved, by the veins that stood out in his neck as he heaved the heavy sacks onto the cart. It was ridiculous. She was a grown woman and yet her traitorous stomach kept tying itself in knots whenever she looked at him.

He glanced over and spotted her. Something in his expression softened and, barking orders to his men, he tossed the sack in his arms over to one of them and strode towards her.

"What is it, lass?" he rumbled. "What's wrong?"

"Nothing," she replied. "I just wanted to let you know that the villagers from Hemkirk have just arrived. They've taken up your offer of sanctuary after all."

His dark eyes flicked in the direction of the gates. "Good. That's good."

"Um. There's something else," she continued. "Agnes said that it was the storm yesterday that changed their mind. They saw the same stormlights that Seamus and Brina did. Out in the bay, only it sounds as though they were far stronger near Hemkirk and there was lightning that struck the ground out there."

That got his attention. He frowned, jaw tightening. "Where exactly?"

"I don't know. The beach. Some of the islets out in the bay. But I want to go and check it out."

"No," Cailean said sharply. "Absolutely not."

"What? Why not?"

"There's another storm coming," he said, gesturing at the sky which was black and angry. "Ye saw what the last one did. I willnae risk ye—or anyone—on a half-remembered tale and superstition."

"It's not just a tale," she insisted. "You *know* it isn't."

His hands clenched and unclenched. "No," he said, shaking his head. "Ye are *not* going, Rose. Not until the weather improves. That is final."

He turned and stalked off, shoulders rigid, gait clipped. Rose glared after him, teeth clenched in annoyance. With a huff, she spun and stomped back to the castle, not stopping until she reached the study where she slammed the door behind her and threw herself into the chair. Who did he think he was ordering her around?

But, she had to admit, she could feel the storm that Cailean predicted beginning to break. The shutters on the window rattled and another curtain of gray rain came sheeting down, turning the view through the window misty and vague.

Her senses tingled. The air felt charged, full of an ominous potential. Her MacFinnan blood stirred. The instinct that had guided her all her life was pulsing now, hot and urgent. This was no ordinary storm.

She had to get to Hemkirk. She knew it in her bones. Whatever secrets this island was hiding, this was her chance to discover them.

Snatching up her cloak, she wrapped it tightly around her shoulders and left the study. She slipped through the corridors with silent steps, avoiding servants and loitering guards, thankful for the noise of the gathering storm that covered her footsteps. She paused on entering the courtyard, looking around for Cailean. She could hear him and his men still battling to load the carts on the other side of the stables, but they were not in sight. Good. She hurried across the courtyard without being spotted.

The horses nickered as she entered the stable and shifted uneasily, unnerved by the thunder that rumbled overhead and the patter of rain on the roof.

Only one of them seemed unfazed. Snip, the sturdy mare who had carried her the other day was munching lazily on a bale of hay attached to her stall. Rose approached and stroked her muzzle. "You'll take me, won't you, girl? And you already know the way."

The horse whinnied softly as if in agreement. Moments later, Rose had her saddled and was leading her out into the yard. The wind tugged at her hair, and thunder rolled over the sea. Rain obscured everything beyond a few feet.

She swung up into the saddle and, pulling her hood up over her head, she guided the horse down the slope, away from the keep. Toward Hemkirk. Toward the truth that awaited her there.

>>><<<

THE WIND LASHED the courtyard like a vengeful spirit, sending Cailean's hair whipping around his head and rattling the shutters on the keep's windows as if hungry to get inside. With an annoyed growl, he clenched his fists, raw and red from hauling timber. Would there never be a let up? His people had barely recovered from yesterday's storm and yet here another one was, hot on the tails of its predecessor. What had they done to anger the gods so?

Around him, his men moved in a frenzy, lashing woven covers over the wagons, securing supplies in the storehouse, and shouting to one another over the rising gale. When this was done, he bellowed at them to get inside but as they obeyed, he didn't follow. Soon he was the only one left in the courtyard, but he didn't move as the wind tore through and freezing rain began to fall in earnest, pelting into his face like tiny shards of glass.

Anger and frustration roiled inside him, every bit as wild as the gathering storm. In fact, it fit his mood perfectly. He'd been unsettled ever since Rose had told him what she'd discovered about the stormlights and that unease had not abated since. In fact, it had only grown worse. Gods. Curses. Magic. How was he supposed to deal with such things?

He shook his head, wiping a hand across his face. It would do no good standing here like this. He jogged across the courtyard and into the keep, slamming the big doors behind him and cutting out the worst of the wind. The din of conversation came from his right, indicating that his people were beginning to congregate in the great hall as they often did to wait out the storm.

He almost joined them but then hesitated on the threshold and didn't go in. He couldn't face his people's questions right now. No, what he needed was something else entirely. So he strode away, deeper into the keep where it was quieter and darker, the only sounds distant and soft.

Finally, he fetched up outside a closed wooden door. He raised his hand to knock but hesitated. He suddenly felt as nervous as a lad. What was wrong with him? He'd not left things well between him and Rose and he regretted barking at her the way he had. He'd not been able to help himself. The thought of her riding out into the storm—into danger—had twisted his guts with terror and that terror had transmuted into anger.

Rose's angry expression had been enough to tell him exactly what she thought of his edict against her riding to Hemkirk, but at least she'd done as he asked. At least she was safe. Now all he had to do was make her see it was for the best.

He rapped on the door. There was no answer.

"Rose?" he called. "Lass? May I come in?"

When there was still no response, he pushed the door open and cautiously stepped inside.

The study was empty. The fire had burned down to embers, the chair was pushed back as if she'd risen in a hurry, and her cloak was missing from the peg. A sudden stab of alarm sent his pulse racing. Leaving the study, the strode through the keep.

"Go check Lady Rose's room," he snapped at a passing servant. "And see if anyone has seen her in the last hour."

Instinct told him that Rose would not be found in her room. Nor in any other part of the castle. Had he thought she'd accepted his ban on her going to Hemkirk? Pah! He should have known better!

He strode to the main doors and threw them open. The wind

snatched them from his grasp, sending them crashing back against the outer wall of the keep with a boom. Cailean hurried down the steps and over to the stables, the door banging open as he stepped inside.

Inside, the air was thick and warm with the scent of hay and horse. His eyes scanned the stalls. His own mount was there, shifting restlessly, but the fourth bay was empty.

His stomach clenched. Damn the woman! Why could she *never* do as he asked?

"My laird?"

He spun as a stable hand carrying a bucket of oats stepped inside, seeming surprised to see him there.

"Where is she?" Cailean growled, his voice low and dangerous.

The lad swallowed thickly, his throat bobbing. "Where is who?"

"Lady Rose."

"I... I dinna know, my laird. I havenae seen her."

Cailen pointed at the empty stall. "Which horse is missing?"

"Snip, my laird."

Of course it was. The sure-footed one. The one Rose had ridden the other day. He felt like punching something. That stubborn woman had looked him in the eye only hours ago and then *defied* him. And now she'd gone and ridden out into the teeth of a storm—alone.

He slammed his fist into the stable wall, the wood rattling in protest.

Fool of a woman.

"Help me get Arrow saddled."

The stable lad hurried to obey. When it was done, he led the horse out into the courtyard.

Glancing towards the keep, he saw Catriona emerge onto the steps, looking around for him. "Go to Maggie, now!" he shouted to her. "And stay inside!"

"But—"

"Now, Cat."

She scowled at him but obeyed without further word and he mounted up, the wind tearing at his cloak. The fat drops of rain thickened into a deluge as he galloped through the gates.

The storm had arrived. And Rose was out there in the heart of it.

Chapter Fourteen

Rose used to like walking in the rain. Back home, when it was raining she would often take a stroll around the lake, watching how the surface danced and shimmered as the raindrops hit it. Elise had told her she was crazy, but she had always found it relaxing.

Now though, she was beginning to wonder if Elise hadn't been right all along. Walking around the lake in the soft, gentle showers that they often got back home was vastly different to riding through this wild, angry maelstrom that seemed intent on ripping her from the saddle and dumping her in the mud.

And yet, it was exhilarating too. The storm was alive with power and potential. It sang along her senses, stirring her blood. It was so raw. So present. No past. No future. Just the vast powers of the earth singing along her nerves.

Poor Snip though was *not* sharing Rose's enthusiasm. The horse's head was hanging down as she plodded along the muddy track looking thoroughly miserable. Rose patted the beast's neck.

"Sorry, girl. I promise you a nice extra big bag of oats when we get back. How about that? And maybe some apples if I can pilfer them from the kitchen. Eh?"

Snip flicked her ears and carried on plodding.

Rose's hood had blown back ages ago and she'd given up trying to keep it in place. Now her hair was plastered to the sides of her face and droplets kept running down her back, making her shiver. Still, they had made good time, despite the weather. Rose had needed no maps to know where she was going. Her destination pulled at her like a lodestone. She was pretty sure she could find the place even with her eyes closed.

The path sloped down through two high banks topped with stunted trees. She was close now—she recognized the bend in the track where the gorse bushes thickened and the ground dipped toward the low stone wall that marked the boundary of the village of Hemkirk.

Finally, she rode in among the first of the houses. The place was eerily deserted. No candlelight shone from the windows and no voices could be heard from within the buildings. Even the dog that had barked at her and Cailean last time they were here was gone. The wind had ripped one of the doors of the wooden houses open and now it banged incessantly in the wind.

Rose pulled the horse to a stop in the muddy street between two houses and gazed out at the bay. The wind was so fierce now that it squeezed tears from the corners of her eyes and whipped her hair out behind her like a banner. She shaded her eyes with one arm—and then she saw it.

Out in the bay, the waves were a lashing gray maelstrom. They thrashed against the rocks that littered the shore, sending up spumes of white foam. Breakers roared as they crashed onto the beach, leaving behind streamers of seaweed and bits of flotsam as they retreated.

And above it all, dancing across the surface of the water, was light. It was not jagged or actinic like lightning but rather formed a shimmery curtain of opalescent green, blue, and purple that flickered and danced like an aurora.

The hairs rose on the back of Rose's neck.

"Stormlights," she murmured.

She could feel the power in that light. It was vast and alien, not part of the magic that thrummed through the bedrock of this island. It was something... other.

And it was angry.

She dismounted and led the mare into an abandoned cottage. Taking off the saddle, she quickly rubbed her down, and then ducked back outside into the tempest. Rain streamed down her face, chilling her skin and blurring her vision, but she didn't feel cold. Not really. Not anymore.

All she felt was the power of the storm.

Her boots slipped on the mud and slick stone as she walked down to the water and followed the curve of the shoreline. Waves crashed against the jagged rocks, foaming white and wild. The bay loomed just ahead, shrouded in mist and glowing with an eerie shimmer that pulsed like a heartbeat.

A narrow spit of rock stuck out into the bay like an accusing finger. She picked her way along the beach until she reached it and then stepped up onto the black rocks, slick with seaweed and rain. Lightning forked overhead, illuminating the dark sea—and the shimmering light down in the depths. Rose walked right to the end of the spur of rock and gazed down at the thrashing sea. A pale-green light spiralled just beneath the waves, moving like something alive.

She stared down at it, mesmerized. Some deep part of her whispered a warning. She was very close to the edge, and all that lay beneath her was the thrashing waves. One tiny slip, that's all it would take, and she would be gone into the grasping water. But she seemed unable to move back. The pulsing of the power filled her, and the light in the depths held her in a spell.

The storm faded from her mind. The thunder, the rain, the wind—all of it melted away beneath the song she now heard. Not with her ears, but with her blood. A hum in her veins. A call in her bones.

And old magic. Ancient. Hungry.

The stormlights began to move, the green glow to gather in the water below her. The lights swirled and flickered in a hypnotic dance, like smoke trapped under glass. She found herself leaning forward, watching its slow dance.

It seemed to coalesce into a shape—a figure?—before breaking apart and swirling once more, beautiful, bright movement in the darkness.

"Who are you?" she whispered, the words snatched away by the wind and scattered out over the thrashing waves. "Why are you hurting the people of this island?"

There was no answer. At least, not one spoken aloud. Yet she heard a response all the same. Inside her head she heard a voice, like the roll of waves against a distant shore.

Come to me.

The voice was like silk and thunder all wrapped into one. It wound around her, through her, promising warmth and sweet oblivion. It seeped into her, filling the empty places in her heart she didn't even know were there.

Come to me.

She took a step closer to the edge until her toes were sticking out beyond the lip.

Join me. Be part of my song, daughter of the Isles. I will end your suffering.

All thought vanished. There was only the irresistible pull of the stormlights and the roar of the water.

She lifted one foot, prepared to take the step that would send her down to join the lights—but a hand seized her wrist.

She jerked in surprise, spun—and found herself staring into Cailean's storm-dark eyes.

The spell of the stormlight shattered.

Rose gasped, her eyes snapping wide. The world came rushing back in—the roar of the wind, the rain pounding her skin, the cold. She staggered back from the edge, her knees buckling as realization struck her like a blow.

She had been about to jump.

Around them the storm's fury redoubled. Waves crashed against the rocks they were standing on, sending freezing spray over both of them. The wind howled, and to Rose's mind it sounded like thwarted fury.

Cailean didn't hesitate. He reached down, got his arms around her, and lifted her into his arms. Fighting through the spray and wind, he carried down the headland and back into the village while the sea screamed behind them.

He shouldered open the door of the nearest cottage, kicked it shut, and dropped the bolt, cutting out the scream of the wind.

Only then did he set her down.

He was drenched to the bone, his clothes plastered to his big frame, and water was running from his hair in rivulets. His presence seemed to fill the room every bit as much as the storm outside did.

She wanted to run to him. To throw her arms around him. To bury her face in his shoulders and revel in the solid, reassuring safety of his presence. But something stopped her.

Cailean's expression was tight and his eyes flashed with something that went beyond anger into cold, hard fury.

"Do ye mind telling me," he growled, his voice sounding like part of the wild storm outside, "what in God's name ye thought ye were doing?"

ROSE STARED UP at him and it was all Cailean could do to keep hold of his anger. He wanted to shake her. He wanted to rage and rant and tell her how stupid she'd been. But he also wanted to hold her, to pull her into his arms and let the feel of her wash away the terror that had squeezed his heart when he'd seen her standing on the rocks.

She could have drowned, been washed out to sea. He could have lost her and that thought was strong enough to snap him in half.

She wrapped her arms around herself. "I... I don't know what I was doing." She shook her head as though trying to clear it of disquieting thoughts. "It's like... like I didn't have control anymore. Something was calling to me. There was a voice..."

Cailean scrubbed a hand through his wet hair. That hand was trembling. Hell, his whole body was trembling. With anger. With fear. With relief.

"Aye, well perhaps next time ye hear a damned whisper in yer head try not to follow out into a storm, especially when I've expressly told ye no!"

She flinched in the face of his anger. "But you came for me."

"Of course I did."

Did she really expect anything else? Did she really think he would let her go riding off into a danger alone? Did she not understand what she meant to him? Did she really not know how he felt?

He turned his back on her, afraid of the look in her eyes. He needed something to do, or he'd go mad. His knees thumped to the floor in front of the hearth and he began fumbling with the stacked wood inside.

Flint. Spark. Smoke. Flame.

Focus.

Behind him, Rose hadn't moved. He could hear her breathing, shaky and shallow. He wanted to rage. He wanted to *hold* her. And that war inside him was tearing him apart.

Finally, he got a spark going. He leaned forward, blowing on the flames until they took. Then he rocked back on his heels, watching as the fire blossomed, pushing away the worst of the cold and sending flickering light through the room.

The house he'd brought them to was a modest dwelling with just this single room. An iron tripod for cooking stood to one side of the hearth and there was a straw mattress in the corner. That was it.

Cailean wondered whose house this had been. Someone who had succumbed to the sickness? Or someone who had left this village and was now holed up at Dun Mallach, safe and warm? He chose to believe the latter.

Rose edged closer to the hearth, sinking down next to him.

Her teeth were chattering. He got up, pulled the blanket from the mattress, and handed it to her. She took it with a grateful nod of thanks and pulled it around her shoulders.

Cailean lowered himself to the floor, but was careful to keep a distance between them. Neither spoke and Cailean contented himself with staring into the flames, listening to their hiss and crackle as rain lashed the world outside.

"Thank you," she murmured at last. "For coming after me."

He didn't know how to answer. Words felt too small for the storm still raging in his chest.

"Was it worth it?" he asked at last.

She turned her head. "What do you mean?"

His gaze flicked to hers. "Did ye find what ye came out here to find?" *What you risked your life for? What you scared the seven hells out of me for?*

Her gaze went distant, and she turned to look at the shuttered window, beyond which the storm raged. "I don't know," she said softly. "There's something here, Cailean. Out there. Something powerful and angry. Something that wants revenge and will do anything to get it. It... it almost had me."

There was fear in her voice, and it made him want to reach out and pull her to him, to whisper that everything would be all right. But he held himself back. The truth was, he didn't know if everything was going to be all right. He hadn't been able to promise that for a long time. All he knew was that he would do anything, *anything*, to stop this woman from getting hurt.

"Why?" he asked hoarsely. "Why would ye put yer life at risk like that?"

Rose's eyes seemed huge in her pale face, firelight dancing in their depths. Her look was raw and unguarded and Cailean saw emotions there he'd never expected to see. Self-doubt. Regret. Vulnerability.

"Because I didn't want to let you all down," she said at last. Her voice was barely above a whisper, almost drowned out by the hiss and crackle of the flame. "I'm a MacFinnan spellweaver, remember? I have powers others don't. There is a reason I was given those powers—to help those who can't help themselves. What good am I if I can't even do that?" She turned to stare into the fire, hugging her knees against her chest. "I didn't want to fail."

Cailean wasn't sure how to respond. How could she think she was a failure? How could she think that anyone would think that of her? Yet he understood her doubts. He knew what it was like to carry the weight of expectation around your shoulders. He knew how it felt to hold the lives of others in your hand. It was a heavy weight to carry and Rose MacFinnan's was heavier than anyone's.

"I'm beginning to agree with yer sister Elise," he said at last. "And I've never even met her."

Rose looked at him. "You are?"

"Aye. Doesnae she say ye work too hard? That ye push yerself too much? She is right. And ye are too hard on yerself." He shook his head. "Lass, ye have done more towards ending this sickness in the short time ye've been here than any of us have been able to do in over a year."

"But it's not enough, is it?" she countered. "Drew and the others are still lying comatose in the infirmary. Who knows how many more will fall sick because of my inability to figure this damned thing out? How many more will die because of my failure?"

"Lass," he said. "Rose. Ye are *not* a failure."

"Yes I am!" she yelled. "Don't you get it? This is the only thing I've ever been good at! Everything else in my life is a disaster! I couldn't even save my damned marriage! Now I'm even failing at this, the one thing in my life that I could actually do!"

She was close to tears and it almost ripped Cailean's heart in half to see it. Dear God, did this woman *believe* all this? Did she really think these things about herself? Did she really not see the brave, extraordinary, brilliant woman he did?

"Ye canna save everyone," he said quietly.

She blinked. "What?"

He pulled his knees up to his chest and wrapped his arms around them just as she'd done. He stared into the fire, watching the flames dancing and flickering. "Ye canna save everyone," he repeated, his voice soft. "That's a lesson I learned the hard way."

Rose was silent for a moment. "You mean, your wife?"

He let out a long breath. "Aye, I mean my wife." Normally, when he thought of Mary, a hard stab of pain went through his chest and he usually changed the subject. He didn't like talking about her. He didn't like *thinking* about her. The pain and guilt was too much. But this time that piercing pain didn't come. Instead there was just a deep, dull ache, and he found he didn't want to change the subject this time.

"I thought I could do anything," he said. "In my time as laird, I'd beaten off raiders from the mainland, from Ireland, from Norway. I'd given them such a hiding that they hadnae returned to our shores for years. I'd introduced new farming methods from the Continent and improved my people's yields. I'd strengthened the old alliances with Skye and Islay. Oh, aye, I could do anything. I was Cailean MacNeil, master of all!" He huffed out a breath, flexing his fingers where they were clasped around his knees. "But then Mary fell ill. I brought in the best healers coin could buy. I prayed and gave offerings to the old gods and the new. I did everything I could think to do, but none of it did any good. I couldnae save her."

"Cailean…" Rose said softly, reaching out.

He didn't flinch from her touch, but he didn't look at her either. His voice was hoarse. "I carry it with me, every day. That I couldnae keep our daughter from losing her mother." He looked down at his hands, fingers curled in tight. "I thought being laird meant I had to save everyone. And when I couldn't, it near destroyed me."

Rose's fingers found his and squeezed. "I'm sorry, Cailean."

He turned his head to look at her. "I dinna tell ye this in order to garner sympathy. I tell ye this because I dinna want ye to make the same mistake I did. I dinna want ye to let the weight of responsibility choke ye. Ye are *not* a failure, Rose MacFinnan. Dinna ever think ye are."

A faint smile curled her lips. "You are a better man than you give yourself credit for, do you know that?"

"And ye are far braver than ye know, Rose MacFinnan."

Their fingers were still entwined, warm against the cold of the storm. Cailean looked down at them. He had not touched another woman since his wife had died, with the exception of their one kiss. He'd closed off his heart for Catriona's sake and for his own, unwilling to risk such hurt ever again.

But Rose MacFinnan's fingers in his own felt *right*. Being in her company felt right. Here they were, trapped in a hut in the middle of a storm, both drenched to the skin, and yet he didn't want to be anywhere else.

He stroked his thumb across her hand, such a tiny, delicate touch, but it sent sparks through his blood. Rose's lips parted and a slow breath escaped her. She tightened her fingers on his for a second, but in the next instant, she snatched her hand back and moved away slightly, putting more distance between them.

Cailean felt suddenly cold, despite the roaring fire. "I'm sorry, lass," he said. "I didnae mean to—"

"It's fine," she said without looking at him. "Honestly, it's fine."

It clearly wasn't fine. He had clearly overstepped the mark. He cursed himself for a fool. Damn it!

"Rose, listen—" he began, but she cut him off.

"You terrify me."

Cailean blinked. "I'm sorry?"

She was still staring at the fire, hugging her knees as though trying to keep herself together. Without looking at him, she said, "When my marriage broke down, I swore I would never, ever, make the same mistake again. I would never allow myself to feel like that ever again."

Now she did turn to look at him. "But you…" she said, and her voice was barely a breath now. "You make me feel *too much*, Cailean. And it terrifies me. *You* terrify me."

Cailean stared at her. Was she saying what he thought she was? His heart was suddenly racing. He had to swallow a few times before he could speak.

"I swore the same," he said, voice thick. "After Mary. But with you I feel like I'm waking up after a long winter. I dinna understand it. I dinna know what to *do* with it. But I canna ignore it either."

She gazed at him and the silence between them pulsed. Then slowly, hesitantly, she reached out, her hand grazing his. The touch was light. Barely there. But it undid him.

He shifted closer, until their knees touched, and reached up to brush a strand of wet hair from her face. His thumb lingered at her cheekbone, and she leaned into his hand as if it steadied her.

He couldn't stop himself any longer. His heart was thumping like a drum in his chest and his hand against her cheek trembled slightly.

He kissed her.

Not gently, not hesitantly—*hungrily*, like a dam breaking and letting loose all the pent up desire that had been building for days. Rose responded with equal heat, rising to meet him, her hand curling into his shirt, pulling him closer. Their mouths met again and again, the storm outside forgotten, the fire crackling loud in their ears.

Cailean broke the kiss with a ragged breath, resting his forehead against hers, trying to find his footing in the whirlwind of want and tenderness that swept through him.

"I should be angry with ye still," he murmured, voice rough.

Rose gave a breathless, shaking laugh. "I know."

"But I'm not," he said. "I'm just… afraid of what comes next."

"So am I," she whispered. "So am I."

Chapter Fifteen

THIS ALL SEEMED so unreal, like she'd slipped into a dream. Had Cailean really just said what she thought he had? Did he really feel the same way she did? Rose hardly dared breathe in case this moment shattered around her like glass.

She was afraid. Oh God, she was afraid! She was terrified of the feelings that he stirred in her, feelings so unexpected that she felt like she was struggling to catch up with herself, to make sense of the storm inside her.

She was newly divorced for pity's sake! She should *not* be feeling this way. And yet she couldn't help it. Cailean, and what she felt for him, seemed more real, more visceral than anything she'd felt before.

He sat beside her now, silent and watchful, as if waiting for her to decide the next move. Firelight flickered over the hard edge of his jaw, the riot of emotion in his dark, dark eyes.

Rose was tired of *thinking*. She was tired of trying to do the right thing. Tired of trying to be good. Just this once, she wanted to let go, to act on instinct. So, giving in to what she'd wanted to do for what felt an age, she leaned close and pressed her lips against his.

He stilled for a heartbeat, a sharp intake of breath against her mouth. Then he kissed her back.

Rough, sure, desperate. His hands cupped her face, one sliding into her damp hair, holding her close. The blanket slipped from her shoulders, forgotten. The storm faded into the background, just a distant, inconsequential roar that had lost all meaning.

Only this moment mattered.

The kiss deepened, Cailean's lips hot and insistent against hers, full of hunger and need. She gasped against his mouth as he grabbed her hips, pulled her into his lap. She wrapped her arms around his neck, tangling her fingers in his luscious hair and trailing them across the hard muscles of his shoulders, wanting to feel every inch of him against every inch of her.

His kisses tasted of salt and heat and something she couldn't quite define, something that lit an ache deep in her belly and drew a moan from her lips. Oh God. She wanted him. She wanted him so badly it made her muscles ache and her stomach constrict.

But he suddenly broke the kiss. Breathing close by her ear, he murmured, "Tell me to stop and I will."

"Don't," she whispered, her voice ragged. "Please... don't."

His eyes slid closed with a low groan. He caught her lip between his teeth and then they were kissing again, her hands all over him, his hands all over her, and Rose could no longer tell which way was up, which way was down, or whether anything existed in the world other than this man and the fire he was lighting inside her.

She didn't know who started pulling at whose clothes first. She just knew that suddenly they were shedding garments until they were both right down to the skin and Cailean was pushing her onto her back in front of the fire and following her down, kissing her neck, her ears, her collarbone until she arched and gasped beneath him. She'd yanked off his shirt and now her eyes roved over the ridges and contours of his hard body, the firelight casting dimples of shadow and light across his muscular frame.

It was a body that spoke of hardness and strength, and yet his touch was as soft as gossamer as he trailed the tips of his fingers along her sides, across her belly, and down to the core of heat between her legs. She gasped as he lowered his head and took one of her nipples into his mouth at the same moment that his fingers sank into the heat of her.

Fire ignited within and she gasped and arched, screwing her eyes shut tight and tangling her fingers in his hair. Oh. What was he doing to her? This was... this was... she had no name for what it was.

"Cailean," she gasped. "Don't stop. Please don't stop."

He didn't. His tongue licked and sucked at her nipples and his fingers worked her core with expert precision, knowing exactly where to stroke, where to apply pressure and how much, and Rose felt herself beginning to come apart.

She had expected him to be good, but she had never expected him to be *this* good, able to read her body like a book and give her exactly what she needed.

He raised his head and looked at her, his eyes like pools of ink as he watched her, full of desire and heat. "Let go," he murmured as his fingers continued their work. "I want to see ye shatter."

And Rose did. With a cry, she tipped over the edge, felt herself clenching around his fingers, and crashing down the other side of a tingling, blissful wave.

Her eyes fluttered closed as she surrendered to the sensations coursing through her and when she opened them again, she found Cailean looking down at her, his hair falling forward to frame his face.

"Beautiful," he murmured. "Ye are so beautiful."

Rose just reached up, laced her hands behind his neck and pulled him down into a kiss. She was not sated. Despite what he'd just done to her, despite the climax that had just sent her soaring, she wanted more. She wanted *him*. All of him. Every last inch.

Her kiss was wild and hungry, full of longing and need. Cailean responded in kind, his lips crashing against hers, his tongue slipping into her mouth and dancing with her own. Rose tangled one hand in his hair but with the other she reached down, skimming her palm along the hard lines of his chest and belly, down between his legs where she found him hard and ready for her.

His breath hitched as she began to stroke him gently, slowly, the tips of her fingers barely touching him, but raising goosebumps along his skin all the same.

A low growl sounded deep in his throat. "Dear God, woman, what are ye trying to do to me? If ye dinna stop I'm going to have to take ye right now."

His words sent a thrill right through her. That ache was back again, deep in her core, that ache that only he could satisfy.

"Then what are you waiting for?"

It was all the invitation he needed. He rose onto his hands and knees and positioned himself above her. Dark eyes fixed on her, he nudged her legs apart with his knees. Then slowly, not breaking her gaze, he lowered himself on top of her. Rose shifted to meet him, and he suddenly jerked his hips and thrust into her, burying himself up to the hilt.

Rose gasped as she felt him fill her, felt herself stretching to accommodate every inch of him, felt the shudder that went through his body as they joined.

And then he was moving. Deep and slow at first, he moved inside her, and Rose found herself matching his rhythm, her fingers clawing at his back, feeling the bunch and release of the muscles in his back and buttocks.

The sensations that flooded her were like nothing she'd ever felt before. She was no untouched virgin and had been with men before, but this... this was something else. If was as if Cailean's body had been made to fit hers, and as they found their tempo, moving together as firelight painted their bodies with light and shadow, every nerve in Rose's body seemed to come alive.

Tingles raced across her skin. The hair on the back of her neck stood on end. Shudders of something like electricity zinged through her blood.

"Dear God," Cailean breathed, his breath hot on her neck.

"This feels... ye feel like heaven, lass."

She didn't have the breath to answer him. She could only gasp and moan as their tempo increased, as Cailean began to move faster, thrusting into her with increasing force, each movement sending hot spears of bliss rocketing through her body. She writhed under him. Her nails dug into his back. She gasped out his name as she began to burn.

Fire sizzled along her nerves, roared through her blood, and suddenly she was being consumed, losing all sense of herself as burning ecstasy obliterated her. She arched her back, yelling his name as she was finally, utterly consumed.

Cailean gasped out a breath, his body shuddering as he too reached his climax, her name falling from his lips in a groan of pure, sated pleasure.

Rose's awareness shrank and for one long, seemingly infinite moment, all she knew was the sensations of shuddering bliss that rocketed through her and the sound of Cailean's breath by her ear. All else ceased to exist.

But gradually, oh so gradually, she came back to herself. Her chest was heaving and as the euphoria faded a little, a heavy, contented lassitude replaced it, leaving her feeling whole and sated.

Only seconds had passed although it had felt like a lifetime and Cailean's weight still pressed her into the rug beneath them. She ran her hands down his back, delighting in the sensation of his slick, sweat-covered skin and the sound of his ragged breaths. *She* had done that to him. She had given this strong, gorgeous man such pleasure that he was still recovering from it.

He lifted his head from her shoulder, and she found herself looking into his storm-dark eyes.

"Rose," he murmured, the word feeling like a caress across her skin. "I... I... That was..."

He seemed at a loss for words so Rose merely lifted her head and kissed him again. Gone was the heat and passion that had consumed them earlier. This time the kiss was soft and slow, and all the sweeter for it. When it broke, Cailean blew out a breath and rested his forehead against hers.

"I dinna wish to move," he said, his voice low and gruff. "I could stay in this moment forever. With ye."

Rose cupped his face in her hands. Her heart swelled with a sensation she couldn't name. "Me too," she whispered. "Oh, Cailean, what's happening to us?"

His eyes searched her face. "I dinna know, lass." He gently kissed the tip of her nose. "But I like it." Finally, he moved, rolling off her and settling on his back by her side, tucking one hand behind his head and staring at the ceiling.

Rose felt cold without his warmth and found she didn't like being away from him, even though he was only a few inches away. She rolled onto her side, tucking her body alongside his and his arm came up to pull her close, his hand resting on the swell of her hip.

She settled her head against his shoulder, and he turned his head to look at her. There was a world of meaning and longing in the way he looked at her, and Rose found that ache forming deep in her stomach again.

What were they doing? This was madness. It could never work between them. And yet, she found that nothing, *nothing* in her life had ever felt more right than this. Around them the storm still raged but inside, all was still. Rose could hear the gale battering the village and the wind moaned down the chimney, making the flames dance and spit. But inside, it didn't touch them.

It was as if time and the world outside had been suspended. The MacFinnan spellweaver and the MacNeil laird were gone and they were just Rose and Cailean, two people exploring something that neither of them had expected.

He smiled, his fingertip tracing lazy spirals on her hip. "What are ye thinking, lass?"

Rose smiled faintly. The warmth of his touch made it hard to think clearly, let alone speak.

"I was thinking," she said softly, "that this shouldn't be happening."

Cailean arched a brow but didn't pull away. "And yet, here we are."

"Yes." Her voice was barely more than a whisper. "Here we are."

He shifted so he could see her better. His eyes searched hers. "Does it frighten ye?"

"It terrifies me."

He nodded. "Me too."

That surprised her. The mighty Laird MacNeil, afraid? But she saw the truth of it in the tightness around his mouth, in the vulnerability that flickered in his gaze.

She exhaled slowly, placing a hand on his chest over his heart. "Everything in my life has always been about control. Plans. Safety. I never imagined… this."

He let out a low breath. "I never imagined *ye*, Rose MacFinnan. Not in my life, not in my arms."

She blinked rapidly. His words struck something inside her, tender and raw. The fire popped, sending sparks dancing upward, and the wind howled again outside, but within their cocoon, the world narrowed to the space between them.

His hand moved to her face, thumb brushing over her cheek. "Whatever this is, it isnae madness. I've known madness, lass. But this?" His voice dropped, rough with emotion. "This feels like sanity."

She leaned into his touch, her lips brushing the inside of his palm. "Then why does it feel like the rest of the world is going to come crashing in the moment we open that door?"

Cailean gave a short laugh, quiet and a little sad. "Because it probably will."

Rose didn't want to face what awaited them beyond the door. But they had no choice. They might be just Rose and Cailean inside this room, but beyond it they were still the MacFinnan spellweaver and the MacNeil laird and they had duties they could not escape.

Rose settled into his embrace, content to listen to the soft hiss of his breath and feel the rise and fall of his chest beneath her cheek. Gradually, the howl of the wind began to quieten.

"I think the storm is passing."

Cailen sighed. "Is it wrong of me that I dinna want it to?"

She huffed a quiet laugh. "If it is, then I'm wrong too."

She pushed herself up to sitting. The fire had died down to embers but as the storm clouds broke, sunlight was beginning to leak around the shutters on the windows.

"We should get back," she said reluctantly. "They'll be wondering where we've got to."

"Let them," Cailean grunted. Then he sighed, rising to sit beside her. "Aye, ye are no doubt right."

But neither of them moved. They were sitting incredibly close, only an inch between them, but it was still too much for Rose. She wanted to edge closer, to touch him again, to never stop touching him. But time and the world were slowly reasserting themselves.

Cailean reached out and cupped her cheek with one of his big hands. "Come," he said softly.

She nodded and he leaned in, kissed her softly, then rose to his feet and pulled her up after him.

Slowly, reluctantly, they dressed. Rose found herself stealing glances at Cailean as they did so, feeling a shot of disappointment each time a piece of clothing hid more of his body. Once they were dressed, Cailean doused the embers of the fire and crossed to the door. There, he paused.

His hand hovered over the latch and Rose could see reluctance in every line of his body. She understood it. She felt the same way.

He glanced at her. "Ready?"

No, she wanted to say. *I'm not.* But she forced a tight nod. "Ready."

He pushed the door open, and they stepped out into a fresh,

sparkling world. The storm clouds had departed far out to sea. Rose could still see flashes of lightning in them. But directly above, the clouds had broken and now the late-afternoon sun was beaming down, making the puddles sparkle like mirrors. There was a fresh smell in the air, like morning dew, and Rose pulled a deep, invigorating breath down into her lungs.

Cailean held out his hand and she took it as the two of them walked through the village to the house where she'd left her horse. Inside, they found both Snip and Arrow happily drowsing, heads hanging and tails swishing lazily. They raised their heads and whickered as she and Cailean entered, hoping for a treat.

Cailean led them both outside and began checking their saddles and stirrups while Rose turned and gazed out to sea. It looked calm now, peaceful, so different from the raging tempest it had been only a short time ago. There was no evidence of the dark entity she'd encountered when she'd walked out onto the promontory and even when she sent her senses tentatively questing towards it, she found no trace of the dark malevolence that had lurked beneath the waves.

Was it gone? She didn't think so. Biding its time, more likely. She shivered, remembering that voice in her head, that power that had so easily bested her.

She hadn't realized she was trembling until Cailean's arms wrapped around her from behind and pulled her close. "Easy, lass," he rumbled. "I've got ye. I willnae let it harm ye."

She leaned back against him and closed her eyes. The feel of his hard chest against her back was solid and reassuring and she felt the fear recede to be replaced by a fierce kind of determination. *I will best you*, she promised whatever lurked in the water. *We will best you.*

With Cailean by her side, she felt like she could do anything.

They mounted and set off back up the trail towards Dun Mallach. As they rode, evidence of the storm littered the road beside them: fallen branches, piles of leaves, runnels of water trickling down both sides of the path.

"How do you think the keep fared?" Rose asked him as they moved.

"The keep will be fine," he replied. "It's built to withstand far worse. The villages though? That's another matter. There will be more repair work needed after this."

She nodded, accepting this in silence. He sounded weary, as if the weight of the lairdship had settled around his shoulders once more. She longed to be back in that hut with him, the storm cutting them off from the world.

She found herself dropping back a little, allowing Snip to trail behind Arrow so she could watch the way his body swayed with the movement of the horse, his shirt pulling tight over his broad shoulders, his plaid hanging loose across his chest and across his knees. Only a short time ago, that strong, powerful body had been atop her, giving her the most amazing pleasure. She felt her cheeks heat and her stomach tighten.

"Ye are staring, lass."

She blinked. Cailean was looking at her over his shoulder, one eyebrow raised in amusement.

"I am not," she retorted. "*You* were watching me."

"Aye," he agreed. "I was. I canna seem to help it."

Her cheeks heated even further, the warmth spiralling all the way down through her belly and to the spot between her legs.

"See anything you like?" she said in a teasing voice.

"Aye, something I like very much," Cailean breathed. His eyes shone with desire and something else, something more than just lust, something... deeper.

Rose pulled her gaze away and concentrated on guiding her horse. They rode in silence, a deep companionable silence, but all the way back she found herself glancing at him. She couldn't seem to keep her eyes off him. Each time, she found him looking back at her and the two of them would break into stupid grins, like a couple of moonstruck teenagers.

This was *not* supposed to be happening. Falling for the man she'd come to help was not part of the plan.

Is that what this is? she thought. *Is that why I can't seem to breathe when he looks at me? Is that why I'm craving his touch so much? Is that it? Am I falling for him?*

She had no answers. She only knew that she didn't want this journey to end. She didn't want to reach Dun Mallach. She wanted it to remain just her and Cailean. Forever, if possible.

They did not hurry back, and the sun was sinking towards the horizon when they reached the keep. Rose felt her stomach sink as it came into view and from the slight slumping of Cailean's shoulders, she guessed he felt the same.

The gates were standing open and as they rode closer, a group of people came running out towards them. Rose made out Maggie among them.

Cailean pulled his horse to a halt, suddenly alert. "What is this?" he muttered.

The group hurried up to them. "My laird! Rose!" Maggie cried. "Thank the gods ye've returned. Ye must come now! Quickly!"

A shot of alarm went through her at Maggie's urgent tone. Cailean's hands tightened on the reins.

"What is it?" he demanded. "What's happened?"

Maggie wrung her hands. Her skin was pale, her hair coming loose of the normally meticulous braid she tied it in.

"It happened so quickly!" she cried. "There was nothing we could do!"

Cailean's nostrils flared. His skin paled. "What's happened? Answer me, woman!"

"It's Catriona!" Maggie wailed. "She's contracted the sickness!"

IT WAS ALL Cailean could do to remain upright as he tore through the keep towards Catriona's room. He felt like the world was tilting beneath him and blackness roared at the edge of his vision, threatening to send him crashing to his knees.

No. Oh God, please no!

Terror like he'd never known clutched his heart with icy fingers, making it difficult to think, to breathe, to function. Dimly, he was aware of Rose and Maggie sprinting along behind him, but this was a distant awareness.

He raced up the stairs two at a time and burst through the door to Catriona's room so hard he sent it smashing back against the wall. Sister Beatrice rose from where she'd been sitting by the bed. She looked as pale and worried as Maggie.

"My laird—"

Cailean's eyes flew to the bed.

Catriona lay on her back, hair spread out in a halo across her pillow, eyes closed. Sweat beaded her brow, and the sheet was rucked up where she'd been tossing and turning.

He flung himself to her side, going onto his knees by the bed. He grabbed her hands, clenching them tight in his own.

"It's all right, sweetling," he said softly. "I'm here. I'm here."

His daughter made no response. Her brow was furrowed and her head moved from side to side as if she was having bad dreams. Her hands were hot and as he reached out to place one palm against her forehead, he felt the fever there, burning through her like flame through kindling.

No. No. No.

"Sweetling?" he said. "Cat? Can ye hear me?"

There was no response and Cailean's heart began to beat so fast that he was sure it was going to burst out his chest. Not her. Anyone but her. Oh please God, no.

Rose lowered herself to Cat's other side. Cailean flicked a glance in her direction and found her eyes wide, her skin waxy. She pressed two fingers to Catriona's neck then swallowed thickly.

"What happened?" she asked, turning to Beatrice and Maggie. Her voice shook a little.

Beatrice pressed her hands together at her heart in the prayer position. "We were in lessons," she said. "Studying the Gospel of Mark when Catriona suddenly said she didnae feel very well. Next thing I knew, she's swooning out of her chair and running a fever the like of which could set parchment alight."

"When was this?"

"Earlier this afternoon, during the storm," Maggie replied. "It came on so suddenly. We didnae know where ye both were. We sent out riders to look for ye but they couldnae find ye."

Guilt punched Cailean in the stomach with the force of a hammer blow. He glanced at Rose and saw the same emotion mirrored in her wide, horror-filled eyes. They had been in the hut. Together. He'd been with Rose, indulging his lust instead of being here when his daughter needed him most.

He felt sick. He had to grip the edge of the bed to fight the sudden wave of dizziness that swamped him.

Gods, not Cat. Please not Cat.

Rose took a deep breath and closed her eyes. For one, two, three heartbeats, she breathed steadily. Then she snapped her eyes open. When she did, Cailean saw the guilt and horror were gone. Instead, a fierce determination burned in her bright gaze. This was no longer his Rose. It was the MacFinnan spellweaver who sat before him now.

"Beatrice, Maggie, clear the room," she commanded in a tone that brooked no argument. "Go check on the other patients. Leave Catriona to me."

The two women shared a look but neither dared raise an objection, and they quickly strode from the room.

"Cailean, look at me," Rose said. Reluctantly, he tore his gaze away from his daughter's sweat-soaked features and looked at Rose. She reached across the bed and laid her hand atop his and Catriona's. She squeezed and he felt strength and determination in that grip. "She is *not* going to die, do you hear me? I will not allow it."

He swallowed. "What are ye going to do?"

"I'm going to put her asleep, into the same deep sleep as

Drew and the others." A low growl escaped her throat, and she turned her head to study Catriona's writhing form. "And then I'm going to find a way to end this curse and make whatever sent it wish they'd never been born."

Her voice throbbed with anger. Releasing Cailean's hand, she placed both of her palms flat against Catriona's chest and closed her eyes. The air in the room suddenly seemed tighter, closer, like the charged air before a thunderstorm. Catriona let out a long sigh and relaxed. She stopped writhing, and the furrow left her brow. Her breathing seemed to come a little steadier.

Cailen cupped her face. "Cat? Sweetling?"

There was no response. He turned to Rose. "Can she hear me?"

Rose shook her head. "I... I don't know." She gulped in air. "Oh God, Cailean, I'm so sorry."

"Sorry?" he said, looking at her sharply. "For what? None of this is yer fault."

It's mine, he thought. *All of this is my fault. I'm supposed to protect her and I've failed, just like I failed to save her mother.*

A cold spear of despair stabbed through him, so sharp and biting that for a moment it took his breath. Rose raised a hand as though she would reach out to him but then let it drop.

"Let me know if there is any change," she whispered before climbing to her feet. "I'll be in the study if you need me."

Cailean held her gaze. Unshed tears shone in her eyes and Cailean had to look away in case it undid him. A stew of emotions roiled within him just beneath the surface and if he weren't careful they would come bursting out and he would be lost. He couldn't let that happen. Catriona needed him strong, in control.

So he didn't reply to Rose's words, merely nodded dumbly. He felt her pause behind him as though she wanted to say something else but then heard her footsteps crossing the floor and the door closing softly behind her.

The room felt colder, emptier with her gone.

Cailean clasped his daughter's hands in his own and bowed his head, resting his forehead on his hands and screwing his eyes closed.

Please save her, he prayed. He didn't know who he was praying to. To Beatrice's Christian god? To Maggie's pagan ones? He didn't know and he didn't care.

Please save her. I will do anything you ask. Please. I'm begging you.

But he got the feeling nobody was listening.

Chapter Sixteen

ROSE GAVE UP tossing and turning in her bed, threw back the covers, and went to sit in the chair by the window. Dawn was breaking out over the ocean, the sky clear and the sea calm, but Rose's emotions were anything but. She'd not slept. Now she pressed the heels of her hands against her eyes to try and keep in the emotion that tightened her chest. It did no good. The tears came anyway, leaking from beneath her eyelids and running down her cheeks.

This could not be happening. It couldn't.

Images of Catriona's tortured expression flashed through her head, and her stomach knotted with dread and despair.

Why her? Why a nine-year-old girl? What had she ever done to deserve this?

Rose knew it was futile to ask such things. Through the years of treating sickness, she'd learned that there was no rhyme or reason to it and that it could strike at anyone, young or old, fit or unfit. Asking such questions only drove you mad.

Yet she couldn't help it. The despair she'd seen etched on Cailean's face broke her heart. He didn't deserve this either.

Rose thumped her fists down on the arms of her chair in sudden fury. It was better to feel anger than the sick sensation that bubbled underneath it, the sensation that would rise up and swallow her whole if she let it.

Guilt.

Was this her fault? Had she caused this? The rational part of her mind wanted to deny it. Yet some deeper, more instinctive part whispered that this was because of her. Because of what she'd done that afternoon.

Her thoughts went flitting back to that moment on the headland. That moment with the storm crashing around her and the waves lashing the rocks and that voice in her head whispering, *"Come to me."*

But she had not. Cailean had stopped her. And in response, she'd felt a burning anger from whatever lurked beneath the waves. Anger led to vengeance.

Was *this* that vengeance? Was Catriona being punished for what she, Rose, had done?

The tears came again, and she leaned forward, curling over her stomach as the sobs wracked her. She wasn't strong enough for this. How had she ever believed she was? She was just plain old Rose MacFinnan, and despite everything she'd tried to do to help these people, she had failed.

Now Cailean's daughter was going to pay the price for that failure.

No, she thought. *She won't. I won't let that happen.*

She wiped away her tears, straightened in her chair, and took a deep breath. From her seat she could see the sea in the distance at the bottom of the hill, looking quiet and tranquil now that the storm had passed. The sea. It all started and ended with the sea.

And in particular, with a *goddess* of the sea.

"Lir!" Rose bellowed, rising to her feet. "Lir! Attend me! I want some answers, damn you!"

The sea goddess had brought her here, asking for her help. Well, now she needed some help herself.

She turned in a circle, her fists clenched at her sides. "Lir!" she bellowed. "Where are you?"

There was no response. That ember of anger deep in her belly began to burn again, flaring to life and washing away Rose's grief. Instead, fury filled her veins. She was tired of being used. Lir had asked for her help but had offered none of her own. Well, enough was enough. It was time for answers, and if Lir wouldn't respond to Rose's call, then she would *make* her.

Rose's gaze flicked to the desk and the platter that held the crumbs from her breakfast. But it wasn't the platter she was looking at.

It was the knife that sat on it.

Her nostrils flared, the anger burning hotter. Oh yes, there was a way to make the goddess answer. It was dangerous, appallingly so, and she had been taught never, ever to try such a thing. She no longer cared.

She had promised Cailean she would save Catriona, and she intended to keep that promise. No matter what it took. She glanced out of the window at the waves beating against the shore in the distance.

Then she grabbed the knife, clasped it hard in her fist, and strode out the door.

CAILEAN PLACED THE flowers he'd picked from the meadow on the mound at his feet and knelt, the grass wet with morning dew against his bare knees. He bowed his head, allowing his hair to fall forward to curtain his face. All night he'd sat by Catriona's bedside, but as dawn came and he'd found himself falling asleep in his chair, he'd forced himself to come here, to face what he'd been avoiding.

Around him, the wind hissed, making the tall grasses wave and sending whispers through the branches of the trees. To Cailean they sounded like accusing voices.

Traitor, they whispered. *Betrayer.*

He lifted his head and looked at the mound in front of him. A tiny alder tree grew from the head of it, bravely battling the wind.

There was no name to mark who lay beneath, no carved cross or other marker.

But Cailean didn't need any of that. The name of the person who lay here was carved across his soul.

"Mary," he whispered, barely able to speak the word. "I'm sorry. Forgive me."

The cold weight of guilt settled on his shoulders, heavier than an anvil. He had loved his wife. He had promised to hold to her for his entire life, but he had broken that promise. And when their daughter had needed him the most, he'd been in the arms of another woman.

Rose's face flashed through his mind. With it came that lifting of his soul he felt whenever she was near, that brightening of the world around him. Just for an instant. In the next, the guilt crashed back in and that lightness was replaced with self-loathing.

Dear God, what sort of man was he? What sort of man took his pleasure with a woman while his daughter lay ill? What sort of man put his own lust before the needs of his people?

Dark despair washed through him, closing his throat.

"My laird?"

He looked up to see Sister Beatrice standing nearby. Alarm spiked in his belly. "What is it? Is it Catriona?"

"Nay, laird," Beatrice replied, holding out a placating hand. "Maggie is with her. There has been no change. She's sleeping soundly, thanks to Rose."

Thanks to Rose. Just the sound of her name sent a tremor along his skin. Oh, how he ached to be with her now. How he ached to feel her arms around him, ached to hear her telling him everything was going to be all right. And that only made him feel all the guiltier.

"Then what do ye want?" he snapped more forcefully than he intended. The last thing he needed right now was any of her preaching.

Instead of replying, she knelt on the ground by his side, ignoring the mud that dirtied her pristine white habit.

"She was a fine woman," she said. "We all miss her."

Cailean did not respond. He was in no mood for talking, especially not about his wife.

"She was strong-willed, decisive, a fit match for the laird of Barra," Beatrice continued. "But do ye know what impressed me the most about her? The way she put others' happiness before her own. Her daughter's. Yers."

Cailean scowled. "What are ye getting at? If ye have something to say, sister, spit it out."

"Do ye think Mary would want ye to be unhappy? Do ye think she would begrudge what ye have found with Rose MacFinnan?"

Cailean looked at her sharply. "What are ye talking about?"

"Oh, I think ye know. I may be a nun now, but I wasnae *always* wedded to God, ye know. I have some experience of matters of the heart, and even if I didnae it wouldnae be too difficult to see what ye feel for her. It's written in every line of yer face whenever ye look at her."

Cailean opened his mouth for an angry retort, to tell Beatrice to mind her own business, to tell her that she didn't know what she was talking about. But his anger drained away under her knowing gaze. There was no judgment in her eyes, only a steady, deep compassion.

He hung his head. "What am I going to do, Beatrice?" he whispered.

Her hand caught his and clasped it. "Firstly, ye are going to let go of this guilt that sits like a shadow in yer eyes. Ye loved Mary, we all know that. But it isnae a betrayal to let another in to yer heart."

A shudder went through Cailean. He felt like weeping. He felt like bellowing. He felt like roaring his frustration at the sky. But all he did was squeeze Beatrice's hand in response.

Was she right? He didn't know.

"And if I canna?"

She fixed him with a stern glare. "Then ye will have lost

something precious, something most of us never find in our lifetimes. And it will shrivel ye inside. Ye wish to be a good laird? A good father? Then ye need to be happy. Open yer heart, Cailean MacNeil. Allow the sun to shine inside. Allow Rose MacFinnan in."

Cailean didn't know how to reply. These were the last words he'd expected from her. He'd expected her usual words of fire and brimstone, proclaiming that what had happened to Catriona was some sort of judgment from God and that it was his fault for giving into the sin of lust.

But it wasn't lust, he realized suddenly. Not lust. Something else entirely.

It was love.

ROSE IGNORED EVERYONE who waved to her or called her name as she descended along the winding path down the hill through the village.

Cailean's work crews were out helping to clean up the mess from the last storm. Rose stepped around crates of supplies, piles of blown debris and collapsed rubble, and kept herself focused on her destination.

She reached the bottom of the hill and kept going, picking her way through the tussocky grass and then down the sand dunes, onto the beach, and right up to the water. She didn't stop until the cold waves were lapping around her ankles, soaking the hem of her dress.

"Lir!" she screamed into the wind. "Answer me, damn you!"

There was no response except the hiss and whoosh of the waves. Rose's nostrils flared, and a hot surge of anger went through her. Fine. She would rather it hadn't come to this, but she was left with no choice.

She lifted her hands and, gripping the knife in her right hand, she sliced the blade against the palm of her left, wincing at the sudden sting of pain. Curling her fingers, she made a fist with her left hand and squeezed. A trickle of bright red droplets ran down her fist and drip, drip, dripped into the sea.

"Lir!" she bellowed, accessing her power and sending it rushing through the waves with the power of her blood. "I summon you! Answer me!"

Blood magic was the most dangerous form of magic. Since she'd been a child, she'd been told never, ever, to use it. It bordered on dark things and was seductive in its power. Rose had never used it. She had never even considered it until now. But she'd do anything, anything to help Catriona. To help the people of Barra.

To help Cailean.

She waited. Around her, the day was becoming bright and breezy, with fluffy clouds scudding across the sky like sheep. It seemed peaceful, but Rose wasn't fooled. She knew all too well the fury and darkness that lurked beneath the seemingly peaceful scene.

Suddenly, the feel of the air changed. There was a boom as of a door opening and closing and then a gust of wind battered her so strongly that it almost sent her to her knees. It dissipated as quickly as it had come, and when it was gone, a voice spoke by Rose's side.

"Ye called?"

Rose turned her head. Lir stood beside her, silver eyes fixed on her, hair blowing in the wind. Although the goddess's smooth face was expressionless, Rose could feel the annoyance coming off her in waves. Lir, it seemed, didn't take too kindly to being ordered around.

Well, too bad.

"I did."

Lir glanced at the Rose's sliced palm and the blood still dripping from it. "Blood magic?" she said, curling one elegant eyebrow. "Ye of all people should know how dangerous that is.

There are others who might have answered such a call, others who ye would *not* like to meet."

"I wouldn't have had to take the risk if you'd bothered answering when I called!" Rose snapped. "Or in fact, if you'd given me any help at all rather than just dumping me here and leaving me to fend for myself!"

Lir cocked her head, seeming slightly puzzled by her outburst. "I didnae leave ye without help, Rose MacFinnan. All the help ye need, or ever will need, is right by yer side. Ye know this, I think, even if ye willnae admit it, even to yerself."

Cailean. She was talking about Cailean. His face flashed through her mind, but she pushed the image away ruthlessly. She would not be distracted. Nor would she let this goddess tie her in knots.

"You know what I'm talking about," she growled. "You knew the sickness was caused by a curse all along. Why didn't you just tell me? It could have saved a lot of trouble and heartache."

It might have saved Catriona, she thought. *It might have stopped Cailean's heart from breaking with guilt and despair. It might have...*

She stopped the thought. What-ifs and might-haves would only drive her crazy.

For the first time, an expression crossed Lir's porcelain face that could only be described as... regret? Sadness?

"Ah, Rose MacFinnan," she breathed. "Now we get to it. Now we get to the truth of gods and goddesses. We might seem all-powerful, but we are not. Ye of all people must understand the limits of power. I, like all my kind, am bound by rules, and I did all I could within the limits of those rules."

Rose narrowed her eyes at the goddess. One of their *rules* was that they couldn't lie, but that didn't mean they couldn't bend the truth to suit their needs or only reveal what they needed to in order to get their own way. There was more to this, she was sure, more that Lir wasn't telling her. She began to see why Cailean was so mistrustful of gods and goddesses.

She shook her head. "All right. Let's forget that for now. Lir, I need your help. I need you to tell me the truth about what's happening here. I need you to tell me the truth about whatever that being is in the bay near Hemkirk. It's a god, isn't it?"

Lir looked away, her expression troubled, and Rose knew she'd guessed right. "Aye," Lir said softly. "It is one of my brethren."

Rose's breathing quickened. "I was told a strange tale. That tale spoke of a god and a goddess who were once lovers. The story said the god grew jealous when the goddess chose her people over him and swore to take revenge. The story says that the stormlights seen in the ocean are his anger. That's what the story says. But it's not a story, is it? It's true."

Lir did not answer for a long time. Her silver eyes were fixed on the ocean, gazing out at the horizon where the sea met the sky. Her expression was one of such sadness that it stole Rose's breath. It was strange to see such a human emotion on such an inhuman face.

"Aye," she whispered at last. "It's true."

"And was that goddess yourself? Are *you* the one in the story?"

Lir turned to face her. "Nay," she said. "It wasnae me. But ye are close to the truth, Rose MacFinnan, so close ye could reach out and touch it."

Lir sighed. "The goddess who was the sea god's lover was a goddess of the earth. Of the field and hedgerow. Of the rivers and the mountains. It was she who brought prosperity to the people of Barra. She loved them as they loved her. But aye, the sea god, her lover, grew jealous. He didnae like the fact that she loved her people more than she loved him. He demanded that she forsake them and give herself over wholly to him. But she refused, and they fought. The cataclysm it caused almost broke Barra in two. But the goddess won out, and to safeguard her people, she imprisoned her lover beneath the seabed in an unbreakable prison. So long as she endured, so would the jail. Yet, she loved him still, and without him by her side, she began to wither from grief. Years passed and the goddess's power began to wane. Finally, worn down by years of loneliness and despair, the goddess faded until she was no more than a whisper on the breeze, less than a memory to her people. And when she finally left the world, her power went with her. The protective magic that had once guarded Barra was gone. As a result, the sea god's prison began to break, and he was able to touch the world again."

The silver eyes found Rose's. "*That* is the curse on Barra. He is breaking free, and his lust for vengeance hasnae dimmed over the centuries. He blames the people of Barra for robbing him of his love. Should he break free, he will destroy them all."

She fell silent, staring at Rose, awaiting her response. Rose had no words. What was she supposed to say to that? What *could* she say? It was a fantastical tale, the kind of thing told around a flickering fire on a cold winter's night. And yet, she knew every word of it was true. She felt it in her bones.

Something nagged at her, a suspicion that had been growing as she listened to Lir's story and saw the expression on the goddess's face. "The sea god and the earth goddess," she asked. "Who are they?"

Lir lifted her chin and fixed Rose with an almost defiant expression. Despite her vast age, the goddess suddenly seemed very young.

"My parents," she said at last. "My mother is gone, but my father remains trapped in his prison. If he escapes, he will wreak his revenge, and everything my mother died for will have been for nothing. Ye must *not* let that happen, Rose MacFinnan."

Rose stared. "Me? You expect *me* to fix this? I'm a healer, damn it! I cure colds and fix broken bones. I ease people's arthritis and deliver babies. I don't have the power for this!" It was her turn to fix Lir with a challenging stare. "But *you* do. You're a goddess, for pity's sake! You have the power. You have to reseal your father's prison!"

But Lir was already shaking her head. "I canna. Did I not tell ye we have rules? Were I to touch my father's prison, it would free him instantly. My mother used earth magic to create it but I inherited my father's power. I am aligned to the sea. Should I touch the earth magic, it would shatter. In this, Rose MacFinnan, I am as powerless as a newborn babe."

Lir's voice shook a little, and Rose blinked in surprise. *She's frightened*, she thought. *She's terrified of her father breaking free and what he might do.* Lord above, what could be so terrible that it frightens a goddess?

But she already knew the answer to that question. She'd seen it in the countless graves on the outskirts of Hemkirk. She'd seen it in the dark power that had struck her when she'd tried to heal Drew. She'd seen it in Catriona's twisted expression as she writhed and thrashed.

She closed her eyes, trying to draw strength from somewhere, from anywhere. Who was she to think she was up to so monumental a task?

"Lir," she said, her voice sounding pitifully weak against the crash of the waves. "What do I do?"

The goddess's expression softened. She reached out and took Rose's hand, her touch cool and soothing, like the soft sighing of the sea against a golden shore.

"Ye already know what ye have to do," she replied softly. "Ye have always known, deep inside."

Rose stared into those silver eyes and felt something shift inside her. Something loosened. Something floated free. It took Rose a moment to realize what it was.

Acceptance.

Lir was right. From the moment she had discovered that magic was the cause of the sickness she had known, ultimately, what it would take to beat it. Deep down, in some place she never normally went, she had recognized the cost she would have to pay.

And suddenly she knew what she had to do.

With it came an odd kind of peace. She squeezed Lir's hand and let it go.

"Thank you," she whispered.

Then, without a word, she turned and left the goddess on the shore, climbing the dunes towards Dun Mallach and everything that awaited her there. Yes, she knew what she had to do.

But first, she wanted to say goodbye.

Chapter Seventeen

SHE FOUND HIM standing on the battlements, hands resting on the crenellations, staring out to sea. She'd gone first to Catriona's room but, not finding him there and being told by Maggie that she'd ordered him to go and get some rest, she'd scoured the keep.

The whole castle was strangely subdued. Everyone had been affected by the news of Catriona's illness, and the warriors and household staff alike wore haggard expressions as they went about their business.

It was two anxious warriors who told Rose where to find him. They were keeping a worried eye on him from below, hanging around at the base of the steps that led up the battlements, in case their laird should need them. Rose thanked them and climbed warily up the steps.

Coming out onto the walkway that spanned the top of the curtain wall, she had to squint against the sunlight reflecting off the sea in the distance and shade her eyes as she scanned the battlements. She found him almost immediately, gazing out to sea, his form nothing more than a silhouette against the brightness.

She walked over to him. "Cailean?"

He turned, and the despair written across his face almost stopped her heart. But his expression softened when he saw her.

"Rose," he breathed, and took a half step toward her. "Where have ye been?"

She waved away his question. "That's not important. What is important is that I know how to break the curse."

His eyes flared with hope. "What? How?"

"I spoke to Lir. Hemkirk is the key. That's where this all started, and that's where it will end. I have to go back there."

"Then I'm coming with ye."

"No," she said, shaking her head. "Your place is here, with your people. With your daughter. Not chasing shadows with me."

"There is naught I can do here," he replied, his storm-dark eyes meeting hers. "Ye think I can turn my back on ye now?"

She raised a hand as if to touch him but let it drop. There were maybe three or four paces between them, but it felt like a hundred miles. "You have to."

His nostrils flared. "What is it ye are planning? How will ye break the curse?"

She shrugged, trying for a nonchalance she didn't feel. "I'll use my powers."

"Yer powers? But that didnae work before." His eyes narrowed in suspicion.

Don't ask me any more, she thought. *Don't make me lie to you.*

"That's because I didn't fully understand it before. Now I do. Now I know what it will take." Now she did step forward, laid her hand on his arm. "You have to trust me, Cailean. Can you do that?"

He gazed down at her, and she saw a storm of emotion in his eyes. Emotions that mirrored her own. She wanted to step into his embrace so badly she could barely breathe. She wanted to tell him how she felt about him so much that the words burned in her chest. But she could not. She had known from the start that nothing could come of what had happened between them. Speaking such things now would only hurt all the more.

He opened his mouth and then closed it again. His throat

bobbed as he swallowed. "Ye know I trust ye," he said at last. "I would trust ye with my life just as I trust ye with my daughter's life."

His words filled her up inside, like the warmth of a fire on a cold evening. She doubted he realized just how much they meant to her. Catriona was the most precious thing in his life. He would die for her if needed. And he trusted *her* with Catriona's life. Nothing he could have said could have meant as much.

She felt tears pricking her eyes and blinked furiously to stop them from falling. Cailean was there in an instant. All the awkward reserve that had existed between them snapped, and he took her face in his hands and brushed away the tears from the corners of her eyes with his thumbs.

"Oh, my dear lass," he said. "Please dinna cry. I canna bear it." He gently kissed the top of her head. "What is it? What's wrong?"

I'm terrified is what's wrong, she thought. *Terrified that I'll fail. Terrified that I won't be able to keep my promise to you. But most of all, I'm terrified that if I do succeed, I'll never see you again.*

She forced a wry smile onto her face. "In case you haven't noticed, things have been a little... difficult around here of late."

His lips quirked. "Aye, ye willnae get any argument from me on that."

It took all the strength she had to step back from him, to put space between them. "There are some preparations I need to make before I leave for Hemkirk. I'll ride out this evening."

"Not alone ye willnae."

"You have to stay here, Cailean. I—"

"Damn it, woman," he growled. "Must ye always argue with me? In case ye have forgotten, *I* am lord of this island. What kind of leader would I be if I let ye face this alone? What kind of father would I be if I didnae do all I could to help secure a cure for my daughter? This isnae up for discussion. I'm coming with ye."

Rose opened her mouth to argue and then snapped it closed. She recognized that look on his face, the one that said he'd made up his mind and there would be no changing it. And besides, she *wanted* him with her. She needed his strength if she was going to be able to face this.

"All right," she breathed. "Fine."

He nodded tightly. "Good. Then we'll leave at midday."

Rose let out a long, slow breath. Midday. A few hours away. Just enough time to make her preparations, do the rounds of her patients, and say her final goodbyes.

She nodded. "Midday it is."

Chapter Eighteen

"...AND THAT'S HOW the giant Tur An Rog beat the invaders and kept his family safe for all time," Cailean concluded.

As expected, Catriona made no response. To any untrained eye, she would just look as if she was sleeping peacefully. Her expression was smooth, and her forehead unmarred by any lines of worry or unease. Her chest rose and fell gently, and her hands were clasped together on her stomach. To any untrained eye.

But Cailean knew his daughter's face better than he knew his own, and that look of peaceful sleep didn't fool him. She was gone far away, retreated so deep inside herself that what remained was only a shell. Every time he looked at her, his heart clenched with mindless terror. What if she never woke? What if she remained like this forever?

"Seems an age since I heard that story," Maggie commented from where she was checking some of the patients on the other side of the room. "Not since I was a lass. It used to be one of my favorites."

"It's one of Cat's too," he replied. "Do ye think she can hear me?" He tried to keep his voice calm, assured, but he heard the tremor in it all the same.

Maggie straightened, her expression softening. "I'm sure she can, my laird. And I'm sure her da's voice soothes her as she sleeps."

Cailean hoped Maggie was right. He reached out and gently brushed his thumb across his daughter's cheek. "I have to go away for a little while, sweetling," he said softly. "Yer Aunt Rose and I think we may have found the cause of the sickness and a way to stop it. But I'll be back before ye know it and then we'll take Patch out for a ramble together, eh? I know where there are mushrooms just coming up in the woods."

He leaned down and kissed her lightly on the forehead. Patch, curled up by Catriona's feet as ever, got up, turned around a few times, and then slumped back down, head on his paws.

"Ye take good care of yer mistress until I get back, ye hear?" he told the little dog.

Maggie finished checking Drew's pulse, pulled the sheet back up to the man's chin, and came over to Cailean.

"I'm sure Patch, Beatrice, and I can manage while ye are gone, my laird," she said, fixing him with a shrewd stare. "But I would be happier if I knew where ye were going."

"That isnae something ye need to worry about," he replied. "Ye will just have to trust me." The last thing he wanted was anyone following him out there and falling prey to the angry god in the same way the people of Hemkirk had.

Maggie clearly didn't like this answer. Her brows pulled down into a scowl. "Of course I trust ye," she snapped. "Ye are our laird, aren't ye? But when dealing with the old powers, ye need to be careful, take precautions. *They* canna be trusted."

Cailean looked at her sharply. "How do ye know where I'm going has anything to with the old powers?"

Maggie rolled her eyes. "Look at me, lad. Do I look like some untried maiden to ye? I'm old, my laird, and I've seen a thing or two in my time. I know that Rose spoke to Lir again. I felt her presence. And that after that the two of ye have been as tight-lipped as clams. It doesnae take a seer to work out what's going on."

Cailean sighed, wiping the back of his hand across his forehead. He slumped on his stool, elbows resting on his knees, hands dangling.

Maggie laid a hand on his shoulder. "I've known ye since ye were a bairn, lad," she said softly. "There was a time when ye used to talk to me when things were bothering ye."

Cailean looked up, met Maggie's eyes, and realized that she too was worried. Worried about him. About Catriona. About what he and Rose were planning to do. He wasn't the only one with a lot riding on the success of this mission, he reminded himself.

"Rose and I are going to Hemkirk," he said softly. "That's where the source of the sickness lies."

Maggie gasped out a breath. "So ye've found it then? The totem?"

Cailean shook his head. "It isnae a totem." His eyes met Maggie's. "It's a prison."

Haltingly, he told Maggie of what Rose had discovered. He told her about the stormlights, about what Lir had told Rose and that they planned to seal this prison so the god could not escape.

Maggie's expression became more and more troubled as he spoke. By the time he'd finished his tale, she was as pale as a landed fish. "Ye canna do this!" she cried. "There must be another way!"

Cailean blinked, taken aback by her reaction. "There is no other way, Maggie. I would have thought ye'd be pleased we know of a way to combat the sickness."

"Not like this!" she cried. "The price is too high! This clan needs ye, my laird. Catriona needs ye. And we need Rose too. We canna let ye sacrifice yerselves like this!"

Cailean rocked back in his seat. "Sacrifice? What do ye mean?"

Maggie wrung her hands. "Ye intend to seal the prison of a god! Only the strongest magic can achieve such a thing. Blood magic. Sacrifice. And that sacrifice must be made willingly." She shook her head. "Dinna do this, Cailean. There must be another way!"

Sacrifice? Bood magic? What was she talking about? Rose

hadn't mentioned anything about blood magic.

Cailean suddenly went cold. Of course she hadn't. Of course she'd made light of it, made it seem like her magic would be enough as it was. Because if she'd mentioned anything about a sacrifice, she knew he'd stop her.

He jumped from his chair and strode to the door, heart suddenly hammering. "Take care of Cat!" he yelled as he slammed the door behind him.

As he ran from the infirmary towards the keep, he could hear his blood roaring in his ears and feel his heart thumping against his ribs. Only the strongest magic. Blood magic. Sacrifice.

No. She couldn't. He wouldn't let her.

Reaching the keep, he raced up the stairs and pelted along the corridor until he reached her room. He pushed the door open without knocking and burst inside.

Rose turned in surprise from where she was standing by the window, holding a hairbrush in one hand. "Cailean? It's not midday yet."

"When were ye going to tell me?" he growled. "Or weren't ye going to bother?" *Were ye just going to leave me?*

She paled a little but defiance flashed in her eyes. "I don't know what you're talking about."

"Dinna lie to me, woman!" he bellowed, grabbing her arms. "Maggie explained it all. She explained that there is only one way to reset the old magic. Blood. *Yer* blood. Or do ye deny it?"

Her expression tightened. For a second she looked as though she was considering lying, but in the next instant, the defiance went out of her and tears gathered in her eyes instead. "There's no other way, Cailean."

"There's always another way!" he roared. "Dear God, did ye really think I would let ye do this?"

"You can't 'let' me do anything," she said softly. "This is my choice, Cailean. This is what I came here to do."

"I dinna give two shits what ye came here to do! I willnae let ye do this, Rose. I canna!"

"Even if it means saving your people? Saving your daughter?"

He recoiled as if she'd slapped him. "That isnae fair."

Her shoulders slumped. "I know it isn't. But it's the truth. The old magic has to be reset, Cailean. It's the only way to stop the sea god from breaking free and destroying Barra. But the old magic was woven by a goddess, a being way more powerful than I am. The only way I can even hope to match that power is by making a bargain. And the only thing that will be acceptable is a life. My life. My blood. That is how these things work."

Cailean stared at her, appalled. How could she speak of such things so calmly? Like she was discussing the weather? His heart was thumping so hard he thought it might break his ribs.

He strode over and placed his hands on her shoulders. "Please," he said. "Dinna do this." He knew he sounded like he was begging but he didn't care. Hell, he'd go down on his knees if that's what it took. He was filled with a cold, gut-wrenching fear that filled his veins with ice and made it difficult to think. No. Not her. Please, God, not her.

He cupped her cheek in his hand. "I'm sorry, Rose. Forgive me."

Then, before she could react, he slid his hand down, took hold of the thong around her neck, and snapped it with one quick yank. A key dangled from it. He strode out and pulled the door shut behind him. He'd locked the door before Rose had even realized what was happening.

She began thumping on it from the other side. "Cailean? What are you doing? Let me out this minute!"

Cailean pressed his forehead against the door and closed his eyes. That weight was back around his neck again, feeling heavy enough to crush him. "I canna lose ye," he said, unsure whether Rose could hear him through the thick wood. "I love ye, Rose MacFinnan."

Then he curled his fingers around the key and strode off down the corridor, ignoring Rose's muffled shouts from behind him.

Chapter Nineteen

ROSE'S KNUCKLES WERE red and sore from pounding on the door and her voice hoarse from shouting. How long had it been since Cailean had locked her in here? An hour? Longer? And still nobody answered her shouts.

Cailean had clearly given orders. Bloody infuriating man! How dare he lock her in here? How the hell dare he?

She rested her forehead against the wood, sucking in great heaving breaths. She was furious but her fury was being drowned out by a deeper, stronger emotion.

Fear.

Cailean MacNeil, she knew, was going to do something stupid.

I love ye, Rose MacFinnan.

Those had been the last words he'd spoken to her. His voice had been muffled by the door between them but she'd heard them all the same. Every time she thought about it, her breath caught in her throat and her heartbeat ramped up a notch. She'd been aching to hear those words. Only now did she realize that. Only now did she realize that she felt exactly the same way about him. *That's* what this ache inside was.

She loved Cailean MacNeil.

And now she might never see him again.

She sank down onto the bed and put her head in her hands.

Think, Rose, think.

She had no doubt where Cailean had gone. Even now, he'd be riding to Hemkirk. She knew it as surely as she knew the sun would rise tomorrow. It was his duty, he would think, to sacrifice himself for his people.

Think, Rose, think.

She had to get out of this room. She had to stop him. If he didn't come back...

Barra would be left without a leader. Catriona would be left without a father. And she... she would be left without the light that lit the dark corners of her life. She could not do that. It was unacceptable.

Think, Rose. Think.

There was no breaking down the door. The window was too narrow to fit through. So what did that leave her?

Her eyes fell on the fire burning in the hearth. A mad idea came to her. It was risky, desperate. But desperation was all she had.

Grabbing a bit of parchment from where it sat on the small desk, she rolled it then carried it over to the fire, sticking the end into the flames. It didn't catch fire but began to smolder, giving off an acrid white smoke. Blowing gently on it, and shielding it with one hand, she carried the burning ember over to the door and put it down by the crack underneath. Getting down on hands and knees, she began blowing on it, sending white smoke curling under the door and into the corridor outside.

Next she sprang up and ran to the window. Throwing wide the narrow shutters, she cried, "Fire! Help! Fire!"

People looked up from where they were crossing the bailey and came running. Rose pressed her back against the wall at the side of the door, putting her sleeve over her mouth to keep from inhaling the smoke. She did not have to wait long.

Footsteps pounded in the corridor and she heard the sound of coughing. A moment later, keys jangled in the lock and the door burst open, revealing Mable and a contingent of guards carrying buckets of water.

Rose seized her chance. Shouting a quick apology, she jumped over the burning parchment, pushed past Mable and the guards, and bolted down the corridor. She didn't stop until she'd reached the stable and then only long enough to bark a command to one of the stable hands to saddle Snip.

By the time she was leading the horse out of the stable and into the courtyard, Mable and the guards had gathered outside and had been joined by Maggie and Beatrice.

Rose ignored them, swinging up onto Snip's back and pulling the mare around to face the gates.

One of the guards stepped forward, taking hold of Rose's stirrup. "We canna let ye leave, my lady," he said. "Laird's orders."

"I don't give a fig for the laird's orders," she growled. "So let go, damn it!"

He didn't. His grip only tightened.

Maggie stepped forward. "Let her go, Tom."

"But the laird—"

"The laird wasnae in his right mind when he gave that order," Maggie cut in. "He was weighed down by grief and worry. If ye wish to see yer laird again, ye will let the MacFinnan spellweaver go."

The man swallowed thickly, looking from Maggie to Rose and back again. He nodded, releasing her stirrup and stepping back.

Maggie looked up at Rose. "Bring him back to us," she said hoarsely. "Bring *both* of ye back to us. We need ye."

Rose nodded tightly. "I'll do everything in my power," she said, knowing it wouldn't be enough.

"Then may the gods go with ye," Maggie said.

"And may Christ protect ye," Beatrice added, making the sign of the cross.

Rose nodded to the two women. Then, before she could lose her courage, she set her heels to Snip's flanks.

"Yah!"

She sent the mare galloping out of the gates. Her hair streaming out behind her, she crouched low over the horse's withers, urging all the speed she could from the mare. Urgency bit at her heels. Gripping the reins tighter, she bared her teeth in a savage snarl. She would get there in time. She would save him. She was a MacFinnan spellweaver.

It was time to discover what that really meant.

CAILEAN STOOD ON the beach, the abandoned village of Hemkirk behind him, gazing out at the waves. There was no evidence of the stormlights now and the bay looked serene, peaceful. Nobody would believe that something so evil lurked beneath the waves.

And yet Cailean knew it was there.

He could feel it. Something... off in the caress of the breeze and the whisper of the waves, like a faint carrion stink almost beyond the range of his senses. Now that he knew it was there, it was impossible to miss, and he wondered why he hadn't spotted it before.

Because you didn't have Rose MacFinnan at your side before, he told himself.

He jerked his thoughts away from her. He couldn't afford to think about her, not now. Not if he wanted to find the courage to do what he'd come here to do.

Slowly, methodically, almost making a ritual of it, he stripped off his weapons, his boots, his plaid, until he was left in just the linen shirt that fell to mid-thigh. He dropped his clothes onto the damp sand, knowing he'd never need them again. Bending, he retrieved his dagger, took it from its sheath, and clamped it between his teeth. It was the only thing he was going to need.

Then, clenching his fists and screwing up his courage, he strode down to the water's edge and waded in. The water was cold enough to steal his breath, but he didn't falter as he walked first to waist-high, then chest-high, until finally he felt his feet go out from under him and he began to swim.

To his left was the headland where Rose had almost thrown herself into the water. He kept parallel to this as he swam with sure, powerful strokes out towards the spot where she'd heard the god's voice speaking to her.

Now that he was moving, all his doubts, all his fear vanished, to be replaced by a cold, hard determination. Everyone had their fate after all, and this was his. He'd always known he might have to give his life for his clan. He had thought that would be in battle against raiders or at sea fighting pirates, but the how didn't matter. He was the laird. This was what he was born for.

He reached the rough location of where Rose had seen the stormlights and stopped, treading water and looking around. A few seals bobbed nearby, watching him curiously with their dog-like faces, and a few gulls screamed at him, unhappy with his intrusion. Other than that, all seemed normal.

Except it didn't *feel* normal.

That sense of wrongness had increased and now he could feel it brushing against his skin like an ink stain blighting the waves.

Who are you?

The voice flowered in his head with enough force to make him gasp. He almost dropped the knife but clamped his teeth down at the last minute.

I'm Cailean MacNeil, he thought back. *And I'm here to stop you.*

There was silence for a long time but that sense of wrongness intensified and now Cailean could feel it pulsing through his body like heat from a bonfire. It felt like... anger. Fury.

You are one of them, the voice said. *The betrayers. The ones who took my love from me.*

I took nothing, Cailean replied. *And yet you have taken much from me. My people. My friends. You will not have my daughter.*

Soft laughter. *And how will you stop me?*

Cailean clamped his teeth down on the dagger and dived.

Beneath the waves he entered a strange world of twisting kelp and dappled sunlight. The seals, intrigued by his presence, swam closer, their liquid eyes full of curiosity. He ignored them.

Some twenty feet below him lay the seabed, covered with rounded boulders, waving kelp, and beds of sea grass. But his eyes were immediately drawn to something else. Flickering lights in pearlescent blue and green shimmered across the seabed, like the lights seen in the northern sky in winter.

Stormlights.

They were enchantingly beautiful, flashing in a myriad of hues like a butterfly's wing. He found himself watching them, unable to look away. He began to understand how Rose had been so mesmerized the other day.

Soft laughter again. It seemed to echo from all around him. *You are stronger than most. There aren't many who can resist. It will be interesting to destroy you.*

Cailean ignored the voice. Instead, his eyes scanned the sea floor. There! Amidst the waving kelp he spotted something, a crack that split the seabed. It branched and twisted like a jagged piece of lightning, and it was from this crack that the stormlight was spilling.

The god's prison.

Lungs screaming for air, Cailen took the knife from between his teeth and clasped it in one hand. Blood magic was needed, Maggie had told him. A sacrifice. Well, so be it. He was descended from the people who first worshipped the goddess. He had to hope that connection would be enough. That his blood would be enough. He had nothing else.

He pressed the blade against his wrist, feeling the sharp edge part his skin.

Then suddenly something grabbed him by the wrist, yanking away the hand holding the knife. A voice called from above, a voice that washed over him like a summer breeze.

"Cailean!"

The force around his wrist pulled, there was a surge of power, and suddenly he was being yanked upward. He lost his grip on his knife, and it went sinking out of reach. He broke the surface and gasped in a great, whooping breath.

It took a moment for him to get his bearings and when he did, he spotted a familiar figure standing on the headland, staring at him with wide, fear-filled eyes.

Rose.

The sight of her nearly stopped his heart. Something surged within him, a sensation that filled him from head to toe, a feeling that banished all the fear and doubt he'd been feeling and replaced it with a quiet joy.

Rose. His Rose.

But he let none of his feelings show in his voice.

"What are ye doing here?" he roared.

"What's it bloody well look like?" she roared back. "Stopping you from doing something monumentally idiotic. Now get the hell over here!"

Cailean hesitated. He'd come here to seal the prison with his blood. If he went to Rose now, he knew she'd stop him. He could not allow that. He could not let anyone, even Rose MacFinnan, divert him from this path. Yet what choice did he have? He'd dropped his knife and the rest of his weapons lay on the beach where he'd discarded them.

With a growl of frustrated exasperation, he began swimming towards her. He reached the rocks and clambered up. Rose grabbed his arm and helped to pull him the rest of the way.

He straightened and faced her. She looked disheveled, with her hair in disarray and her clothes spattered with mud. But even so, she was the most beautiful thing he'd ever seen.

But all he said was, "Ye shouldnae be here."

Her eyebrows rose. "*I* shouldn't be here? *You* shouldn't have locked me up!"

He winced. "Aye, maybe not, but I couldnae think of any other way to stop ye from following me."

"Damn right I would have followed you! Cailean, what the

hell do you think you're doing? Were you really going to… going to…" She didn't finish the sentence. She pressed one hand over her mouth and blinked rapidly as though fighting back tears. "Damn you," she whispered. "How could you do that to me?"

Cailean's heart broke at the sight of her anguish. The last thing he wanted to do was hurt her. But this was the only way he could see to save his daughter. Didn't she, of all people, understand that?

"I'm sorry," he replied softly. "I'm sorry it has to be this way. I wish it could be different. I wish I had more time to spend with ye. But I have to save my daughter. I have to save my people. If my blood is the way to doing that, then so be it."

"Not your blood! Dear God, Cailean, not yours! What were you thinking? Don't you know what it would do to Catriona and your people if they lost you? Don't you know what it would do to me?"

Her eyes flashed and her fists clenched at her sides. "I can't lose you, Cailean. I love you!"

CAILEAN'S EYES FLARED wide as Rose spoke those words. He went very still. Around them, the breeze plucked at Rose's hair and clothing, and the sea hissed against the headland. The raucous cries of seabirds filled the air. But between them, all was still.

"What did ye say?" Cailean whispered.

She gazed up at him. "I love you, Cailean MacNeil. I need you. Which is why I won't let you do this. I won't lose you. I can't."

He blinked slowly, as if trying to figure out if this was real or just a dream. She placed her palms flat against his chest. "*Now* do you get it? Now do you see why I came after you?"

He cupped her cheek with one hand. "Is this real?" he whispered. "Never did I think… never did I dare to hope…" He swallowed thickly, his throat bobbing.

She shook her head. "I know it's crazy. When Lir brought me here, she said I might find what I've been looking for. I didn't know what she meant at the time, but I do now. It's you, Cailean. *You're* what I've been looking for."

His eyes slid closed. He pressed his forehead against hers and she breathed deeply, breathing in the scent of him. He was here. He was alive. That's all that mattered right now. They could figure out the rest from there.

"What are we going to do, lass?" he whispered.

And that was the question, wasn't it? No matter what they felt for each other, they both still had their duty. She'd vowed to end the sickness that afflicted this island and Cailean, she knew, would do whatever it took to save his people and his daughter.

Frustrated rage welled up inside her. Was their love to be destroyed before it could even begin?

There has to be another way, she thought. *There has to be.*

She pushed away from Cailean. He watched her warily, his stance tense as though readying himself to stop her from doing anything stupid.

"What are ye thinking, love?" he asked softly.

"I'm going to speak to him."

"No, ye are not!" he snapped. "Ye know what happened last time! He isnae to be trusted, Rose. He will try to snare ye!"

"I know that. And last time you were here to bring me back. You'll just have to do the same again, won't you?" She huffed out an exasperated breath. "I have to try. What else can I do?"

He stared at her and she read a hundred different emotions in his eyes. Longing. Desire. Helplessness. But most of all, fear. Fear for her. For his daughter. For what this might cost. But there was also a weary kind of resignation as well.

"All right," he breathed. "I'll be right beside ye."

She leaned into him, breathing in his reassuring, sea-and-sky scent. "I know you will."

Taking a deep breath, she lowered herself to her knees. She

closed her eyes and sent her senses questing outwards. She felt the god immediately. His presence slammed into her like sledgehammer, battering at her senses. Rage. Frustration. All-consuming hatred.

Give him to me! The voice boomed through her head like thunder. *Son of the betrayer's line! I will tear him apart! I will bathe the waters with his blood! I will make them all pay for what they did to me!*

It was so powerful it almost flattened her. She pressed her fists against her head and screwed her eyes shut tight, battling against the raging torrent of the god's power. It was like standing in the path of a hurricane, like staring into the heart of a volcano. She'd never felt such rage and grief. Such suffering.

You cannot have him, she said to the voice. *He was not the one who trapped you. Your lover did that.*

Because of the poison he and his kind poured into her ear! And now she is gone and I am alone! You think to seal me back in here, spellweaver? Ye dinna have the power! Ye are just an insect against my might. Ye willnae give me the MacNeil? Then I will take ye instead! Come to me! I will drown ye!

Something washed through Rose's mind. Gone was the rage, the frustration, the hatred. Instead, something soft and soothing filled her. In her mind's eye she saw cool dark caves washed by the gentle sigh of the waves. She saw forests of kelp waving gently in the breeze, multicolored fish darting between their fronds. She saw moonlight on a dark ocean as still as glass. She saw tranquility. The peace of oblivion. All she had to do was dive in and it would be hers. No more cares. No more worries.

She felt her will fading, all thought and desire being washed into the endless sighing of the waves. It would be so easy to give in. So easy to step forward, to dive into the deep, dark water and let it close over her head…

"No!" a voice spoke by her ear, and she felt a firm grip take hold of her arm. "Come back to me, Rose, come back."

A face floated into her mind. A handsome, beloved face, and all of a sudden the god's compulsion shattered.

"Cailean," she whispered. She didn't open her eyes but she reached out and grabbed him, placing her own hands over his where he held her firm. Then, using him to anchor her, using his presence to stop her from losing herself again, she sent her senses out towards the god once more.

His rage and frustration battered against her but this time she had Cailean's presence to keep it at bay, had his love surrounding her like a cocoon. The god tore at her, trying to find a way past her defenses, but could find no way in. Instead, Rose grasped hold of his fury and followed it to its source, sending her senses questing down into the cracks in the seabed that marked where he was attempting to escape his prison.

The god quailed, trying to flee her now, but she would not let him go. She rode his fury, deeper, deeper, until she saw what lay beyond it. Loneliness. A deep, soul-crushing despair. He had been trapped for centuries, full of grief and sorrow for his lost love, believing that he was alone.

But he wasn't.

A memory formed in Rose's mind. It was an image of Cailean and Catriona. They were in the courtyard at Dun Mallach, Catriona trying unsuccessfully to get Patch to do some tricks while the little dog kept dancing around in circles and pulling on the hem of Catriona's dress. Cailean watched, arms folded across his broad chest, an amused smile curling the corners of his mouth. And in his eyes shone a deep, unadulterated joy. The love of a father for his daughter.

And suddenly Rose knew what she had to do.

With a gasp, she withdrew her senses, untangled her awareness from that of the god, and opened her eyes. Her outward senses came rushing back and she swayed on her knees. Cailean's hands on her shoulders steadied her.

He crouched, his dark eyes intense as he studied her face. "Are ye all right, lass?"

She swallowed a few times before she could speak and then nodded. "I know what we have to do, Cailean. We have to let him out of his prison."

Chapter Twenty

Cailean stared at her, appalled. "What? Ye canna be serious!"

Rose shook her head. "It's the only way. I thought his prison had to be resealed but it's not that at all. If we do that it will only be a matter of time before he starts to break free again. A sticking plaster over a wound. But we need to *treat* the wound. That's the only way to save everyone on Barra."

No. She'd lost him. "I dinna understand."

She went up onto her knees, placing her palms flat against his chest and he kept a firm grip on her shoulders in case she swooned again. Her dark eyes found his, sparkling with that determination he'd come to expect from her. "The sea god isn't angry, not really. He's full of grief and loneliness. He thinks the way to deal with that is through inflicting his pain on others. But what if we could ease his grief and loneliness?"

"And how, exactly would we do that?"

"By showing him he's not alone. That he's not lost his love. At least, not all of her."

Cailean studied her face, watching the way the light danced across her features and the wind swept her dark hair back from her face. He shook his head. "No," he said. "This is the god talking. He's bewitched ye like he did the other day. He's trying to get ye to free him. I willnae allow it."

"That's not what happened," she replied. "Do you trust me, Cailean?"

And that was the crux of it. He had always known that the work of a MacFinnan spellweaver was far beyond him. Physical enemies he could fight. Mundane problems he could deal with. But this? Gods and goddesses and magic? This was far beyond his ken. So now they came to the heart of it: Did he trust her? Could he put aside his distrust of all things mystical and put his faith in this woman?

The answer was far easier than he'd imagined. If she'd asked him this when she first arrived, the answer would have been no. Never. But that had changed. By slow increments his doubt had been eroded. Bit by tiny bit, his skepticism had died. Of course he trusted her. He would trust her with his life.

He released his grip on her shoulders. "Ye already know the answer to that, lass. If ye say this is what must be done, then this is what must be done." He climbed to his feet and held out a hand. Rose took it and he pulled her up. "But I will be right here, guarding yer back."

A bright smile lit her face before she let out a long breath. "Ready?"

"No. I'll never be ready. But let's get started all the same."

Cailean took his place at her side. Rose turned to face the waves. She closed her eyes, clasping her hands at her breast. She made no grand gestures, murmured no spells, but Cailean felt it immediately when she accessed her power. A warmth stole through him, full of peace like a summer breeze. It was so different to the god's angry power.

For long moments nothing happened. Then all of a sudden Rose staggered and the sea lit up with stormlights of opalescent green and blue so bright Cailean had to throw up an arm to shield his eyes.

When he looked again, a man was standing on the headland, watching them. He was tall, taller than Cailean, with the broad shoulders and muscular arms of a warrior. Pale-blond hair waved around his head as though stirred by an unseen current. A sword that looked to be made of shell or pearl was strapped to his hip.

Cailean stepped forward, putting himself between Rose and the newcomer. He didn't have any weapons but he wouldn't let that stop him. This creature would *not* harm her. Not while he had breath in his body.

The man regarded them in silence. He looked remarkably human, for a god. It was only the eyes that gave him away. Instead of having iris and pupil, they were pure orbs of silver, like liquid metal.

Rose gripped Cailean's arm and came to stand by his side. She lifted her chin, faced the man. "I'm—"

She got no further. The man raised his arms and a tempest roared to life around them. The wind began to howl, buffeting them both and sending their hair and clothes streaming. Cailean staggered against the force of it, one hand steadying Rose to help her keep her footing. The sea began to churn. The waves turned choppy, topped with white breakers, and began to slam against the headland with enough force to send up gouts of freezing spray.

"Listen to me!" Rose yelled into the wind. "I need to speak to you!"

But the god didn't listen. Throwing his arms to either side, he flung his head back and screamed at the sky in a voice like thunder. "Danu, my love! I am come to avenge ye!"

Clouds began to boil across the sky, obscuring the sun and turning the day into twilight. Above them, a roiling storm front formed like a dark bruise and Cailean felt the hairs along the back of his neck stand on end with its power.

"We have to get out of here!" he yelled at Rose.

But she shook her head. "No! I have to get him to listen!" She took a step closer to him, fighting against the wind that almost bent her double.

Cailean went with her, not releasing his grip on her arm. "Rose, this is madness! He willnae listen!"

"He must!" She fixed her gaze on the figure at the center of the maelstrom and bellowed with all her might to be heard over the howling wind, "Mannan, listen to me!"

To Cailean's surprise, the man's head snapped around, his silver gaze narrowing as it fixed on Rose. "What did ye call me?"

"That's your name, isn't it?" Rose said. "It hasn't been forgotten. There are still those on this island who remember you, who invoke your name for protection when they take their boats out on the sea."

Mannan's lips pulled up in a sneer. "Ye think that will placate me? A few whispered invocations from a few cowering mortals? After what they did to me? After they came between me and my love and condemned me to an eternity of loneliness?"

Rose shook her head. "No, I know it's not enough. I know what drives you. I feel your despair, Mannan, I feel your grief. But you're *not* alone. There is another. You were imprisoned before Danu could tell you, weren't you?"

The god's eyes narrowed in suspicion. But, Cailean noticed, the storm around them lessened just a little. "What are ye talking about? What other?"

"Danu bore you a child, Mannan. You have a daughter."

The god stilled. The storm fell out of the air as if it had never existed, replaced instead by a silent, eerie calm. In the sudden stillness, Cailean could hear his heart beating in his chest, his blood roaring in his ears. He rocked onto the balls of his feet, ready to move in any direction should Mannan lash out at Rose. But the god did nothing, only stared as if lost for words.

But in the next instant, the storm howled into being once more, ferocious and full of rage. "Ye lie!" the god bellowed. "I will crush ye all!"

Rose flung her head back and shouted at the sky, "Lir! I summon you!"

She clenched one of her fists, reopening a scab across her palm and little droplets of blood dripped down her wrist, to be snatched away by the wind and deposited into the white, churning waves.

There was an almighty boom as of a heavy door opening and closing and suddenly another woman stood by Cailean's side. She was tall, willowy, with long hair and eyes of silver.

Lir.

"Stop this, Father," the goddess said.

Mannan's eyes widened. "Who... who are ye?"

Lir walked towards him, her hair and long dress untouched by the wind, her feet barely seeming to touch the bare rock of the headland. She halted several paces from her father and regarded him steadily.

"Ye know who I am. I'm yer daughter."

Emotions ripped across Mannan's face, all too human in their intensity. Cailean saw shock, disbelief, heart-rending longing.

"My... my daughter?"

Lir nodded. "Ye were never forgotten, Father. Nor mother either. Not while I walk the earth. I am the green in every wave, the surf along the shore, the rain upon the mountains. Through me, Danu lives."

Cailean watched Mannan closely. His senses tingled with the energies he felt stirring around him, but he wouldn't let it distract him. He didn't trust either of these creatures and he watched both of them, alert for any movement that might indicate they posed a threat to Rose.

But neither Mannan nor Lir were looking at him. Their attention was fixed wholly on each other. To Cailean's eyes, father and daughter looked like two stalking cats, sizing the other up and trying to figure out if they should be friends or enemies. Did immortal beings even feel the same emotions as humans? Mannan had displayed rage and grief and all the darker human emotions, but what about the lighter ones? Was this creature even capable of feeling love for his daughter?

Around them, the storm continued to rage. The wind howled and sea lashed the sides of the headland with its fury. Yet they seemed trapped within a pocket of preternatural calm, the tableau frozen as Mannan and Lir stared at each other.

Then suddenly, Cailean saw it. An expression crossed Mannan's face and something filled his eyes that Cailean might not have recognized had he not felt it himself. But he knew exactly what that emotion was. He'd felt it the first time he'd held Catriona and she'd looked up at him with those big eyes of hers, curling one tiny hand around his thumb. It was a feeling that had never left him but only grew stronger with every passing moment.

The love of a father for his daughter.

Something seemed to snap within Mannan. His shoulders slumped and the storm calmed. He bowed his head, pressing a hand to his forehead.

"Forgive me," he whispered. "I did not know. I did not see."

His great shoulders heaved with silent sobs. Something broke in Lir now too. With a strangled cry, she ran across the rocks and threw herself at her father, wrapping her arms around him. Mannan's brawny arms encircled her too, holding her close as both said things to the other that Cailean couldn't hear.

Perhaps the sea god and Cailean were more similar than he cared to admit. He too knew the all-encompassing grief that could swallow a person whole and send them spiraling into a deep, dark pit where the only things left to cling to were bitterness and anger. But, unlike the sea god, he'd had Catriona to keep from falling into that pit entirely. Perhaps with Lir's help, Mannan could claw his way out of that pit too.

Rose squeezed his arm, and he turned to see she had tears in her eyes. She leaned against him, seeming exhausted. He pulled her close, putting his arms around her and kissing the top of her head. It wasn't just Catriona that kept him from the pit now. He had Rose too. He had a second chance at happiness he never dared hope for. He didn't intend to let it go.

At the end of the headland, Mannan and Lir broke their embrace. They turned to face him and Rose and walked towards them. Cailean tensed, edging slightly ahead of Rose, his fingers curling at his hip where his sword ought to be.

"There is no need for that," Mannan said, seeing the gesture. "Ye have no need to fear me, Cailean MacNeil. I see now what damage my vengeance has wrought and at what cost to ye and yer people. For that I am sorry. I will do what I can to make restitution. See."

He raised a finger and a vision enveloped Cailean. He was suddenly back in Dun Mallach standing over Catriona's bed in the infirmary. Her eyes were closed, Patch curled at the bottom of her bed. The little dog suddenly raised his head, ears pricking. Then he leapt to his feet, tail wagging, and jumped on Catriona's chest, peering intently at her face. A moment later, Catriona's eyelids flickered, and she slowly opened her eyes, blinking and looking around. Patch yelped excitedly, rasping his tongue all over her face.

"Ugh!" Cat cried, trying unsuccessfully to push the little dog off. "Geroff!"

A heady rush of relief flashed through Cailean, so strong that his legs went weak. He reached out to touch his daughter's face but of course, he wasn't really there, and she didn't notice his presence. He heard a gasp and looked up to see Maggie and Beatrice standing on the far side of the infirmary, looking around with awed expressions. Every one of the sleeping patients was waking up. Even old Drew, who'd been ill for so long, blinked his eyes open, stretched his arms over his head, then pushed himself onto his elbows, looking around with a grumpy expression on his face.

"By the seven hells," he muttered, "I'm bloody starving."

Then a rushing sensation filled Cailean's head and he was suddenly standing back on the headland, Rose by his side. From the awed expression on her face he guessed she'd seen the vision too.

"Was that real?" Cailean demanded of Mannan and Lir. "Or another of yer tricks?" He couldn't keep the anger from his voice, fear that it wasn't real putting a bite into his tone.

"It was real," Mannan replied. "Yer people will recover. The sickness is gone. On this, ye have my word. What's more, I pledge myself to Barra in my love, Danu's name. I will watch over ye to make restitution for what I've done. I will bring ye calm seas and good fishing. Such is my vow."

Cailean didn't know what to say to that. This creature had brought such suffering to his people. Was he just supposed to forgive that? He wasn't sure he had it in him. But he could try.

He nodded tightly. "Keep yer word and I will consider it settled between us. I will ensure yer name isnae forgotten on Barra."

The god inclined his head, sealing their bargain. Now Lir stepped up, coming to stand in front of Rose.

"Thank ye," she said softly. "I knew ye would find a way." Her gaze skipped to Cailean behind her. "And I knew ye would find what ye were looking for along the way. I am in yer debt. Call on me. I will answer."

Rose nodded, tears shining in her eyes. "I will."

To his surprise, Lir bowed to him and then Rose, before taking her father's hand. The two of them walked to the end of the headland and dove into the water, disappearing into the waves and disappearing from view.

Cailean blew out a shaky breath and ran a hand through his hair. "Is that it?" he asked. "Is it over?"

"It's over," Rose replied, her voice sounding just as shaky as Cailean's.

"Ye did it," he breathed. "Ye really did it."

She shook her head. "No. *We* did it. I couldn't have done any of this without you, Cailean. You kept me grounded, kept Mannan's power from taking me. And without you and Catriona, I wouldn't have worked out what I had to do."

Cailean reached down and cupped her face in his big hands. His chest filled with love for this woman. How could he bear to let her go? Now that she'd fulfilled the task that Lir had set her, she would leave, return to her own time. The thought was like a cold blade slicing through his gut. He couldn't let that happen. It would be the end of him.

He took a deep breath, steeling his courage. "Dinna leave me," he whispered, the words coming out in a desperate plea. "Stay with me, Rose. Will ye marry me?"

ROSE STARED AT Cailean, unable to quite believe he'd just said those words.

Will you marry me?

She could see everything he felt for her dancing in his eyes and knew it must be mirrored in her own. It crackled in the air around them, this undeniable pull between them. Rose wasn't sure what it was called. Chemistry? Attraction?

No. It was love. Simple as that. She'd fallen in love with Cailean MacNeil and now she couldn't bear to think of leaving him, of returning to her lonely life in her little cottage by the lake.

Will you marry me?

Was it possible? Could she really stay? Could she really marry him?

Cailean's eyes suddenly clouded with uncertainty. "Rose?"

She closed her eyes, took a juddering breath. The word *yes* danced on the tip of her tongue, demanding release. She wanted nothing more than to build a life with this man and grow old with him by her side.

But she'd thought that once before and look how that had turned out. She was newly divorced. How could she countenance jumping into another marriage?

You might be newly divorced, she told herself, *but your marriage ended a long time before that. And life is too short to not take chances.*

She looked up at Cailean. This was how it was meant to be, she thought. This all-encompassing ache, this need to be with somebody like they were the air you breathed. *This* was love. She had never felt it before. Not with Dennis. Not with anyone.

Perhaps ye will find what ye were looking for all along. They were the words Lir had spoken to her that day when she'd come to fetch her. Now Rose knew what she'd meant. She'd been looking for this. For him. For a place to belong.

And now she'd found it.

"Yes!" she gasped. "A hundred times yes. I'll marry you, Cailean MacNeil."

A smile of pure joy lit his face. "Say that again, lass," he breathed. "I didnae hear ye properly."

"You big idiot," she laughed. "I said I'll marry you. Was that loud enough for you? Or would you like it louder still?" She threw back her head and shouted at the sky. "I love Cailean MacNeil and I've agreed to marry him! Will that do?"

He scooped her into his arms. "Aye, lass," he breathed. "That will do." Then he bent his head and kissed her.

The ride back to Dun Mallach passed in a blur. Snip followed along behind while Rose rode on Arrow with Cailean. She sat in front of him in the saddle, leaning back against his solid, reassuring bulk while he kept one arm clamped protectively around her waist.

That was just fine with her. She couldn't seem to stop touching him. Or looking at him. Or kissing him. Every so often she turned in the saddle and their journey came to a grinding halt while they kissed.

So it took a long time to get back to Dun Mallach, but finally, the keep came into view. As they neared the gates, two figures came bursting out, one small and four-legged, the other two-legged with flying red hair.

Cailean pulled Arrow to a halt, a low gasp escaping him. He swung his leg over the horse's back, jumped to the ground, and knelt just in time to catch Catriona into a hug as she cannoned into him. He wrapped his arms around her and squeezed her tight as Patch danced around excitedly.

"Oh my sweet girl," Rose heard Cailean murmur. "Thank all the gods that ye are all right."

The sight of the two of them brought tears to Rose's eyes. She dismounted, knelt in the mud by their sides, and threw her arms around them both. After a second, Cailean's arm shifted to include her in the three-way hug and Catriona turned to bury her face in Rose's shoulder.

She had no idea how long the three of them remained like that. She only knew that she was reluctant to let either of them go. But finally, Cailean released them both.

"How are ye feeling?" he asked his daughter, his eyes scanning up and down as though searching for any sign of sickness.

Catriona shrugged. "Bored. Sister Beatrice wouldnae let me out of the infirmary but it's so dull in there! I snuck out when she wasnae looking." She sounded very proud of this fact.

Cailean shared a look with Rose and the two of them burst out laughing. It was the laughter of relief, the laughter of hope restored after despair and Rose felt it blast through her like a gale, taking with it the last of her doubts.

"Catriona," Cailean said, putting his hands on his daughter's shoulders. "Rose and I have something to tell ye." He glanced at Rose and took a deep breath. "We are getting married."

Rose didn't know what kind of reaction she'd expected to this news, but the exasperated eye roll Catriona gave them wasn't it.

"Papa, that's not news," she said in the all-knowing tone of a nine-year-old. "Of *course* ye are getting married. I did see ye kissing, ye know."

Cailean blinked, taken aback, and glanced at Rose. She merely shrugged. She had forgotten to tell Cailean that little detail.

Catriona clapped her hands together. "I've already got it all planned out! There are going to be games and competitions and dancing. And I'm going to be bridesmaid of course." She gave Rose a defiant look. "Aren't I?"

Rose laughed. "Of course you are! I wouldn't have it any other way."

"That's good then. Me and Patch have been practicing. He's getting very good at it."

"Getting good at what?"

"Carrying the train, of course! After all, he is going to be brides-dog."

Rose found she had no answer to that.

Chapter Twenty-One

"OKAY, READY?" ELISE said. "Pick a card, but don't tell me what it is."

Catriona, sitting cross-legged in front of Elise, nodded and then pulled a card from the deck, glancing at it before she pressed it against her chest.

"Right, put it back and I bet I can guess which one yours is."

Obediently, Catriona put the card back in the deck. Elise proceeded to shuffle them and then lay them out in a pattern on the rug between the two of them. She picked up a card and held it out.

"Was this your card?" It was the four of hearts.

Catriona's eyes went wide. "Aye, it was! How did ye do that?"

Elise waved her fingers dramatically. "Magic."

Jenna, who was sitting in the window seat, rolled her eyes. "Don't listen to her, Cat. That wasn't magic at all, just sleight of hand. Anyone could do it."

"So ye could teach me?" Catriona asked, excitement in her voice.

Rose smiled to herself as she sat at the dressing table while Mable fussed with her hair. It felt so good to have her sister and niece here. She wasn't sure she would have been able to do this without them. Lir kept her promise and dutifully brought Elise through time so she could be present today and brought Jenna over from the neighboring island of Skye where she lived with her husband, Arran MacLeod.

To say that they were both surprised by her story was an understatement. As Elise had pulled herself out of the tidal pool that Lir had used as a portal, it was probably the only time Rose had seen her younger sister speechless. Jenna too had been shocked that her rule-following, risk-avoidant aunt had agreed to travel to the fifteenth century. And not only that, now she'd decided to stay.

Mable stepped back. "All done. I hope ye like it."

Rose squeezed the maid's hand in thanks then turned to the others. "Well? How do I look?"

"Awesome!" Catriona cried. "My papa willnae know what's hit him!"

Rose couldn't help but smile. Catriona was already picking up Jenna and Elise's turns of phrase. She just hoped the pair didn't teach her any swear words. She wasn't sure how she'd explain that one away to Cailean.

"I think Trouble has got it just about right," Elise said, using the nickname she'd given Catriona. "You look awesome, sis."

"Like a proper fifteenth-century lady!" Jenna added. She gave Elise a mischievous smile. "Sure you don't want to come and join us, Elise? I can really picture you in one of my dresses."

Elise scowled. "No, thank you. There is no way you're getting me living in this time. It's bad enough that I have to come here if I want to visit the pair of you. No internet? No coffee shops? No indoor plumbing? Not a chance." She shivered at this horrifying thought.

Jenna laughed. "You get used to it. You'd be surprised what you can get used to when the trade-off is finding your soulmate."

A disgusted look crossed Elise's face. "Ugh. You sound like a Disney movie."

Rose chuckled at their banter. Oh, how she'd missed it. She perhaps hadn't realized quite how much until now.

There was a knock on the door. Mable went over to answer

it, revealing Drew MacRae standing there, looking dapper in his tartan plaid and with his hair and beard freshly combed. It was strange to think this was the same man who'd been at death's door when she first arrived. Now he looked whole and hale and years younger than his sixty years.

He cleared his throat. "Erm... I've been sent to tell ye... that is, I've been sent to ask... if ye are ready, the ceremony is ready to begin."

Rose felt a thrill go through her. She wasn't sure if it was nerves or excitement or both. She rose to her feet. "Thank you, Drew. We're on our way." She said it calmly, even though her stomach was suddenly tying itself in knots.

"Well," Elise said, climbing to her feet and pulling Catriona up after her. "Let's get this show on the road, shall we?"

"Ready?" Jenna asked, laying a hand on Rose's shoulder.

Rose took a deep breath. Oh God. She was really doing this. It was really happening.

"Ready."

She'd asked Elise to give her away. Unconventional, maybe, but nobody in Dun Mallach had batted an eyelid. After all, she *was* a MacFinnan spellweaver, and eccentricity went with the title. Elise gave her a wink and came to stand beside her. Jenna and Catriona took up their places behind, carrying bouquets, while Mable took hold of Patch.

The little dog had been put on a leash, and he was *not* happy about it. But the last thing Rose needed was him deciding now was a great time to play chase-the-hem while she was in her wedding dress. He pulled and yapped, excited at all the commotion.

"Patch, behave yerself!" Catriona scolded and, for a wonder, he calmed a little. Catriona bent and hung a wreath of flowers around his neck.

"Brides-dog indeed," Rose said with a laugh.

They stepped out of the room and made their way through the corridors of the castle. As they walked, Rose thought of how strange this had all seemed when she'd first come here. It had felt alien, far removed from everything she knew. But now, as her eyes skimmed across the tapestries on the walls, the beams across the ceilings, the plaid runners that covered the flagstones, it didn't feel strange any more at all.

It felt like home.

They reached the doors to the great hall and paused. Drew was waiting there to announce them, and as she reached him, he turned and announced their arrival to the guests waiting within. Music sprang up from the quartet that Cailean had recruited, and Rose felt her heart skip a beat.

This was it. The moment she'd been dreaming of for the past few weeks as preparations were made. She could hardly believe it had finally arrived.

Stepping inside, she saw that the great hall was crowded with people, some of whom she recognized, some of whom she didn't. Maggie and Beatrice were there, grinning like a couple of excited schoolgirls, along with Old Seamus, his daughter Brina, and a huge gaggle of grandchildren. Others she didn't know, as many had come in from other islands to mark the wedding of the laird of Barra.

As she and Elise took the first step down the aisle, her gaze immediately sprang to Cailean. He was waiting for her in the place where the high table normally sat but which had now been cleared away and replaced by a woven arch covered in late-blooming flowers. His eyes found hers across the intervening distance, and her breath caught in her throat. Decked out in the MacNeil plaid, with his dark hair framing his face, he was enough to take her breath away.

She found herself grinning every bit as stupidly as Maggie and Beatrice had been, and he gave her an answering grin, boyish and full of joy.

"Who is *that*?" Elise murmured as they began walking down the aisle.

Rose tore her gaze away from Cailean to see that Elise was

eyeing the man standing at Cailean's side. He was younger than Cailean with wavy blond hair so pale it was almost white. He wore clothes even finer than Cailean's and had a bearing that spoke of easy confidence. She'd met the man yesterday, when he'd arrived from Islay to stand as Cailean's best man.

"That's Jamie Donald," Rose said. "They call him the Lord of the Isles. He's Cailean's liege lord."

"Is he now?" Elise said in a musing tone. "So what's that? Some sort of king?"

"I don't think it quite works like that. I think it's more that he's first among equals."

Elise said nothing more, but Rose could see her glancing in Jamie Donald's direction as they walked. Oh dear. She recognized that look in her sister's eyes. The poor man didn't know what he was in for.

But all such considerations were pushed from her mind as they reached the end of the aisle. Elise eyed Cailean as she held out Rose's hand towards him.

"You take good care of her, you hear?"

Cailean's eyes shone. "Oh, I will. On that ye have my word."

Elise gave a tight nod and stepped back, shooting Jamie Donald a curious look as she went to stand next to him.

Cailean took Rose's hand and squeezed. "Rose," he breathed. "Ye look stunning."

"You don't scrub up too badly yourself," she replied, squeezing his hand and giving him a smile. God, she couldn't seem to stop smiling.

"Ready, love?"

"Ready."

Together, they turned to face the person who was to marry them. This was to be a handfasting, a traditional Scottish wedding rather than a Christian one—to Beatrice's disgust and Maggie's delight. So rather than a priest, they had asked for the most experienced person on Barra in such matters, one who had one foot in the old religion and one foot in the new. It just so happened that they both knew her.

"My, look at ye two," Agnes of Hemkirk sighed. "A more suited couple I dinna think I've ever seen." Her eyes almost disappeared into their nests of wrinkles as she smiled. "Let's begin."

She raised her arms above her head and called in a voice louder than anyone would expect from so diminutive a woman, "Ye all know why we are here, aye? We are here to handfast the laird and the spellweaver, aye?"

"Aye!" came the roar from the guests, followed by a loud bout of cheering.

Agnes stepped forward, a length of red and green tartan, the colors of Clan MacNeil, in her hands.

"Ye come before us in love, in trust, and in hope for the days ahead," she said. "Do ye offer yourselves freely, without fear or force?"

Cailean looked at Rose, his thumb brushing across her knuckles. "Aye," he said. "With all that I am."

Rose smiled, heart fluttering. "Yes," she whispered. "With all that I have."

Agnes nodded, eyes bright, and began to wrap the tartan around their joined hands, binding left to left, heart to heart.

"By this cord, yer lives are bound. As the fabric weaves together threads, may yer days be woven with patience, with laughter, with strength. May the storm pass over ye, and the sun return, again and again."

"I love ye," Cailean murmured, low so only Rose could hear. "And I'll stand beside ye, now and always."

Rose's breath hitched, her free hand rising to touch his cheek. "And I love you. Even through time itself."

Agnes gave a quiet smile and then called loudly, "So be it! What is tied in love, let none undo."

It was done. As the final words echoed around the great hall, the crowd broke into a chorus of clapping and cheering loud enough to lift the rafters.

Cailean bent his head and kissed her, sure and steady—and with a passion that gave a hint of what would come later—which only made the guests cheer all the harder.

Rose leaned into him, into the kiss, forgetting the guests, forgetting the hall, forgetting the entire world. There was only the two of them and this timeless moment.

That is until Catriona said quite clearly, and in a perfect imitation of Elise's diction, "Ugh. That is *gross!*"

Rose couldn't help it. She burst out laughing. "Oh, come here! I'll show you gross!"

Pulling Catriona close, she threw her arms around her and planted the wettest, noisiest kiss she could manage right on her stepdaughter's cheek.

ROSE DIDN'T REMEMBER much of the celebration after that. Everything became a whirlwind of eating, drinking, dancing, chatting, and generally having more fun than she could ever remember having. One thing she realized was that her adopted people *really* knew how to party. Sure, they worked hard to scrape a living from Barra's harsh landscape, but they made up for it whenever there was a celebration to be had. What was the term? Work hard, play hard?

But as she sat at Cailean's side at the high table, watching the banter and the dancing, the drinking contests, and the friendly arguments, she knew the people of Barra had something to celebrate that went far beyond a mere wedding. They were finally closing the door on a dark chapter in their lives and opening a page on a new one. It was clear that her marriage to Cailean meant a lot to them. All day people had been coming up to her to give her their blessing and to give Cailean dire warnings of what they would do to him if he didn't take good care of her.

Cailean had borne this with good grace. It seemed that teasing the groom was also a part of Scottish wedding tradition.

Rose sat back, letting forth a long, contented sigh as she looked out over the throng of people enjoying themselves. Catriona was dancing with Jenna while Patch bobbed around their feet. Maggie was waxing lyrical about something to Beatrice while her sister sat there with her arms folded and a scowl on her face. Rose definitely didn't want to know what *that* conversation was about. Elise had gradually shifted along the seats at the high table and now she sat next to Jamie Donald. The Lord of the Isles certainly didn't look very lordly right now. In fact, he looked a little terrified as a clearly drunken Elise waved her goblet around as she tried to explain the rules of ice hockey.

"Do you think we should rescue him?" Rose said to Cailean, nodding in their direction.

Her husband glanced over at his liege-lord and then raised an eyebrow. "Rescue him? He looks to be having the time of his life. I'm sure he can handle yer sister."

"Hmm. You don't know Elise," Rose muttered. She snuggled back against Cailean and heaved another sigh.

"That was a big sigh, love," Cailean observed.

She shrugged. "I'm just happy, that's all."

"I'm glad. So, no regrets then?"

They were handfasted rather than married, and in Scottish tradition that meant they stayed together for a year and a day. After that, if they found they'd made a mistake, they were free to go their separate ways or formalize it into a permanent union.

Cailean had insisted on this arrangement for her sake. After the ending of her marriage to Dennis, he didn't want to pressure her into another. She loved him for that. But she also knew, absolutely knew, that after the year and a day was up, she wouldn't be going anywhere. This was where she was meant to be. This was her home now. *He* was her home.

"No regrets," she said softly. "Not now. Not ever."

Something stirred in his gaze. His hand, resting on her shoulder, tightened, and a little tingle went through her. His eyes darkened, and that tingle inside her intensified, becoming an ache deep in her belly.

"I dinna think anyone would notice if we slipped away," he said softly.

"I don't care if they do," she replied, her voice suddenly husky.

He pushed his chair back and rose to his feet, pulling her up after him. Without a word, he took her hand and led her to the door—accompanied by a chorus of whistling and heckling, showing that their escape was *definitely* noticed.

Cailean turned at the door, gave a theatrical bow, then led Rose out, pulling the door closed behind him. As soon as the door was shut, cutting off the noise of the celebration, he was on her.

He pushed her against the wall, kissing her fiercely, curling his hands into her hair and exploring her lips with his own. She kissed him back just as ferociously, wrapping her arms around his neck and slipping her tongue into his mouth. A deluge of heat and desire swamped her, deepening the ache in her belly and lighting a heat between her legs.

"Take me upstairs," she groaned into his mouth. "Right now."

He smiled against her lips. "Yer command, my lady."

He swept her into his arms, lifting her as though she weighed hardly anything at all. Cradling her tight, he carried her up the winding stairs and to the chamber they shared, kicking the door open and then pushing it shut with his hip.

Somebody had been in the chamber before them. Candles had been lit on almost every surface, filling the room with warm golden light, and bunches of dried lavender gave the air a delicious scent. A fire crackled in the hearth to chase away the autumn chill, and on the low table sat a decanter of wine, two goblets, and a covered platter of food. Even the covers on the bed had been turned down.

"Remind me to thank Mable," Rose said.

"Aye," Cailean agreed. He set her on her feet and looked

down at her. Candlelight danced in his dark, dark eyes. His lips parted, and a soft breath escaped him.

"I can hardly believe ye are mine," he whispered. "I keep thinking this is a dream and I will awaken in a moment."

"Then it's a good dream," she replied. She went up on tiptoes and kissed him. It was a soft kiss, just a delicate brush of her lips over his, but he shivered at the touch.

"Ah, lass," he whispered, running a thumb across her cheek. "Ye have such power over me. What is it ye wish of me, my lady?"

She smiled wickedly. "Oh, I think you know exactly what I wish."

An equally wicked smile quirked his lips, and the look in his eyes intensified. "And I am helpless but to obey."

He dipped his head and pressed his lips against hers, softly, gently, as chaste as the kiss she'd just given him. But Rose's restraint snapped. Reaching up to cup his face in her hands, she kissed him back, and this time it was *not* chaste. It was full of fire and passion and need. She wanted him. Oh God, how she wanted him!

And Cailean responded. With a groan, his hands went to the small of her back, pushing her against the hardness of his body, his mouth exploring hers with a desperate hunger. She wrapped her arms around his neck, and he slipped his hands under her backside, lifting her up as she wrapped her legs around his hips.

In this position, she could feel the hardness of him pressing against her, and knew he was as desperate for her as she was for him. Still kissing, he carried her over to the bed and laid her on the cover, following her down. His lips moved to her neck, her earlobes, her collarbone. Rose writhed and gasped, the ache deep within her becoming almost overwhelming.

They began tearing at each other's clothing, throwing the garments on the floor in their haste to get at each other. Cailean rose onto his knees, naked and glorious above her, and her eyes devoured him hungrily, tracing the hard planes and angles of his chest, down to where his manhood stood stiff and proud.

She gasped, unable to form words, hoping he could read in her body language what she needed.

He did. He bent his head and took one of her nipples into his mouth as he positioned himself between her thighs, nudging her legs apart with his knees. Arching her back beneath him, Rose moaned as his tongue licked and teased her nipple until it hardened.

"Now," she whispered. "Please."

He obliged. Dropping his weight on top of her, he raised his head and stared deep into her eyes as he thrust his hips and drove himself deep inside her.

Rose cried out with pleasure, with the delicious sensation of him filling her, and gripped his shoulders with her fingers.

He watched her as he began to move, driving into her slowly at first but with increasing speed as he found his tempo. The fire inside her intensified. She was helpless to do anything but gasp and shift beneath him, tilting her hips to meet his thrusts as they matched their rhythm. It was too much. Too much. Surely she was going to burst into flame. Surely she was going to burn from the inside out.

But she didn't. Instead, fire began to sizzle along her nerves, beginning at the place where their bodies met, and radiating outwards. It was a pleasure that bordered on pain, so intense she began to lose herself, to come apart beneath this onslaught of sensation.

"Cailean," she gasped, her moans and cries becoming quicker, higher, as the sensations began to overwhelm her.

He grunted in response, his movement becoming hard and fast and frantic, slamming into her with enough force to make the headboard slam against the wall. Rose didn't care. All she cared about was this inferno that was lifting her up, up, up until finally it engulfed her and she was obliterated into a raging torrent of ecstasy.

She might have cried out his name. She might have shouted her pleasure to the ceiling. She didn't know. She was dimly aware of Cailean shuddering as he reached his peak and then collapsing on top of her, his weight pinning her to the bed.

It felt an age that she lay there, clinging to him, feeling the euphoria burn through her, feeling her muscles turn weak and lethargic with draining ecstasy. But finally, Cailean raised his head and looked at her.

"I love ye," he said, his voice thick with emotion. "My soul loves ye. My body loves ye. My heart loves ye. My Rose."

She felt emotion clog her throat as well. She tilted her head slightly and kissed the end of his nose. "And I you, my Cailean."

He rolled away from her, pulling her into an embrace, and she laid her head against his shoulder. A sleepy lassitude filled her, but as she felt herself begin to drift, her power suddenly surged inside her. Blinking, she sent her senses inward. Something had changed. Something…unexpected.

It took her a moment to discover what it was. There. A tiny, infinitesimal spark of life, deep inside her. Her eyes widened with realization, and she felt her heart begin to beat a little faster. Joy swept through her, and tears sprang to her eyes.

"Rose?" Cailean asked. "What's wrong, my love?"

"Nothing is wrong," she answered. "Quite the opposite, in fact."

She took his hand and laid it on her belly. Confusion lit his face for a moment, and then his eyes widened.

"But… but how… how can ye know?"

She raised an eyebrow. "I *am* a MacFinnan spellweaver, you know."

Cailean's were full of wonder. Then the biggest grin she'd ever seen on him curled his lips.

"Ha!" he crowed, punching the air. "Goal!"

Rose laughed. That was another of Elise's phrases he'd picked up.

"And I know the perfect way to celebrate," she said. She wrapped her arms around his neck and pulled him down on top of her.

THE END

About the Author

Katy Baker was born in London to an English mother and an American father. She grew up a stone's throw from Hampstead Heath which remains one of her favourite places in the world. During her twenties she spent several years living in San Francisco where she developed an abiding love of bagels before returning to her beloved London. She lives in south London with her husband and a very grumpy bulldog.

Katy's books explore the intricacies of human relationships with plenty of spice thrown in. What would life be without a little spice?

Website:
www.katybakerromance.com

www.ingramcontent.com/pod-product-compliance
Lightning Source LLC
LaVergne TN
LVHW011934070526
838202LV00054B/4634